Kill, or They Die

Max Holden

COPYRIGHT

DEDICATION

To Scotland, the part of the UK where I was raised and which sowed the seeds of what I am.

To England, the part of the UK I call home.

FOREWARD

'Kill or They Die' is the second book in the Harry Logan series after 'Logan's Rules'. Harry Logan books stand on their own. However, I recommend you read Logan's Rules first for contextual and 'spoiler' reasons.

As a Brit, I write in UK English because this is what I know.

I have used some Scottish-cum-slang words in as limited a way as possible but also in sufficient amounts to give the reader a feel for the characters and their version of the English language.

** Warning **

This book contains bad language, as and when appropriate to the characters within.

I refrain from gratuitous violence in my writing. However, this book does contain scenes of sexual and physical violence necessary to the story.

I do hope you enjoy.

ACKNOWLEDGMENTS

I'd like to convey my thanks to everyone who helped me with this book.

In particular, can I acknowledge:

- Eileen, my long-suffering and patient wife, has to be at the top of this list.

- Accuracy International for their advice and support regarding sniper rifles.

- Yet again, I appreciate this book's Beta Readers: Andrea, Kevin, Dawn, Karen, and Jeff.

CONTENTS

	Chapter Name	**Page #**
	Glossary	vii
1	The Auld Monarch	10
2	Taigh Locha	16
3	Anti-Guest Preparations	24
4	Self-Preservation	29
5	First Guests	36
6	Mountain Rules	42
7	Panic!	53
8	Abducted	56
9	Intruders	65
10	Unleashing the Demons	72
11	Preparations	86
12	Job Offer	92
13	Poor Little Girl	99
14	Chedworth Manor	107
15	Matching	120
16	Uncle Jack	125
17	Catching Up	133
18	Take Your Medicine	144
19	Access	150
20	Game On	157
21	Ace of Diamonds	162

22	New Friends	164
23	Meeting	171
24	Pleasure, Not Work	178
25	Foiled Plan - Fortunately	184
26	Preparations	188
27	Torpedoing the Convoy	198
28	Family Weekend	205
29	Answers	217
30	Confession	230
31	Darling Lover	238
32	Power Games	245
33	The Plan	248
34	Ambushed	255
35	Re-Negotiation	363
36	Exchange	267
37	Kill Tom!	271
38	A Setup	277
39	Spring Cleaning	283
40	Full Circle	287
41	Notice	302
42	Payback	308
	Epilogue	
	Small Request, Big Favour	287
	About The Author	287

GLOSSARY: CHARACTERS & TERMS

It was necessary to use a few pseudonyms in this book, to ensure the flow of the story.

Harry Logan: aka Barrie Greywell at the Taigh, aka Arthur Fox at the residential unit.

Jessica (Jess) Lloyd: aka Tessa (Tess) Greywell at the Taigh, aka Oakleigh Woods while on the run.

Thomas (Tom) Lloyd: aka Ronald (Ron) Greywell at the Taigh.

Mrs Mathews – aka the Bulldog at the residential unit.

Fedor Kotova – aka Leanid Koslov.

Nessie (Agnes) and **Chick** (Charles) MacPherson, Auchtershiel Hotel proprietors

Where this takes place in Scotland, the use of colloquial Scots can be difficult to understand, so I've toned down the usage. However, for a smidgen of authenticity, I've kept some examples in the text. I trust these are delivered in such a context that they are understood. My Beta readers had no problems, but just in case, I hope these most common ones help:

a' = all,

ain = own,

blether = chat,

cannae = cannot,

dae = do,

'em = I'm,
gillie = game-keeper,
meh = my,
noo = now,
o' = of,
oot = out,
pehs = pies,
saft = soft,
toon = town,
wi' = with & oot = out (wi'oot = without),
ye = you,
yer = your.

1. THE AULD MONARCH

While it wasn't freezing, the mid-April weather in the Scottish Highlands was still bitter. Jessica Lloyd and Harry Logan lay prone in their hide, observing the magnificent stag in the distance. They'd been lying on the ground for quite some time, barely moving. The cold seeped into their expensive hunting gear, and they started to feel uncomfortable. It was the nature of this morning's training.

She needed to make a highly accurate shot to ensure the stag was dealt with cleanly. No one wants a suffering, wounded animal, or even worse, one that needs to be chased before being dispatched. From this distance, it was no easy task. She'd set the AX308 rifle sights and had taken a wind reading for the shot. Her finger squeezed the trigger through the first pull, almost ready. Finally, Jessica gently squeezed the trigger fully. Even with the large suppressor, the deadened explosion was loud enough to echo throughout the surrounding hills.

Harry and Jessica had come here almost six months ago with her brother Thomas to escape their inner-city life. Living in this harsh environment over the winter was life-changing, bringing the already close friends further together.

Harry was the eldest of the three, 'the old codger', as the other two fondly referred to him. The youngest, Jessica Lloyd, had recently turned 20. Her elder brother, Thomas, was only a few years her senior. Harry, in his late 30s, seemed old, or at least that was the ongoing joke.

Harry met the street-wise siblings, Jess and Tom, on the streets of London when they were all living rough. Jess was a drug addict who'd run from the social care organisations and personnel, where she'd been repeatedly abused; in every way conceivable. Tom, her elder brother, had chosen a life on the street to be close to his sister, doing his best to protect her from the excesses of that life. He wasn't a big or even powerful man, but he was brave for his sister and did his limited best. Things changed when Harry arrived.

Harry and the siblings had made friends for mutual protection against a common enemy, for a shared purpose. All were vulnerable in that environment. However, together, they could make the best this street-living could offer, which was not a lot.

They were all the family they had, looking after each other as they rebuilt their lives within the underground world of drugs, gangs, and violence. Eventually, it was time for them to make the break, escaping to the highlands of Scotland. This place was the first of their short-term sanctuaries as they built a chain of hiding places and personas before their final destination.

During the preceding winter months, Harry took every opportunity of gaps in the extreme weather to venture out on his runs in the hills and glens around their house. He'd regularly come upon this stag and his herd and took advantage of their nervousness. While stopping and quietly admiring the creatures, he could test and hone his stalking and silent running skills while finding another route around them to avoid being heard or smelled. If they didn't notice him, no one would.

The Auld Monarch was a cunning beast and had occasionally spied Harry. Harry ensured this creature didn't consider him an innocuous part of the countryside. This beast was too valuable a prize for it to be complacent with humans.

The stag, a great hart, surveyed the land around, overseeing his herd below. He was a mature male red deer, probably close to 190kg, the weight of two large men. During the last winter, Harry and his two companions had watched him sporting a Monarch's 16-point antlers that distinguished him from lesser beasts. Up here, a Monarch was a rare sight. Even now, without its mass of antlers, he was still a magnificent creature.

A stag gets its 'Monarch' title from the number of points on his antlers, sixteen in his rare case. During the rutting season, he'd seen off numerous suitors for the attention of his hinds, the females in his herd. Harry could often hear the clash of interlocking antlers echoing around the glen.

The legal hunting season was over. And now, without the antlers, which had fallen off last month, he'd have thought he'd be safe from hunters, assuming he had that level of understanding. The Monarch didn't know there were hunting seasons. And anyway, poachers had no hunting season. If poachers wanted a kill out of season and the price was right, he and his herd were at risk.

Like all highland deer, his herd led a life of being hunted. He knew how to stay alert and watch for foxes and the great golden eagles, the scourge of his young calves in early summer. Now his herd was older, the only predator was man.

The stag jumped in surprise at the sound of the .308 bullet ricocheting off the large boulder beside where it stood. It bolted. It knew the sound from old. Jessica's second shot also ricocheted but on a cairn two feet away. That second shot had two objectives. It gave the stag impetus to gallop faster, and it directed him toward his already running herd which had been spooked by the sound of the gunfire.

Harry eyed his companion, lying alongside him in their ground-level hide.

'Ratty would have been proud of her.'

Today was one of their regular marksmanship training sessions. They'd purloined various weapons from Harry's previous life and masters, this snipe rifle being one.

Jess' shots had dealt with the problem. She'd chased the stag and the herd away from impending danger.

From day one, Jess had a marksman's sharp eye. Unfortunately, her abusive childhood background had made her highly stressed, reactive, and impetuous. Harry's calm and focused training had gone a long way in helping curb and channel those emotions that would have prevented her from being the best of the best.

When the weather had been at its worst, she trained indoors. There, she learned to control her breathing and racing heart while holding her finger on the trigger without any movement until the final imperceptible squeeze. Almost six months on, she was a different person. Although not there yet, she was building the patience and control of a marksman.

Harry was trained by the best sniper in the regiment, possibly in the British Army. Although Harry's sniper skills nestled in the lower echelons of his regiment's marksmen, he was nonetheless a skilled shooter, albeit not the best of the best. He could never be the marksman of his best friend and teacher, but he knew how to teach someone who had an in-built eye and delivery. Jess had the potential to be in that top 1%, as was Harry's teacher, his best friend, and brother-in-law.

In the distance, almost at their 2 o'clock (to you, that's ahead and off to the right), three men popped their heads up. They also had been in a hide, although not particularly inconspicuous. Now the herd had gone and was no longer in reach of their rifles, they stood up and showed themselves. Jess, through her high-power telescopic sights, and Harry, through his spotting scope, watched the three men gesticulate among themselves.

"That's Fat Bob and his friend Gus with another guy," whispered Jess.

Bob was the shorter and very much the wider of the two. The tall, skinny one was Gangly Gus, for reasons one can well imagine. These well-known local poachers were always on the lookout for a quick earner. On the occasions Harry and his two friends visited the Forge, the local hostelry, these two were always there. They were regulars, bar-worthies who invariably propped up the bar.

Bob and Gus were pragmatically dressed for the terrain and time of year. Mind you, in the pub, they still wore their same working attire. It was that sort of watering hole, and they were that sort of people.

The three men in the distance all held telescopically sighted rifles. Jess and Harry watched them contemplate the disappearing herd and their prized trophy, which had now caught up with the hindmost. The two poachers continued to remonstrate with each other. The short, fat man held up his hands and pointed in the rough direction of Harry and Jess, the source of the gunshots.

The third man was three to four inches below Gus' six feet five inches and of medium build. He had the appearance of a rich visitor; expensive coat, breeks, boots, and rifle. All three stared toward Harry and Jess, who were invisible to their eyes, hidden in their hide. Their rich visitor seemed less distraught as he contemplated the direction of the two shots. He raised his powerful field binoculars to the source of the gunfire.

If the man cared to look past Harry and Jess, he'd have been able to see the B&B that was now their new, albeit temporary, home. It was some three miles distant. To the right and below the three men, the loch stretched out below, ending at the home of Harry, Jess, and Tom. On crisp mornings like this, when Harry was out here running, he'd sometimes stop and take in the glorious scenery. It was so different from the noise and dirt of their earlier city life.

The three men had given up trying to identify those who'd interrupted their sport. Their quarry had gone too far for comfort. So, the three men trudged despondently back to the track where Fat Bob's decrepit Landrover was parked.

Harry assumed they, or rather Bob's and Gus' customer, needed something warm inside and around him. Lying on the cold, frost-covered ground for more than a few minutes was hard, even on the toughest and most appropriately dressed hunter. The three men had been there for almost half an hour. Harry and Jess had arrived before them and saw their arrival.

They waited until the three men had long gone before they packed up and headed home. Looking towards their home in the distance, they could see the white smoke rising from the remnants of last night's log fire. While the light of sunrise was sufficient to give them a view of their house, it was helped by the lights in the windows. Tom was already up and would have a hot breakfast awaiting their return.

Today's exercise couldn't have gone better. Jessica was under pressure to save the stag. She needed to make the first shot before the poachers could fire. With the stag on the move, her second shot was much harder. She needed intense speed and concentration to force the stag to speed up and turn it toward the herd.

Harry was proud of her.

Before they headed home, Harry took one final look at where the three men once stood. From there, it was a perfect view of their house.

2. TAIGH LOCHA

Harry Logan, plus his two friends, the siblings Jess and Tom Lloyd, were approaching the end of their first six months running their Bed and Breakfast business in the Scottish Highlands.

Winter had been vicious, thankfully.

It had snowed over the Christmas and winter half-terms, blocking roads and access. The recent Easter break was just as inhospitable. It had snowed. Then, incessant rain, melting the snow, washed away tracks, even causing minor avalanches that blocked roads.

As a result, they'd had no guests to bring in any income. Even better!

When they arrived over five months ago, it was the onset of winter. At that time, the bad weather was coming in fast. They needed to ensure the property was weatherproof and they had sufficient provisions for the forthcoming weather; winter was on its way.

And now, here they were, May was a couple of weeks away. The harsh, austere white and brown landscape had already started its annual change into the greens, browns, and purples of the hillside foliage. The loch, which their large house overlooked, had also changed colour. Gone were the dark shades of grey, with its short, sharp wavelets. Now, there were lighter hues, even blue at times, reflecting the clearer skies in the increasingly glassy water.

The improving weather would soon bring tourists, the secondary industry in this area next to livestock farming.

The locals were readying their rental rooms and properties for the soon-to-come influx of people, assuming the weather held.

Harry, Tom, and Jess had leased their lochside B&B on a three-year agreement. Any shorter would beg the question of why. Any longer would have been a waste of money; not that they were short of a bob-or-two, to use the phrase of the older locals. In truth, they were quite well off.

And yes, Taigh Locha is a rather twee name. However, the tourists, mainly from the Scottish lowlands and England, loved the idea of the name. It translated to English as 'Loch House'. The three merely referred to it as the Taigh, as did the locals.

The three newcomers had chosen this location, by the loch and mountains, for its solitude. It was quiet with little passing trade. There was no through road or any way to circumnavigate the loch except by foot. The road that passed their B&B turned into a single track 100m past the house. It ended about 300m further on, partly round the side of the loch, and still visible from the house. The house's occupants could see what people were doing there. And that was important.

Across the road from the Taigh, lay the four-mile-long loch, on the smaller side by Scottish standards. The house's wide living room bay window offered a stunning view of the loch, adjacent hills, and adjoining small side glens. During the very short and cold winter days, Harry and sometimes the other two would sit and admire the free landscape view. It was at these times Harry wished he could paint. So, he dabbled, mostly unsuccessfully. It was, however, a therapeutic release.

Jess, ever the wind-up merchant, hung his first attempt in the hallway. It was a reminder of his lack of prowess. "This is your starting effort." She replayed one of Harry's favourite sayings. "You have to start somewhere, and knowing where you've come from and where you want to be helps you plan how to get there." To Jess, those words were most profound, helping her rationalise her past to where she was now.

Whatever the case, he dared not take it down to incur that withering Jess look.

A forthcoming painting group had booked out most of the loch-view rooms to capture that view and others. Jess had him sucked into those sessions, assuming they'd still be there, which was most unlikely.

Like many inland lochs, theirs was effectively a widened part of the river that flowed into it at one end and out at the other. The loch was almost 1km at its widest. The fresh running water brought nutrients from the mountains, making the loch live with marine life. So, the fishing was excellent.

The walking around the hills and glens around Taigh was stunning. For the less experienced rambler, it was a godsend. Lower down, there were many easy and well-signposted tracks to follow. The previous tenant had made every effort to make this location a novice rambler's dream.

Higher up the sides of the valley was for the more experienced walker-cum-hiker. There were deep rock-sided gullies and steep hillsides, reached via paths strewn with loose stones and rocks. If that wasn't bad enough, then there was the weather. It could turn nasty, seemingly without notice. A pleasant hike to the top of the hills could quickly turn a challenging walk into a difficult one, sometimes dangerously impossible.

So, for people who wanted an escape into the fresh air and enjoy beautiful and rugged scenery, there was something for most preferences. Since the property was off the beaten track, there was little or no passing trade. Visitors had to make a point of coming, whether to fish, paint, walk, or whatever was their objective. And that was perfect for the trio.

The other side of the loch had a narrow, single-lane road with passing places to reach the main road at the far end of the loch. For anyone intending to reach that main road, it would be quickest to travel the eight miles to the village and then take the 'B' road. Harry drove the lochside route once. It was slow, with steep cliff-like sides, down to the loch. It was a challenging and slow journey. So, few ventured up that narrow road, even though the scenery was not to be missed. However, this area was an integral part of his daily runs.

The Taigh's top floor was a self-contained flat created from a loft conversion in the late 1980s. It freed the three bedrooms on the first floor to become guest rooms for the then-new B&B. At that time, over thirty years earlier, the shared bathroom on the 1st floor was acceptable; to most people anyway.

Over the intervening years, previous owners and tenants had converted the old barn on the western side of the property into two ensuite bedrooms sharing a small kitchen. Similarly, an outhouse at the rear of the property had been converted into a self-contained one-bedroom cottage.

Nowadays, people prefer latrine and ablution privacy. So, the rooms in the house were backup accommodation. Harry, Tom, and Jess preferred the house for themselves, the accommodation layout being perfect for them.

During the almost six months of winter and early spring to date, they spread out. Jess enjoyed the freedom of her 2nd-floor apartment, and the two men each occupied a room on the 1st floor, sharing the bathroom; their ablution accessories were minimal.

However, when the larger group of 'elderly' ramblers would arrive, all three would have to move into the loft flat, with Tom and Harry bunking up in the same twin room. Poor Jess would have to share her ablution facilities, or was it poor Tom and Harry having to navigate around her 'stuff'?

Immediately in front of the house and across the road sat the loch-side wooden boathouse, which partially sat over the water. Inside were two wooden rowing boats and various fishing equipment. The lease banned them from using petrol-powered outboards on the loch, hence both boats being muscle-powered. It made no sense for them to invest in electric power since visitors were not put off by having to row. Also, as part of their lease, they had fishing rights for the loch.

Wholly separate from their house lease, Tom had rented a small, dilapidated farm cottage; pretty much a ruin. There were many old houses-cum-crofts in this area, which, for whatever reason, the previous owners had given up. Theirs was just off the road from the 'toon', two miles away from their house.

It was their emergency secure backup retreat. A major reason for this property choice was that they could access it via a hidden track that ran behind a hill and parallel to the main road.

At the start of their time there, they'd made a concealed, secure, underground room, provisioned for a month with water and food. Should the worst happen, this place would permit them to hide undetected.

It had ventilation, internet access, and cameras inside and out. It was secure from the outside and also from the inside. They had to prepare for all eventualities. The locals naturally assumed that their building material purchases were preparations for the forthcoming tourist season. They used out-of-region labour for the heavy work.

Taigh Locha was exposed to the worst of the winter elements and not a place to visit at that time for anyone with any sense. So, the building and preparation work went on without fuss or interruption.

From previous records, they knew the improving weather would bring people. The B&B, with its surrounding area, was an attractive proposition.

And, for the threesome, preparations were indeed in their final stages. However, it was for their departure. They didn't do sought-after locations, which this place could be in the good weather. They needed to avoid the impending tourist-ridden spring and summer period.

Harry was on the run from his masters, the pseudo-authorities, and several criminal organisations. His two companions joined him in his escape plan to put life on the street behind them. He owed them and loved them as family, but they were his Achilles Heel. If any of those hunting him caught his scent, they'd almost certainly use them to get to him. It was also why they were undergoing self-preservation training.

Harry was military-trained. He was a planner, a strategist, a thinker, one who could outwit and out-think his opponents. As a soldier, that free-thinking combination of skills and abilities made him dangerous to them under their rigid rules and hierarchy.

For his recent quasi-military-governmental masters, those natural abilities were perfect for their requirements. He also had an innate fighting ability to read situations, minds, expressions, and slight nuances in body movement that gave away intentions. His masters' expensive and intensive training honed those natural talents. And he needed them to survive where they sent him.

While under the innocuous role of an army logistics pen-pusher, Harry had a parallel life. He was their most highly trained, covert services, deniable lone operator. He performed best when he was given a job without rules or boundaries. And that suited them perfectly.

He 'executed' the jobs demanded by his masters discreetly and successfully, albeit with some bumps and bodies in his wake. However, he operated to his rules, often to their annoyance. But they'd learned to accept the operator they'd created, warts and all.

Being a child of missionary parents, who taught him honour, care, and right from wrong, had given him a moral baseline. Their demise drove him to the military. And while in the military, experiencing the extremes of life and death, his role conflicted with that baseline, creating in him an internal conflict. That baseline surfaced, and he'd had enough of killing on demand. And that's why he was here, in hiding.

Knowing too much to be allowed to exist as an outsider, Logan's pseudo-governmental masters wanted him back. They would do whatever was necessary to achieve that goal.

In addition to his ex-masters, Albatross Tactical Security, or ATS as was its most common nickname, also wanted him in their sights. ATS was a western headquartered, quasi-military security organisation. It and its people had a notorious reputation. It had justifiably been blamed for many atrocities across the world. It was a pariah in the eyes of the global security circles and by the ever-watchful yet impotent regulation and monitoring organisations.

However, perception depends on what side of the fence you sit. Its customers, usually second and third-world governments, considered their services a necessary evil. Western governments officially shied away from using ATS. It was, however, protected; international politics is all.

Harry had interfered in its activities. Elements within ATS wanted him dead, ideally after a 'chat'; but not necessarily.

And let's not forget those criminal organisations that would have loved to find him and have a similar 'conversation'.

Their first six-month stint at Taigh Locha was coming to a close. They were almost ready for phase two of their escape plan.

Who would think these escapees would be crazy enough to remain in the UK and operate a B&B under their masters' noses? It was risky being open to the public. That's what Harry had planned on.

If controlled, remote, and at the wrong time of year, it would be less prone to gossip than hiding in a house. So far, all had gone to plan. There were no signs anyone had recognised them here.

3. ANTI-GUEST PREPARATIONS

To date, the only direct and external interaction they'd had was a grandfather-son-grandson fishing group, who arrived the previous weekend for a day's fishing. The weather had sufficiently subsided for them to venture out to become their first ad-hoc arrivals.

The visiting fishing trio had been so elated by the success of their day's fishing that they gave the threesome one of their catch, a large pike, as a thank-you for using their facilities. Pike is not an attractive fish. However, in the hands of Thomas Lloyd who'd recently come to learn he was a dab hand in the kitchen, it turned into a gourmet meal.

During the recent inclement Easter break, they'd the occasional carload of families who had ventured out and became lost. It was easy on these roads, especially when some were still closed. Tom had checked out the three fishermen and those passers-by; their credentials came up as innocent. Apart from those few, the binoculars and spotting scopes rarely came out of their cases.

Harry knew this would soon change. All were surprised not to at least have seen more walkers or fishermen venturing out for them to be surreptitiously scrutinised. So far, the inclement weather had been on their side.

There was another reason for the lack of visitors. And that was down to the ministrations of Tom and Jess. In particular, Jess was a maestro at anti-social media and de-marketing. If there was the slightest question about potential visitors, her skills would come to the fore. She'd become adept at ineptly dropping comments about their issues into telephone and social conversations. Jessica Lloyd could dissuade even the most enthusiastic of potential visitors. To one stubborn potential guest, the reference to cleared-up infestations finally did the trick.

There'd been numerous enquiries over the winter. Some had been from previous guests wishing to return. Other requests had come from online review sites that still held the ratings and related comments from the previous occupants. The threesome could only operate this interference for a limited period before suspicions arose. So, they started accepting the most innocuous guests once the siblings' in-depth research had been satisfied.

Their first guests comprised nursing graduates from Edinburgh University who would arrive late that afternoon, perhaps early evening. A week later, walkers from a well-known Glasgow ramblers association would descend upon them. After them, there was a steady stream of guests looking for the fishing, walking, and peace and solitude the Taigh and its surroundings offered.

All bookings had perfect social media credentials, from the threesome's perspective anyway. Their first batch of sanitised visitors were three young women of not much more than Jess' age, who'd just graduated from their nursing courses. They were taking time out before starting their new posts.

The three new B&B-ers had to learn their trade, so these arrivals were particularly scrutinised and passed with flying colours. As ex-students, they'd hopefully not be prima donnas demanding the highest standards of cuisine and attention. And nothing on their heavily used social platforms suggested otherwise.

Tom was particularly keen on scrutinising this group. Apart from his sister, Tom hadn't interacted with another young woman in six months, let alone socialising with a group of them in a confined place.

Jess took great delight in winding him up. "What's about buxom Maggie in the Forge? She's got her eyes on you."

"No way! She puts the fear of god into me!"

Jess would continue with, "and there's that nice girl in the supermarket. She always goes googly-eyed when she sees you."

He'd reply with, "no way am I getting involved with that scrawny, pimply shop assistant. And even if I did find anyone, we're off soon. Now, those three nurses are different. I could suffer the wrath of Harry for an interlude with one or all of them."

"Are you still fantasising about nurses? Thought you gotten over that in your own pimply youth."

He grinned in response. He was in fantasy heaven.

It was Jess who'd picked up the nurses' first inquiry a few days earlier. She excitedly started re-checking their profiles since she was also keen on their company. However, hers was a wholly different agenda from Tom's. She was desperate for normal female chit-chat.

Seeing who she was scrutinising, Tom nudged her over. He justified his actions with a, "for our safety, of course, want to avoid your pro-feminine bias." He then embarked on his intense investigation of their visitors-to-be.

They were excellent from Tom's perspective. At least two were definitely heterosexual. "A heaven-sent offering and good enough for me," he espoused to the others when their visit was confirmed by Jess, not him. She'd dug him hard in the ribs to retain her rightful position on the chair.

For some reason, Tom wasn't as excited about the next arrivals, to whom he referred as, "elderly and doddery ramblers," when he saw they were in their 50s and 60s. "Probably into Morris Dancing, gin rummy, and folk music," he grumped at the other two.

As their departure from their current spell at the Taigh approached, the B&B started to generate a lot of interest. They'd hopefully be long gone by the time the season kicked in. And no, they would not notify the guests well in advance. There could be no external knowledge of their departure; just in case. Obviously, they'd return guests' deposits before their holidays, as well as generous compensation.

The lives of the three depended on a fast and confused exit, so they had no alternative. That time was soon coming, in less than two weeks, hopefully sooner.

Another of Tom's contributions to the trio was their identities. He'd created their new identities for this location and was finalising their new ones for when they were to leave at the end of the month, April.

Harry was somewhat anxious about the delay. He knew from experience that new identities took time. It wasn't just a matter of walking into a seedy backstreet room where some old bespectacled man would take photographs and issue the documentation. These days, everyone's life is online. Many of today's youth live in that virtual world. So, it took time for Tom to create and build out their new personas in support of their new identities.

Harry's name, while living at the Taigh, was Barrie Greywell. This identity gave him a son and daughter in the guise of Ronald (as was Tom) and Tessa (as was Jessica). Of course, the names were similar and done to help the two siblings more easily stay on-story.

A greyed stubble and hair were all it took to add more than ten years to Harry's thirty-seven years. His glasses, used while in public, had the effect of surreptitiously covering his upper face. It was an easy-to-maintain new look.

There was no need to have Tom and Jess in any form of disguise. As far as those hunting Harry were concerned, these two were pretty much off-the-grid.

There was another downside to the imminent arrival of guests. Tom had found a new love while living here. He'd become adept at "that cheffing lark," as Harry called it. Unfortunately, those new skills would have to be put on the back burner when guests arrived. It would be disastrous for the trio to be exposed by an ecstatic guest taking selfies of his food and with the chef. While they had guests, all of them would have to suffer the bland B&B fare their visitors would expect.

But all were agreed, he was a damned good cook, and they ate very well indeed; at least so far.

4. SELF-PRESERVATION

Everything security was down to Harry. But the kids needed to play their part and were learning well. Tom was a natural and fast. While he'd readily picked up the fighting techniques, he was the less enthusiastic fighter of the two. "I'm more a lover than a fighter," he had a want to say.

Jess was nimble and agile, keenly picking up this fighting 'game' as she called it. Jess was the more vicious of the two, and there was the assumption from all three that she would be Harry's natural backup should the need arise.

Harry was an early riser. First job of the day after a light breakfast was his crack-of-dawn hill run. In almost all weathers, he would be out on patrol.

Hill running is hard, especially for someone with his physique. His body naturally lent itself to power, sprint, and stop-start activities, which was where he focussed his training. He was heavy for his above-average height. Little of that was body fat. It was all unobtrusive muscle.

He knew he had to use caution during his twice-daily, five-mile half-circle of the house runs at dawn and dusk. In that terrain, it would be so easy to pull a muscle or twist a joint.

As well as keeping himself fit, those runs were a perfect way to monitor the goings-on around the property's peripheries. He could identify signs in advance of people watching them. No matter how well dug in, they would leave evidence of their presence. After all, it's what he'd been trained to do, and he knew what to look for.

There would be specific locations that professionals would use, and others that amateurs would choose for less than optimal reasons. He checked them all as part of his routine.

On his return from the morning run, there was the mandatory session in the B&B's gym with the kids, as he jokingly called them.

Tom had converted an unused outbuilding before their 'D-day' flight to the Taigh. He'd also arranged for the training equipment they'd need. The most important part of the siblings' training was on the large mat. It was there that Harry trained his pupils in the basics of self-preservation.

Their training wasn't self-defence. That was too limiting for their requirements. Harry emphasised the single most important principle ingrained in him from the off. In a brawl, there were **NO** Queensbury Rules. There was only survival and walking away; perhaps limping or crawling if that's what you could only do. But your opponent stays, no matter the cost, ideally with the least amount of injury.

The siblings were naturally petite. No matter what bodybuilding exercises he gave them, their small frames were not built for strength. Over the past six months, Jess had taken their training to heart, never again to be on the receiving end of others' abuse and fantasies. Tom's agenda was initially straightforward. He wanted to learn as much as he could to protect Jess. He soon concluded it might well be his sister who'd end up protecting him. However, he keenly participated in their sessions and became most proficient in the techniques.

Despite their size, Tom and Jess had to be skilled in close combat, which meant weaponry, in particular, knives. Tom's weapon of choice was his discreet wrist knives. Sometimes called assassin knives, these were retractable knives strapped to the underside of his wrists. The long blades sprung in and out by wrist action.

Harry always wondered if Tom would have the killer instinct to use them.

Jess' preferred close combat weapon was a variation of the Fairbairn Sykes British Commando Dagger, a one-inch shorter blade and handle. She also carried 'Mousey' with her, a short EDC knife, which she concealed in an ankle or thigh sheath. Both had different uses and with Harry's guidance, she became adept with both.

Harry had no fears about her willingness to use these weapons, or any of their others, when necessary. His fear was her ability to control her emotions in a fight, and control.

For most, their small frames were an obvious disadvantage in combat. However, Harry turned that negative into a positive, which together, they built on. Just looking at them, an attacker would be over-confident. That was the siblings' edge. The two had learned their little-lost-boy-and-girl look on the street, honing it into an art. Being outwardly pathetic and terrified should give them a chance if the worst happens.

If they saw an opportunity to fight back, their response had to be fast, vicious, and deadly. Only then, could their lack of size and strength overcome brute force and training; surprise and technique were paramount. They wouldn't get a second chance.

One situation they worked on was an attacker grabbing from behind. With Jess, they'd most likely wrap their arms around her chest and lift her level without stooping. More likely than not, if a male, and usually they would be, they'd take advantage of the opportunity to have a grope of her breasts. He taught her to go limp with affected fear while looking around for something sharp, heavy, or both.

Invariably, there'd be a reason to move her. Once close to an object, he taught her how to prise open holds and attack without quarter. They practiced stamping on or kicking ankles and toes, scoring heels down shins and knees, biting hard to draw blood, backward head-butting, and more, preferably all together, and fast. She'd use anything and everything to make the attacker loosen their hold, if only for a moment. She'd squirm her body position, making it difficult for the attacker to continue with the same hold.

The attacker was now at a disadvantage, if only fleetingly. Then she'd grab that chosen attack object and strike out repeatedly until the attacker was dead or completely disabled. Stunning an attacker and then running away was for a victim of a street crime. It would be professionals they'd face. So, they had to be professional, decisive, and deadly.

The dynamics with Tom would be somewhat different. Being male, attackers would view him as being more likely to cause trouble. So, he should put up a feeble, untrained struggle, then capitulate, perhaps whimper, even cry from the pain they'd inflicted. The attacker would be self-assured. Then their well-rehearsed training techniques would kick in.

Jess was the most adept at picking up these techniques. She proved herself to be ferocious. Harry assumed one of the reasons for her enthusiasm was her playing out, in her mind, her past encounters. Harry focused her ingrained anger, which sometimes quickly surfaced, to be her strongest weapon, not her downfall.

Tom, the gentler of the two, was more reticent, but he tried his best and picked up the techniques, albeit without the enthusiasm and gusto of his sister.

They could only get better over time, but right now, anything would be of help should the worst happen.

****

After their usual post-training sessions, the three would have breakfast in the large kitchen. That morning, they discussed their getaway status before their first arrivals appeared. Tom went through their new identities with them. He'd already built each of them a social media following.

Harry had to remind the siblings, "visitors today, so please remember, both of you." He looked at Jess, "you're Tessa, or Tess from now on. And you," he turned to Tom, "are now Ronald or Ron."

"Yeh, yeh, we know," defended Jess.

"I'm sorry to belabour the point, but for the first time in almost five months, people will live with us, and we have to be vigilant. We can't drop the pseudonyms even in the house amongst ourselves. Remember, I'm your father Barrie Greywell, dad to you two. So, Tess," he said with emphasis, "are we ready for our first visitors?"

Jess, now to be Tessa, gave an update on the three ex-student nurses. She took that group on, not only to wind up her brother but because they were of a similar age to her, albeit a year or two older. She'd built up a rapport with them via the several social media channels they frequented. Everything was ready for the three women to arrive later that afternoon. Their three guests, Susan, Elizabeth, and Karen, would share the outside cottage.

From what Jess had told Harry and Tom, Susan was the organiser. She was the one who liaised with Jess and did most of the talking and online chat interaction.

Harry had to comment, in a pretend uncle-ish sort of way, about the blond, chatty Susan. "She's the figure of one who likes sports. Actually, quite attractive for a kid."

"Back off, old man," retorted a grinning Tom. He had no pretence of a brotherly relationship with her or the others.

Harry then took a backseat to the discussions, happy to have the 'kids' take the lead.

"Elizabeth's the dumpy one, isn't she?" queried Tom, which necessitated a hard thump from Jess.

"She's lovely, you sod!"

"Only joking," he chuckled. "She's female and breathing. And in my state of desperation, she's good enough for me." He dodged Jess' follow-up strike, and justified his comments by, "I've been cooped up with you for six months and desperate for a 'normal' woman to visit." Tom winced from the strike of the third blow, having now painfully figured out the second was a feint. He withdrew out of reach from any others about to head his way.

'Harry's taught her well.'

Jess had the final say about them. "Karen's profile suggests a quieter, studious character. While Elizabeth invariably took part in the chat and banter between Susan and me, Karen mostly kept her own counsel."

Harry looked over to Tom to explain the next group of arrivals, the three 'doddery' couples, as referred to by Tom, who would arrive the following weekend. The group was down for a week of rambling. The group was too large to be housed outside the main house, so some would occupy the first-floor rooms.

"Done some research on the oldies, but it was tough. Most have an active social media presence but to varying degrees. The old guy, the one with the beard," Tom showed a picture of the grizzled face, who was once a smart and published academic, "now he's the most active online. For an old duffer, he's quite an interesting bloke. The others have accounts, but their postings are all about grandchildren and pictures of their walks. And they do like their post-walk boozing. I expect they'll end up at Forge most nights.

Lucky them."

Harry chipped in. "Be careful when they're around, keep out of their pictures. You don't know who might be on their extended contacts list."

Tom's and Jess' profile pictures were anime caricatures. Harry's was just a picture of the loch from the house.

5. FIRST GUESTS

The three young women, the ex-nursing students, arrived in an old beaten-up transit van. It was their simple accommodation during their travels, helping eke out their limited funds. However, every so often, they needed an element of civilization, hot showers, and comfortable beds. That's why they booked into the B&B for one night. Also, being out of season, Taigh Locha was cheap.

Tom, now officially Ron, almost drooled over Susan when they arrived; she loved the attention.

The three women greeted Jess like a long-lost friend, with hugs and laughing all around. Jess introduced her 'family'. "Our every-so-grumpy dad, Barrie, and you've already met my bother, Ron, online."

The two men received from each a, "Hi, I'm Susan Davidson, I'm Elizabeth Swan, I'm Karen James" The three women formally shook hands with Harry. All politely called him Mr Greywell.

Susan, the most vivacious of the three guests, kissed Tom on the cheek. The others shook his hand.

Now seeing them in the flesh, so to speak, and watching their behaviour, Harry could see the different characters Jess explained. Susan was as expected. She was a strong character, the exuberant one, and definitely the group leader.

Karen seemed to be the easy-going one of the three. She was a pleasant young woman who always seemed to find the right words to make people feel at ease. If Harry wasn't in his 'uncle mode' she was one he might like, obviously if she was a few years older. He preferred her dark-haired, sharp features to that of her bleach-blond friend, Susan.

Elizabeth was a bubbly character who seemed to like everything and everyone. Tom was also starting to warm to her.

Whatever they thought about their visitors, they needed to stay on their toes for the next couple of days.

Once eating preferences and other preliminaries were discussed, the three women went off with Jess to check out their accommodation.

"I think we've lost Tess for today," commented a smiling Tom, nodding after the four departing women; he remembered to use her pseudonym. In truth, he knew she needed these female visitors. "It's been hard for her cloistered with the two of us," commented Tom.

At that, Harry got up and made for the door. "I'll leave our visitors in both your safe hands while I'm off to get some groceries," announced Harry, waving the car keys. "Please don't drool too much onto the carpet while I'm away."

"Yeh, right," jokingly grumped Tom.

The local shop, eight miles back from where their visitors had come, had everything they needed for this evening's cottage pie and tomorrow's Scottish breakfast.

On his return, he found the five of them in the kitchen, chatting over Tom's cake and tea.

"So, from where do you hail, and what brings you here?" enquired Harry.

Before any of the women could respond, Jess interjected with, "they're doing the three Ws."

Harry looked at her, then their three guests questioningly.

The young women laughed. Susan piped up, "walking, wine, and whisky holiday. We dropped the fourth 'W', because your bloody loch's frozen."

"It was wonderful. We all had a dip while you were out," blurted out Elizabeth.

"Hence the need for hot tea and cakes to warm up my innards," grinned Karen.

In response to the other part of his question, Susan added, "I'm from Kirkcaldy, Elizabeth's from Paisley, and Karen's a Dundonian. We've lived in Scotland all our lives. We've all done Ibiza, the Costas, and Karen's even done the Riviera. We're Scottish, but none of us have done Scotland."

"University's drained us, and with nae money and three weeks before we start work," interposed Elizabeth, "it seemed a guid idea at the time. Actually, it's been great. Karen's brother was about to sell that van we came in, so we borrowed it for the holiday."

"Yeh," beamed Susan. "It's been brilliant! So far, at least. "We've been doing the Coast 500 route anti-clockwise. Your place is a wee bit off the track, but Jess did us a great deal. Tomorrow, we're off to Skye for a couple of days, finally finishing at the Trossachs."

"Then work," added Karen. "At last, we'll be earning money. I'm actually looking forward to it."

Susan retorted with a grin, "you would."

"You lucky buggers." Jess was envious. "I'm getting Taigh'd out! We've been so busy here preparing for the tourist season, I've not been further than the 'toon', as it's called here, and the hypermarket."

"What hypermarket?" queried Karen. "The only shop we've seen was the village off-licence miles back down the road."

"So, you've seen our hypermarket?" chuckled Jess to a

chorus of erupting laughter.

"Come with us," offered Susan. It doesn't need to be for more than a few days."

Elizabeth and Karen uncertainly looked at each other. Karen piped up, "we live rough, I'm not sure you'd like it. It's awfully cramped, with none of the luxuries you're used to."

Jess kept her thoughts to herself.

If only they knew where I was a year ago, what they've got is luxury.'

"Ach Karen, dinnae be such a stick-in-the-mud. Tessa's been with these fellas, stuck in this house for months. She needs woman talk!" Susan stared them into what seemed submission.

The other two smiled in resigned agreement. How could they say no?

When Jess again looked at Elizabeth and Karen for agreement, their smiles now included their faces. So that was that. Jess looked at Harry for a response.

Harry sensed something between the women. There was a form of tension for the offer, perhaps jealousy. He could see Jess had already bonded with Susan, perhaps to the chagrin of the others. Harry then looked at Tom, who nodded a yes.

"We're all good then," confirmed Harry to all. To Jess, he added, "we'll manage until Tom's group arrives. Go and enjoy yourself."

Susan leaned in and grabbed Jess as they engaged in a table-side up-and-down version of a group hug. The two others patted Jess' back, albeit with less enthusiasm. "That's wonderful Mr Greywell."

Karen still seemed hesitant and looked at Harry and Jess in turn. It was an uncomfortable look.

"You OK?" asked Harry.

Susan interjected into that mood. "If you want to know the truth, the tank's almost empty, and we were about to tap our parents for a few quid…"

Harry laughed.

Jess piped up, "don't worry, I'll pay my way. Looks like I can leave these two at last. And be with normal people, women."

The four women laughed.

Harry added. "That's settled then. Tessa, please be back by Friday. The ramblers arrive on Saturday. Even better, we'll message you a shopping list on your way back here."

The four young women leaped up. This time they performed a full-on group hug and screaming bounce. Jess fished out a bottle of prosecco to celebrate.

Harry couldn't disagree. She'd been doing so well. A few days with female company would do her the world of good. After being under the household and training regime, she now had an opportunity for a blowout.

In the back of Harry's mind was the concern about Jess getting back into drugs. She'd been clean for almost a year now. He had to trust her, as did Tom. Jess was her own woman, and all they'd done was enable her to become clean. It was down to her to stay clean. Jess would be safe with them since there was nothing in their profiles to suggest otherwise.

All the same, after the four women left for the privacy of their rooms, Harry got Tom to go through their profiles again. He even went so far as to make some spoof sales calls from a burner phone to their parents. All was clear and innocent.

He was more worried about the ramblers. The three women were off in the morning. But the ramblers would be there for a four-night long weekend. The three of them would have to be on their guard. The good thing was that they'd be off to their new location soon after. So, hopefully, any exposure or mistakes wouldn't impact their security; too much.

6. MOUNTAIN RULES

Next morning, the three visitors, plus Jess, would be off early; well, early for them at least. Harry would have been long back from his run to say goodbye to Jess. And he daren't be late.

The dawn air was crisp and clear when Harry set out for his run. A light mist hovered over the dark loch. The illumination from the now orange sun had already moved down from the top of the western hills and mountains. It slowly crept toward the bottom of the glen, bringing increasing light as it descended. During his run, the low light of the early dawn grew in intensity, adding shadows, reflections, and colours that reflected over the still loch.

The outlook over the loch, the hills at its side, and the mountains in the distance lifted Harry's heart as he set off. It was an almost clear sky; today would be a glorious run.

About fifteen minutes into his run, he came upon a flock of sheep nonchalantly grazing amongst the heather. During Harry's daily dawn and dusk runs, he often met the local shepherd who kept sheep on the hillsides around the loch. Everyone knew him as 'Auld Wullie the herder' to differentiate him from the other Auld Wullies in the area. In his local, the Forge, he was just Auld Wullie. William McDonald was the only old person with that forename who frequented that pub, so the addition of 'the herder' wasn't necessary there.

When Harry first arrived at his new home here and was out on his runs, the herder didn't offer much more than a grunt of acknowledgement. Harry knew it wasn't out of rudeness or meanness, for which the Scots have an unwarranted reputation. But, when you're poor, and life is hard, you have to be frugal and careful with every penny. That behaviour is not being mean, merely prudence. And, especially around here, there were some very poor, hard-working people.

Nothing is ever wasted!

* Over the weeks, Harry and Wullie transitioned to nodding terms. Once, when Harry was caught in a squall, Auld Wullie and his dog invited Harry to share their makeshift shelter. Although Wullie was poor, highland hospitality required that he share his food with his guest, although that would leave him short. Wullie would not accept any refusal. Few words were spoken at that first meeting. Auld Wullie wasn't one for unnecessary conversation, as he said. Harry was later to find out differently.

After a few further encounters, and knowing that Harry was a regular up there, Auld Wullie made sure he now had an extra cuppa plus a bannock, slice of porridge, or other edible to share for a bit of company and tittle-tattle. Initially, without spare food, he couldn't invite Harry to stop for a 'blether'. Now with sufficient food and drink to be hospitable, he could at last be welcoming to the newcomer.

In return, Harry ensured he brought some food scraps for Wullie's dog. It suited Harry to stumble across the old herder. The man who insisted he didn't like tittle-tattle, loved to gossip. And Harry soon found out that the lonely herder was a useful source of what was happening around them. Through this old man, he could capture all the salient pieces of information without the need to venture too far from their house, well, not too often anyway.

After all their meetings, Harry recognised these sheep as

being Wullie's. Normally, he'd spot the herder in a prominent position overlooking his animals. However, today, there was no sign of him.

Harry continued his run, expecting to come upon the auld man at any time. He wasn't there. Wullie had been herding sheep for longer than Harry had years and knew every nook and cranny of these hillsides. However, he was old, and anything could have happened. Harry continued his run up the hill, becoming more anxious. He'd never seen Wullie's flock without him around. Even worse, Wullie's dog was nowhere to be seen.

He could hear a faint bleating. It sounded like a hurt animal. There were eagles here and other predators, and he didn't interfere with the course of nature. For many, non-interference was cruel, but his parents instilled a leave-nature-well-alone-philosophy in him.

He cautiously approached the crest. He knew there was a cliff edge at the top with a one-hundred-foot drop below. At the top of the rise, he saw Wullie tying off a rope to his quad bike. His dog sat patiently by the bike. Wullie was readying to make the climb down the cliff face.

Now closer, Harry could hear the bleating of a sheep in pain coming from over the edge,

Wullie grunted acknowledgement to Harry as he readied himself for the climb down as if this was an everyday occurrence. The old man never thought to ask Harry to descend in his place. These were his sheep and his responsibility.

Harry suspected Wullie was in his late 60s or early 70s, and what he was about to do was dangerous, even for a young man. "Fallen?"

"Yep."

"Can I help?"

"Nah, 'em good."

"Euthanase her?"

The old man nodded. Harry could see the sadness in the man's eyes. Not just from the loss of earnings, but his flock was his life.

Harry, ever the soft touch, held out his hands for the rope. "Better I do this. My father was a vet, my mother a doctor, and I helped a lot. Done the deed more times than I could remember. And while you might disagree, I'm more able to climb down there."

Harry had told the truth about his parents' jobs and his helping them. It was also true that he was a multiple killer. However, the killing of animals was far from the truth. Dispatching humans when the need arose was easy. But an innocent animal was a different ballgame. He'd not exactly lied about that, but the implication was there.

"Nah, 'em good laddie. Can't be having you doin' meh job."

Harry wasn't having this old man climbing down, so he tried business logic. "And if anything happened to you, who look after your flock? Anyway, I could do with the exercise."

And Wullie was no fool. At his age, he knew that climb was risky. He capitulated to Harry's reasoning, handed over the rope, and offered over a large hunting knife.

Harry refused the knife. He tapped his custom handmade karambit knife he'd picked up while in the Middle East. The sharp curved blade was made from Damascus steel and sat in a leather sheath knife always strapped to his arm when he was out. Because, you never know.

Harry climbed down. When he reached about twenty-five feet, he landed on a wide ledge. Close to the cliff wall, he saw the ewe. It hadn't yet been shorn. Its heavy, thick coat had taken the brunt of the fall. Sadly, its left front leg

45

pointed awkwardly away from its body. There's no luxury of vets and treatment here in the hills, and this ewe was not a prize-winner. Animals were not allowed to suffer here.

It would be too costly for the poor shepherd to fix a broken leg. Auld Wullie knew this. The best solution would be a quick death. He assumed Wullie could recoup some of his lost income from the illegal sale of unregistered mutton and a little from the fleece.

Harry did what he needed to do. It wasn't as easy as he thought it would be. A long, loud howl of pain from the injured sheep echoed around the glen, seemingly taking ages to die down, and then all was silent.

From above, Wullie heard the sheep's distress. A tear rolled down the shepherd's eyes. He shouted down. "Wit's takin' ye so lang, laddie?" The kill needed to be quick, and this newcomer was making his ewe suffer. He should have done the job himself.

"Just tying it up now," shouted Harry from below.

A few moments later, Harry appeared over the edge. "Let's hoist her up."

The shepherd looked at Harry in anger. There should have been blood on him from slitting the sheep's throat. "Ye couldn't dae it, could ye? Ye saft bastard. Noo she'll suffer even more."

"I know, sorry." Harry looked away. There was nothing he could say in response.

"Gentle now," as they both took the strain and raised the injured ewe. Harry estimated the ewe to be about 80kg. Using the quad bike as an anchor and with the 2:1 block and tackle, the lift was easier but still hard. Harry wondered how Wullie would have managed alone.

The sheep bleated from below as the two men carefully raised her. Tears rolled down Wullie's eyes every time she bleated. He knew every jar they made while pulling her up made the pain worse. At last, the sheep appeared at the cliff edge. They gently manhandled her over, then dragged her away from further danger before Harry loosened the rope.

The ewe looked at Harry. Was it his imagination, or did the ewe smile at him? She had an agenda. Ignoring the two men, she got up. And with a slight limp, she walked toward the flock. She spied a luscious clump of tasty grass, stopped, then started to munch without a care in the world.

A great weight lifted from Wullie, his hunched shoulders lifted. He grinned for the first time since Harry had known him. "Ya wee shite, why'd you no' tell us."

Harry shrugged his shoulders and grinned. "Badly dislocated front leg. Reset it. I forgot how hard it could be. Anyway, a bit of rest, and she'll be fine."

"Coffee laddie?"

Harry couldn't refuse. He knew the old man needed to thank him in his way. He looked at his watch and inwardly cursed. Jess would already have left by now.

'Ah well, I'm in trouble already when she gets back, so a bit of catching up with the old fella won't go amiss.'

They both sat on a large boulder while Wullie undid his flask and poured each of them a cup of steaming coffee.

Harry didn't feel the cold while running, and during that descent, working on the sheep, then ascent. Now sitting here, he shivered. It was a little colder than usual. The hot brew warmed his cupped hands, then his insides as it slid down. He looked at the shepherd. There was the usual odd, yet not unpleasant, taste, but it was stronger today.

Wullie saw the look. "Ah, Jeanie, the missus always adds a wee bit extra on cold mornings like this." He gave the hint of a conspiratorial smile.

Harry had his suspicions the wee dram had been locally made, definitely not bought; well, not from a registered retailer. They made small talk as they drank and ate a slice of porridge Wullie shared with Harry.

"Naebody kens a lot aboot you a' by the loch. They're a'ways gassin' aboot ye doon the Forge."

Harry, Jess, and Tom occasionally ventured out for a quiet drink when their own company became too much. The threesome lived about eight miles away from the Forge, the nearest pub, and the area's nightlife. It sat in the centre of what the locals referred to as the toon (more a village than a town).

When they occasionally popped into the Forge, Harry ensured Wullie got a pint o' heavy and a wee swally (a pint of bitter and a whiskey chaser to any non-Scots).

Many of the Forge's locals drove several miles for a social drink, "aff doon the road fir a pint," they'd announce to their wives.

And since there was little traffic on the roads, the likelihood of an occasional drunken accident was rare. Maggie, the matriarchal landlady, knew her business. For those who over-imbibed to being incapacitated, which was not unusual, she'd take their car keys. There'd always be another, less drunken member who'd drive the drunk home. That also meant the local police didn't worry about drunken drivers; unofficially, of course.

The next morning, when a bleary-eyed worthy arrived to pick up his transport, it wasn't rare for him to be sporting a black eye or other injuries from 'walking into a door'. Partners sometimes had no sense of understanding.

Harry brought his thoughts back to the present. "Why would they be talking about us?" he asked. Being recent incomers to the area, Harry knew they were a source of intrigue for the locals, as long as the gossip remained local. So, he just tested the feedback from Wullie.

"Ach, folk like tae blether when there's nothin' else t'

dae." Then he remembered to slow the delivery of his sanitised English for this incomer.

"There's no' any nastiness, just chit-chat." He grinned at Harry. "They all wonder why you strange English would rent a B&B at the onset of winter. I told them, I ken y'all well. It made sense to get everything done afore the tourists arrived. But they still blether on."

Harry grinned at the thought of them around the fire, finding things to talk about. When the three newcomers occasionally ventured into the local-ish village for supplies or even the occasional beverage, the friendly locals would invariably engage them in social interrogation, or, as they would call it, conversation.

Initially, it was, "whar ye frae?" questions about where they were from. Nowadays, it was more a, "how're ye doin'?" They felt the need to check on them, to keep an eye out for these outsiders. Life could be hard in this area during the winter.

Then there was the, "whar's yer faither," to Jess and Tom, asking about Harry, their 'father', when they ventured into the toon without him. In the same vein, they asked about the "wains" of Harry, in reference to his 'wee ains', or young ones.

With the nicest of smiles and fewest words, the newbies gave vague references to being from over the border, giving little away.

Wullie continued. "Now, you're no' interesting at all, and neither's the wee fella." Then he had a chuckle. "Saying that, our Maggie there would love tae get into his pants."

Harry joined in the laugh at the thought of poor Tom with Maggie.

"On the other hand, your wee lassie's a stunner an' far more interestin'. They're a' wonderin' if she was runnin' frae a bloke, maybe a model dryin' oot frae they drugs, even a mental-case hiding frae the doctors."

Wullie paused. He considered Harry for a moment, wondering whether he should say something. He decided he would. "I was doon the Forge a few days ago, and Fat Bob was complaining as usual. He told everyone some poachers buggered up a stag kill. "They were amateurs, couldn't shoot fir peanuts." His customer missed the opportunity of a prize kill. He said they cost him a fortune. But ye can't separate the truth from that man's lies."

Harry knew from experience at the pub that Bob would have used a tirade of expletives as he explained his tale of woe. Wullie was repeating a sanitised version of what was said.

Wullie continued his story. "Then Maggie piped up from behind the bar, "but you're a poacher, why're you whinging about others in the same trade?" Ye know our Maggie, she doesn't take prisoners and likes tae wind everybody up."

The herder chuckled, "Fat Bob told her, "this is my poaching territory. It's not for interlopers to be after my customer's trophy." An' Maggie responded. "Aye, yer right. That's terrible. We can't have that happenin' on your turf. It's just not right!""

"Bob let out a big sigh knowing she was on his side. Then she came out with the corker. "We need to tell the gillie about these poachers. And, even better, you and yer customer were witnesses. You all could point out these interlopers.""

"Fat Bob stammered and mumbled in his pint that he didn't see them. Everyone was pissin' themselves laughing."

"Then Gus, his mate, had to have his tuppence-worth. You know everyone calls him gangly cos he's a skinny bugger. He should be called Gormless Gus coz he hasn't got the brains he was born with. Anyway, he says, "Maggie's right Bob, we should tell the gillie. Those tossers what can't shoot fir peanuts cost us a fortune. He'll be in later, he'll sort it, he will." Then everyone looked at Bob."

"Then Bob says, "no we'll no' do that. We're not aboot to help the gillie. He's buggered us up loadsa times. Keep stumm, OK!" Then changing the topic, he held up his almost empty glass and said to Gus, "instead of blethering shite, your round.""

"Listening to all that talk, I was just thinking who those other poachers might be, or even if they were really poachers?" Wullie looked up at Harry and waited for his response.

Now it was Harry's turn to wonder. Was that a knowing twinkle in Wullie's eye?

'The old bugger doesn't miss a trick.'

Wullie broke the silence. "Those other people saved that stag's life. Been watching that auld stag turn to a Monarch, these months an' the years before. He's a wondrous creature. Glad the buggers didn't get a chance to kill it."

"Probably done a runner now since everyone knows what happened," mumbled Harry over a mouthful of scone.

"Aye." Wullie smirked. "Sayin' that, I often hear shooting in the hills and not the pop-guns the local poachers use. Takes me back to my army days." He glanced over at Harry. "I don't tell anyone what goes on up here, it's none o' my business." He then looked back at his sheep to check they were all good.

"Now here's the interestin' thing. I wis down the Forge a couple of days ago. Fat Bob and Gus were doon the pub again, this time they brought their customer, a posh English fella, the wan who never got the stag a couple of days ago. Their customer's been looking for some good fishing and accommodation and said he'd heard about your place. He wanted to know if we knew you and what you're all like."

"I told him you've a smashin' place there for visitors, your grub's great, and you've boats and gear."

"The posh bloke says in this very posh accent," that Wullie unsuccessfully tried to imitate, "thanks, it all sounds perfect. I shall definitely pop down there first thing tomorrow to check them out.""

"Bob said they'd take him an' he says "that's settled." An' that was that. You're all good." He then chuckled, "so all that business I've passed on to ye, we're now quits, eh?"

But, there'd been no business!

No one came to visit!

Harry thought back to the incident with Fat Bob and Gangly Gus with their customer. He and Jess had been tracking them, wondering why anyone would be interested in killing a stag when he'd lost his antlers. He had his suspicions, but there'd been no further incidents. While the location of Bob's and Gus' hide didn't give a direct view of the Taigh, standing up as they did afterward meant the house was in full view. He remembered those powerful field binoculars.

Stupid! Stupid! He was now in a panic!

Harry briefly thanked the old man for his hospitality and recommendation as he sprang up, then dashed back to Taigh Locha.

"Sassenachs, cannae fathom their minds," mumbled Wullie while he watched Harry sprint down the hill.

7. PANIC!

Harry called Jess from the small 2G mobile he always carried on these runs. Her phone rang out. He then tried Tom, who thankfully answered. "Everything OK there?"

"Why? What's happened? Are you OK? You sound breathless." It was rare for Harry to call while on his runs. With the agitation in Harry's voice, Tom began to feel worried.

Harry was no longer on his paced running patrol but heading back as fast as he could. So, he was breathless. "Has Jess gone? Her phone's ringing out!"

"Yep, already left, said she couldn't wait for you any longer. You're going face Medusa's wrath for not being here. Woe betide you when she gets back!"

"Tom, I think she might be in danger. If so, we all are!"

"What! Shit! She waited and waited for you to say goodbye. The girls said they needed to be off, so they just left, maybe 10 minutes ago."

"Get the car ready! I'm going after her. Get our things ready. D2 is now. I'll be with you in 10 minutes."

He hung up. He needed to focus and plan for the various contingencies. But there were too many unknowns buzzing around his head. He hated it when he wasn't in control. Now he'd have to have to wing it against whatever comes their way.

The old estate car awaited his arrival, engine running, the interior already warm. The 3.0i badge had been removed. To the untrained eye, it was an old jalopy. But this externally perceived rattle-trap could still top 140mph and had been discreetly modified to handle like a saloon track car.

"Tom, pack the emergency bags and get to the security bunker. I think we've been rumbled. I could be overreacting, and it might not be that bad. Or, it could be dangerous, depending on who they are. Get out fast!"

Tom ran back into the house to make preparations. Harry had seen no evidence of others around during his run back. So he knew Tom had some time, but how much was anyone's guess?

Harry jumped in and gunned the engine. The three women and Jess had a 15-20 minute head start. However, they were in an old, slow van that urgently needed petrol. They'd have stopped in the 'toon' garage for a fill-up. In his head, he calculated stopping time and perhaps buying some snacks. He'd not be far behind.

He called Jess' mobile again.

Tom answered. "Found it in the clothes bin. It could have been an accident while she packed, but she's usually more careful with her lifeline to the outside world. Jess and her mobile are never separated."

"Yep, a typical Generation Z," acknowledged Harry absentmindedly.

The news wasn't good, and he was becoming more certain something was wrong.

He pulled in at the local garage. Shuggie, the mechanic-assistant-cashier-attendant-owner told him they left 5 minutes ago. He had a big grin on his face. "They were a' giggling and laughing. Bought a load o' messages. Best sale in ages."

Harry never understood why 'messages' was used instead of groceries and why anyone called Hugh was nicknamed 'Shuggie'. When they'd first arrived, he just smiled in acceptance and went with the flow. Over time, he slowly managed to get some understanding of the local dialect, words, and expressions the more 'local' locals used. However, many explanations still eluded him.

"Jess left her phone, and I need to catch her. Which way did they go."

"Meh god!" exclaimed Shuggie bellowing with laughter. "Meh daughter'd go mental wi'oot her phone. Yid better catch 'em. Saw them take the right fork oot o' toon. Guid luck."

Harry was again off in a flash.

8. ABDUCTED

The four young women were having an exciting time chatting and exchanging banter. Susan drove, Elizabeth sat in the passenger seat, and Jess and Karen were in the back, propped against the side of the van. They used one of their mattresses as a combined seat and backrest.

After about one mile outside town, Susan announced, "I need a pee. Need to stop at the next lay-by, sorry girls."

"Peanut bladder!" retorted Jess from the back of the van. "Some of us had the sense to go before leaving."

"There's a sign," she enthusiastically announced and pointed, "and lay-by coming up, a bit desperate now."

Jess got up and looked over their shoulders to see where Susan planned to stop. "Susan, you can't stop here. There's a man smoking a ciggie next to his fancy car, he'll see you."

Karen also leaned over from the back, and looking through the passenger window as they passed the car and him, she laughed.

"What's so funny about Susan needing a pee?"

"Nah, nah," Karan laughed in between her words. "Have you seen his beard! That cigarette is almost lost in the foliage. I just had a fleeting vision of him disappearing in a forest fire of burning hair."

"See what you mean," Jess chuckled with her. The man had a head of thick curly hair and a Rasputin-style beard.

"I'll just nip into the woods behind a tree. He's facing the fields on the other side of the road anyway."

At that, she pulled up in front of the large car and dashed into the thick undergrowth beside the lay-by. She was right. There was no chance he'd see her. "Dammit!" Elizabeth piped up. "All that talk of peeing, and now I need to go. Gonna have to join her." At that, she climbed out of the passenger door and followed Susan.

Jess chuckled at Karen, "you as well?"

Karen looked back in concern and shook a no.

"Everything OK?" queried Jess.

The nearside sliding door suddenly slid open, banging into its stops. Another man stood there. It clearly wasn't OK. He was big and broad, with GI-style short blond hair that emphasised his one missing ear. "Out!" he snapped at Jess.

Jess looked at him, mesmerised.

"They're police. You need to give yourself up." Karen stared at Jess accusingly.

"Are you stupid! Do they look like police?"

Jess turned back to the policeman, "OK, show ID."

"Get the fuck out now! Or I come and get you."

After hearing his East European accent, she screeched at Karen, "how many fuckin' police do you know that look like him and talk with a foreign accent like that?"

The bearded man with the cigarette arrived and smiled. While also large, he was a little smaller than the big man. He turned and handed a brown envelope to Susan, who'd returned and now stood beside him.

"Thanks." Susan sported a self-satisfied smile engulfing her face.

"Now piss off quick," ordered the smaller man. "You all need to be away fast. He cannot catch any of you. That man who's pretending to be her father is a killer. If he catches you, you're all dead."

Karen glared at Susan. "They're not police. What have you done? Who are they?"

"They are paying £15,000. That's who they are and all you need to know. Don't listen to him, we'll be fine."

Then to the smaller man, she added, "I've family. He won't get near me."

"What's about us? Who's going to help us?" Karen got between the man and Jess and screamed, "leave her alone!"

The big man punched her hard in the face, launching her towards the far side of the van, where she hit her head and lay stunned.

He then made a grab for Jess, who screamed in response, feebly kicking out at him. He got a hold of one leg and pulled her toward him feet-first. "You're a pretty little thing, aren't you? Yes, we're going to have some fun," he leered at her.

"Help me!" Jess screamed at the others. Elizabeth stood behind the two men, gawping at what had happened. She stared at Susan but said nothing.

Karen was coming around and, from what had happened, was too terrified to do or say anything further.

Jess had twigged that the three of them knew what would happen there. It was a setup orchestrated by Susan. The other two had gone along with it, believing they were helping the police or at least wanting to believe the story. After all, it was a lot of money for these three.

Elizabeth pulled back from Jess and the men as if they had Covid. "What happening isn't right. You're not police. You have to go." But that was as much of a resistance she could muster. She was too scared to do anything further in case what happened to Karen might come her way.

Jess was in tears as the larger man dragged her half-curled-up body out of the van by her leg and threw her to the lay-by's edge. She bounced then rolled to the verge, where she lay, sobbing. She was petrified and had now curled up tight to hide from them.

The smaller man pulled out his phone and took a photo of Jess crying at the kerbside. He sent the image with a message. "Got the parcel. When we get the transfer, we'll deal with it." The message came back almost immediately. "Transfer made, she's yours. Enjoy." He gave a thumbs-up sign to the East European. "Money's in."

At that, the bigger of the two ordered, "Colin, open the back door so I can chuck her in. I've got this." He then knelt beside Jess and caressed her back. Seeing her shiver with fear and hearing her pleadings for help that wouldn't be forthcoming from these three other bitches, he leaned in and grabbed Jess by the hair. He meant to yank her up. He was strong, but she was a dead weight. So he had to use two hands.

That was his mistake.

From where she sat in the van, she'd spied her opportunity. When he'd thrown her from it, she ensured she ended up near a large stone. Then exuding terror, she made sure she ended up wrapped around it. Her feeble kicking out and pretence of fear raised his confidence.

Jess sprung to a crouching position, spun round, and with all that momentum and all the force she could muster, she smashed him in the side of his head with a rock. Then again, and again.

She remembered what Harry had said. "Stay calm, play the game, remember your advantage. No matter what happens, wait for the opportunity; there will always be one. Look for a weapon, anything."

He collapsed. Perhaps it was from the injury or shock. She wasn't hanging around to find out. She wasn't able to follow Harry's other mantra, "when you leave, the opponent doesn't get up!" The other man was a few metres away, so she didn't have the luxury to fully incapacitate the injured one.

Susan and Elizabeth stared in shock at what Jess had done to that large man.

Jess screamed at them. She pointed at Susan. "I'm coming for you."

At that, she leapt over the wire fence that marked the boundary between the lay-by and the woods. She ran straight into the wood, zigzagged, then veered right. She dived into a clump of bushes over one hundred metres in, and then waited.

'Harry, where are you?'

She shivered at the thought of what would happen to her if caught. However, she knew, no prayed, Harry would find her; he always did. But how on earth could he? She left this morning, and he wasn't expecting her back until Friday, three days away. She was on her own, with only her training and cunning to protect her from these two men.

Jess cursed that she'd taken Susan's advice about putting her phone in her overnight bag to be safe from being sat on in the confines of that van. Little did she know that her phone was still at the Taigh.

Minutes passed, and there was no sound of any pursuers. There were also too many witnesses in what she thought were her friends. Had they also dealt with them? How involved were they? Perhaps she hurt the man badly? With any luck, they'd have gone. She waited a few more minutes to make sure.

She waited in her hiding space. The wood was deathly silent. There were no sounds, no sign of movement. Jess knew that getting help meant heading further into the wood. She planned to double back to the village, where she'd be safe.

In the distance, she heard the English man's whispering

voice. He wasn't as far in the wood as she was, and he was off to the village side of the wood. Jess heard the Eastern European voice in response, coming from the same direction. They were together and tracking where she initially entered the wood. Good. They were going along her initial flight path. Straining her ears, she could make them out as they headed further into the wood.

Hearing where they were, meant a change to her plan. When they were level with her she'd sneak back to the road. Once she'd flattened one of the SUV's tyres, she'd run back to the village about a mile away. From there, she'd call Harry and explain. He'd be there in moments, long before those two could change the wheel and come looking for her.

So, keeping very low, she slowly and stealthily extricated herself from her hiding place. As she exited her sanctuary, she looked for a weapon, anything. But in the thick undergrowth, nothing was visible.

Then behind her, there was a crack of a twig breaking. Still crouching, she turned, scared of what to expect. Then she saw the source. It was a deer, a doe, about 50m away; a beauty amongst this danger. It hadn't heard her. Jess did not want to disturb the creature. It wasn't because she didn't want to break the moment, but to do with the bolting deer giving her location away.

Jess stealthily headed back out of the wood as planned. Harry's training had paid off. The doe paid no attention to her as she slowly moved away from it.

Suddenly, the doe's ears pricked up. Its head rose and faced her. It had seen Jess and stared.

'How on earth did that happen? I'm down-wind and silent.'

Suddenly it bolted!

"Gotcha!" Colin, the one-eared man, exclaimed as he grabbed her around her chest, pinning her arms to her side.

It wasn't Jess the doe had heard or seen.

"Barys, get over here I've got her."

Barys, the big man, ran to where they were. Caked blood covered the left-hand side of his head and face. It still oozed from the large gashes above his ear.

Jess grinned at her handiwork. "Nice look."

Barys slapped her hard in response to her taunt. "Fuckin' bitch!"

Jess still grinned at him. She spat blood from her mouth into his face. Her burst lip hurt, but she wasn't going to show it.

He slapped her again. "You think this is funny eh," he snarled, pointing to the side of his head. He then mimicked Colin's whisper. "You fell for the simple trick."

"Mind you, more experienced people than you have fallen for that one," chuckled Colin. "He's good, isn't he?"

"He's a fucking twat. A little girl like me bested him. Let me go, and I'll do it again. Everyone will hear the story." Her anger-fuelled speech hid the terror she felt.

"No, they won't. We got the green light. No one will hear from you ever again."

"Over knees for this one?" interjected Barys. He leered at her as caressed the breast not covered by Colin's arms. "Very pretty, very firm. I will like you."

She looked at them, wondering what they meant by the 'over the knees' phrase. Jess expected a further strike, which didn't come. Instead, they forced her round to face Colin. He grabbed her by her upper arms while Barys, now behind her, grabbed her calves. Colin sank backward, dragging her down so she was on top of and facing him. He forced her forward over his knees.

Barys knelt on her calves to ensure her legs were disabled. He slapped her buttocks in a playful gesture.

"Now we have fun. We have all of today to play, maybe longer if you are a good little girl."

She tried to fight, but it was impossible. They were too strong, and she was anyway immobilised.

These two were well-versed in what they were doing and about to do to her.

Now she knew what was about to happen. She screamed. But they were too far in the woods for anyone to hear. Her advantage was gone. She was left with her small, weak body, upon which these two men would feed their lusts.

Barys undid her jeans and pulled them down with her knickers. "You fight me, and this hurts more."

Jess stared ahead into Colin's smirking face. "He will find you. He knows where the girls live. He will track them, then you. He never fails. You are already dead men walking. What you do to me will be insignificant to what he will do to you and your families."

She knew Harry would never touch their families, but it felt good to say that. She was right about one thing, though. When he caught them, and he would, they would pay the price.

"Shut your mouth, you silly bitch. No one will find us. No one ever has. We are too good."

Her fear grew, and she couldn't bear to look at him anymore. Knowing what was to come, she stared into the woods. She relaxed. This would soon be over. She knew what the end story would be and hoped the telling wouldn't be too long.

Colin growled, "Barys, it's arse for you this time. I want pussy. And I don't want your slops over it."

Barys was livid at her for striking him with the stone and also himself for being taken in. Now the little bitch was going to suffer. He knelt behind her.

She felt Barys' hand press hard down on the small of her back as he prepared to enter her.

She lifted her head, glared into Colin's eyes, then spat in his face.

He laughed at her. "I'm next bitch, then you'll pay for that."

She spat in his face again. He pulled himself up into a seating position. Still holding onto her wrists, he punched her in the face.

"Colin, keep her still!" Barys was annoyed at the distraction.

She had done what she could to delay the inevitable, even if it was just for a few seconds.

Jess knew what was coming. Impotent to what was about to happen, she glowered at him; it was all she had left.

9. INTRUDERS

After Harry's hasty departure, Tom sprinted into the house without even glancing in the direction of their estate car burning rubber as it accelerated away. The three of them hoped this would never happen, but typical of Harry, he'd thought of everything. So, they'd planned for this eventuality, but no plans were foolproof.

He hoped Harry's instincts were wrong but couldn't take the chance of delaying. Jess was potentially at risk. And if so, she was out there alone.

This situation could be a false alarm. However, he needed to leave the house secured and ready for return in case it was real when they'd see evidence of intrusion. So, he dashed around, locking windows and doors, making sure he switched everything off.

He checked the operation of their security system. It was discreet; it had to be.

There was little crime around here, so people tended to leave doors and windows open. If there were any thefts, the police knew the likely candidates and would descend upon them; as would the locals. Therefore, any overt security would raise questions.

Harry had arranged external route movement sensors with timers, covering two concentric rings, with AI learning control. Over time, the system learned how and when animal life managed their territories. Basically, if one tripped, there'd be an amber check. A red warning would show if the second ring was tripped in the same arc when the timing dynamics were different from what it expected. As a result, they had few animal false alarms. They also had window and door sensors.

The monitor showed an orange warning. Tom stopped and waited for the next trip. It stayed at orange. It should have turned red if people were coming. So what was that all about? He discreetly peered outside from each of the bedroom windows but saw nothing. Was it just an animal? That'd be too coincidental.

Each of the threesome had grab bags with their most valuable personal items and their new IDs. They weren't 100% ready. However, what they had would have to do. He needed to decide if he should leave now or first pick up the bags and equipment. What should he do? He checked his watch. It was fifteen minutes since Harry had left, and he needed to decide and speed up.

The sound of breaking glass put paid to any uncertainty. The threat was real. They were here, downstairs. He calmed himself and shouted downstairs. "Dad, what have you broken now? You said you were heading off fifteen minutes ago?"

Tom innocently descended the stairs. "Dad, is that you?" When he reached the bottom, something cold and hard pressed against his temple.

In a Mancunian accent, a man ordered, "into the living room, no sudden moves."

Tom slowly turned to face the man who held a gun to his head. He made a small, slow nod and warily made for the living room.

"Keys!"

Tom gestured to the small hallway side table.

"Call the boss," the gunman said over his shoulder to someone behind.

In the corner of his eye, Tom caught the image of a large man passing behind him, heading toward the front door. He heard the door open and the voice of an East

European speak into what he assumed was a mobile or perhaps a walkie-talkie. "Boss, we have the runt. Logan is not here."

"Stand by the fireplace," ordered the man with the gun to Tom.

Tom duly complied. He'd no option.

A couple of minutes later, Tom heard a car draw up outside and the slamming of two doors.

'Two people coming, at least, methinks.'

A smartly, some might say elegantly, attired man entered the room. From what Harry and Jess had said about the incident up in the hills a couple of days ago, this was the same man with Bob and Gus.

Tom watched the gunman say a few words into Mr Elegant's ear, which brought a smirk to his face.

In a middle England, some would say posh accent, Mr Elegant announced, "let's cut to the chase. Harry Logan's not your dad, and we are very pleased to meet you, Thomas Lloyd, or may I call you Tom?" He gave a wry smile. "Since my friend has a gun pointed at you, I'll decide. So, Tom, it is." He said Tom's name with emphasis to make his point; he was in charge.

"Nice one," the man continued, "your careless announcement coming down the stairs confirmed that Logan's not here. That's good news. There could have been some bloodshed otherwise."

He had that sort of self-satisfied smirk on his face that Tom would have liked to punch.

"Oh, and by the way, I'd have expected better security than you had outside. My men found and disabled your sensors."

Tom didn't explain the early warning he got. He was happy to let these men be over-confident. Instead, he challenged the man. "Who are you? What do you want? Why have you broken into my house? I'm going to call the police." The questions and statements flew from the angry man.

Mr Elegant gestured at the big Eastern European man in the direction of Tom. An eager smile appeared on the man's face as he stomped over to Tom and hit him in the stomach.

Tom doubled up and collapsed to the floor, winded. The big man picked Tom up and pinned him to the wall. Tom, still dazed, tried his best to cover himself up from what he knew was about to come. What little defence he put up was almost useless. The big man pounded through every protection.

Mr Elegant chuckled at the grinning and grimacing man delivering the blows, "I'm thinking the little man has had enough. We still need him to be compos mentis for my questions."

The big considered Mr Elegant, then shrugged.

To emphasise his disdain for the people with him, Mr Elegant addressed Tom. "Hate dealing with damned insolent foreigners."

Then back to Tom's attacker, he added, "don't knock the little shit senseless, you oaf. He needs to talk."

At that, the big man smirked at Mr Posh in what looked like a smidgen of defiance, then hit Tom again and again. He'd made his point. He let Tom fall to the ground.

Tom had been badly hurt. He knew he'd cracked ribs, at best. He prayed there was nothing serious internally. Had it not been for Harry's training in riding blows, Tom's condition would have been much worse. But it was bad enough.

The posh man pulled out a gun and walked up to Tom, who was trying to rise to a crouch. "As I said earlier, we have the guns." And, to make the point, the man leaned down and struck him on the head with the barrel of his gun.

Tom, now dazed, fell to one side.

"Get up you little wimp. It was only a tap, but there'll be more to come if you don't comply. The only words I want to hear from you are the answers to my questions. Got it!"

Tom glared daggers at the man but stayed where he was. He knew the beating he took should have made him unable to get up. So, he put on an incapacitated show, which wasn't too far from the truth. In any case, there was no point in a show of physical defiance.

"You two," the posh man snarled at the other two men. He pointed to the settee. "Pick up the little shit and dump him onto that."

Mr Elegant then made himself comfortable in the armchair opposite Tom. He gestured to one of the other men to sit next to Tom. The man sitting next to Tom wasn't massive. He was a little under six feet tall and reasonably well-built. Obviously, he'd kept himself in shape for the job he was hired for. Next to him, Tom's five feet four and slight frame seemed minuscule.

To the other two, he gestured that one stand on one side of him and the other in front of Tom.

"Now that's settled," the elegantly dressed man opposite Tom continued. "Where's Harry?"

"Out."

The gunman glanced up at the man standing and made a small gesture with his head. The reason why the man who'd already struck Tom remained standing now became obvious to Tom. The man hit Tom full in the face.

"Didn't you learn anything? That's a hint of what's to come for non-compliance."

The punch dazed Tom. When he recovered, he put his

hand to his aching jaw and grimaced at the man opposite. Tom changed his expression back to that of the daggers. He sang a play on a well-known song to the man standing, "you might be ambidextrous, but that don't impr...."

Another blow hit Tom on the other side of his jaw. He grinned up at the man, who was about to strike him again but was stopped by the man opposite holding up his hand.

"I need him conscious, you idiot. We can eke this out and take our time."

Then back to Tom. "Perhaps I didn't make myself clear. Let's try again. I want full and accurate responses to my questions. Where exactly is he?"

"Honest, I don't know," Tom forced out a response through bruised and bloody lips and an aching jaw. "He left earlier and didn't exactly say. But we needed shopping, and while he's out, I assume petrol. That's it, nothing out of the ordinary. There was nothing he really needed to say to me."

"We'll see." At that moment, his phone pinged. He smirked. "Love it when a plan falls into place." He typed in a few words, sent, then typed again. Little did Tom know, but the message was to the men who had taken Jess.

Tom was worried. Did he have Jess? Was that the message? He taunted the gunman. "Don't you all realise that you've poked the tiger, as the saying goes."

"Of course we do, you little shit. We've got you and you're our long stick, as the real saying goes. And now, we have Jess, an even longer stick. You're both our leverage on him, so there'll be no nonsense from him."

"Now we sit quietly and wait." The boss gestured to the large man standing to wait by and monitor the window.

There was a deathly silence, except for the clicking sounds from the gunman's mobile as he seemed to exchange messages. The smile on his face widened to a chuckle. He was now a happy man.

After a few minutes, Tom's phone rang. It was Harry.

"Answer it and put it on speakerphone."

After the short chat, the gunman called for the man outside to come in. To the three of them, he warned. "Follow my lead. Keep your mouths shut. Don't give him any opportunity to mix it with you. You might think you're good, but this one's the master. Got it!"

The one sitting next to Tom nodded in complete understanding.

The two others shrugged an unspoken, "if you say so," and went to their posts. One stood by the window and the other waited outside.

10. UNLEASHING THE DEMONS

When they saw what Jess did to one of the men and then ran away into the woods, the three women immediately left the lay-by. Susan wasn't hanging around and pushed the others into the van, shouting that they needed to be away from there.

Without thinking, the other two got in.

"They weren't police! What the fuck's going on with you, Susan?" challenged Elizabeth at the top of her voice. "You said there'd eventually be a reward after the court case. But that was payment!"

"Of course it was," replied Susan. "It's fifteen thousand quid, five each. We've worked hard and can now pay off some of our debts."

"Not like this. We've got to go back. Or at least, we need to call the police, the real police," shouted Karen. "Tessa's in danger. I don't care what they said she'd done. If they're not the police, who are they? I think they might be the bad ones."

Susan growled at her. "We're not going back, and you're not calling no one."

Elizabeth piped up again, "it's blood money. They said they'll hurt her, and you know what that means."

"If you don't want the money, that's more for Karen and me."

Elizabeth remained silent. The deed had been done and there was no going back. She nodded, accepting the arrangement.

Susan felt she needed to explain. "The people who set this up are not pussies. I've been warned to silence. And that means both of you as well. Otherwise, they'll come for us next. They could have done you both there, but that wasn't the deal. OK?"

"How do you know this, know them?" queried Karen.

"My uncle Nev told me. He's in trouble with the bizzies and needs to do a favour for someone to make it go away. That someone is a well-connected, not-very-nice someone. Get it!"

Then, to appease her friends, she added, "bottom line, that Mr Greywell, or whatever his real name is, is hiding from them. What is true is that he is a professional killer and deserves whatever he gets. Jess is bait, and that's all you need to know. Once they've done him, they'll eventually let her go. So, it'll be OK for her, you'll see, as long as she doesn't talk. But he will get his and won't be coming after us."

There was silence between the three since there was nothing more to say. Susan seemed to relax and started singing the Skye Boat Song to lighten the atmosphere because that's where they were now heading, to put all that behind them. She tried to get them to join in as she drove toward the final week of their trip.

The other two looked at each other, then Susan in disbelief. What had happened to her? Susan could sometimes be cold and calculating, but never like this. She seemed to be enjoying this.

At that moment, an old German estate car overtook them and abruptly stopped in front of them. Susan tried to swerve around the car. However, Karen sitting next to her, pulled the handbrake on hard. She recognised Jess' dad in the car.

Harry jumped out. "Sorry ladies. Tess forgot her mobile. She'd kill me if I didn't give it to her." He still wasn't sure if he was right, so took a cautious approach.

He looked through the open driver's window into the back of the van, no Jess. "Where is she?"

No one replied. The three young women were terrified. The killer they'd been warned about had caught them.

"Where is she!" he screamed at them.

"They tried to take her, but she hit one and ran," Karen blurted out.

"Where!"

"The lay-by 'bout two miles back," Karen continued. She was worried about Jess. She also had the agenda that if she or they were helpful, perhaps he'd let them go. "There was a black SUV. Two men. Tess hurt one of them badly. But he got up, blood everywhere. The both of them chased her into the woods."

"It was Susan," accused Elizabeth, pointing to her friend. "She told us they were police. She said you were a killer, and the police needed our help to get Jess away from you before they could take you. We now know they weren't."

Karen also pointed at Susan. "They paid her for Tessa. She sold her to them, the bitch! I'm so sorry. We didn't know."

Harry took his knife out of his arm sheath.

Susan screamed in terror. The loathing she saw in his face made her shudder.

His mouth smiled while holding out his hand. "I'm not going to hurt you, but you deserve it. The blood money, now!"

Susan handed over the envelope.

"Phones and Tessa's things!"

The women handed their phones over, and Karen passed Jess' bag.

"Never come back and never talk about this to anyone. I know where you all live, and I WILL find you." While he didn't mean it, they didn't know that. His real worry was that Jess knew where Susan lived. He knew Jess was probably the kindest, warmest, and most forgiving person he knew. He also knew she'd a dark side that had been abused into her.

Harry rushed back to his car and did a screaming U-turn. He remembered seeing the SUV they described as he chased the women. It was parked in a lay-by further back up the road. He prayed it was still there.

Less than two minutes later, he pulled up in front of the car and slashed the nearside tyre. They'd not leave in a hurry. He ran quietly yet cautiously into the woods. He had to compromise speed for silence and stealth. Not knowing who the two men were, he didn't know what he was up against. He could also be walking into a trap.

Every few steps, he stopped and listened. Then he heard faint screaming coming from deeper inside the wood. It was Jess. He knew that shout of aggression from their many fights. He still couldn't be certain it wasn't a trap. If he was taken out, she'd be at their mercy.

Jess was brave, sharp, and cunning. He knew there was no way she'd be screaming if she knew he was coming into a trap. So, he quickened his pace to as fast as being stealthy would allow him and progressed deep into the wood. Harry pulled a long cord from around his waist and looped it to the circular eye at the end of the handle of his curved karambit knife. It was now a medium-range, repeatable weapon.

He followed the screaming and eventually saw shadows of men and heard movement on the ground with Jess.

She saw him in the shadows behind Colin. She relaxed.

They didn't. They were too engrossed in what they were about to do with their little sex toy.

****

If Barys had been paying attention, he'd also have seen Harry's shadow in the shrubbery behind Colin. However, his focus was on his hard penis and where it was about to penetrate.

Harry swung the cord, with the curved Karambit knife tied to the end, at Colin. The curved knife's razor-sharp edge sliced through the back of Colin's neck. He swung again, slicing open his upper shoulders.

Neither were lethal gashes into his skin. However, those cuts deep into his flesh were enough to distract him.

"What the Fuck!" Colin felt a searing pain, then again. In that moment of shock, he released Jess's right arm and put his hand behind his head. It came back dripping in blood.

Jess was no longer incapacitated. She half turned and lashed out with her now free right hand, tearing at Barys' wound and face with her nails.

Barys roared out in pain and anger and pulled out of her reach. He saw Harry. The moment of lust had now collapsed between his legs.

Jess tore herself free after doing the same to a shocked Colin. She rolled out of the way and quickly pulled up her jeans. She wasn't about covering her honour, it was about freedom of movement.

Harry closed up on Colin. From behind, he stabbed the curved blade into Colin's neck. It would disable him, yet not fatal, assuming he soon had treatment.

Harry now faced Barys, who'd recovered from Jess' vicious lashing out. Doing up his trousers had given Harry enough time to deal with Colin.

Barys smirked. "A leettle knife with a lanyard. How very Breetish Scouts." His words of derision were accompanied by spitting to the ground in Harry's direction as he thrust his hand into his jacket.

Harry threw again.

Barys saw the aim was wide of the mark, so grinned as he methodically extracted his gun. He'd known colleagues who'd rushed the draw only to have it catch in clothing. He was a professional at this game, and his action was smooth.

Harry pulled the taught cord to the left, and the blade slashed across Barys' face, opening it up from left ear to nose.

Barys lost the moment, and Harry was on him. He held his knife to Barys' throat and removed the gun from its underarm holster. Now fully armed, Harry stepped away from both men.

In the meantime, Colin had recovered his composure. But, before he could intervene in the fight with Barys, Jess was upon him tearing, biting, and screaming at him. There was no way she was letting him up. Despite his injuries, he punched her hard and then threw her away. He got up, knife in hand, but was too late. Jess' intervention had given Harry time to deal with Barys and take his gun.

Harry shouted to Colin, "drop it and kick it over here."

Colin looked at the gun in Harry's hand. He knew the gunman's reputation, so reluctantly did as asked, then kicked it over to him.

Harry picked up the knife. Under different circumstances, Harry would have admired the choice of weapon, a Bopoh-3, used by Spetsnaz operators. Its 6.5-inch blade has almost a spear point for good penetration against an enemy wearing heavy clothing. He wondered why a Brit was carrying a knife that few over here would use.

Harry passed the gun to Jess. "Hold this while I chat with your friend over here."

Jess took off the safety, checked it was ready to fire, smiled, and pointed the gun at Colin.

Harry sheathed his weapon and walked over to the big man. The Bopoh would be a better tool for this discussion. Harry hoped this man would attack, giving him the justifiable opportunity to exact the revenge burning within.

While the big man's chance of success was slim, there might be no other opportunity. So he waited and watched. Everyone makes mistakes, eventually. He'd not do that again.

"Name!"

No reply.

"Why are you here? Why take Tessa? What's going on?"

"So, many questions," came his heavily accented response. "Anything happens to us, you get no answers." Barys knew Harry wouldn't kill him while he held the information cards. This would be a negotiation, and he could afford to play for time.

"Eastern European?"

The big man smirked back at the obvious conclusion.

"Ukraine, nah. They're properly trained, not a fat pussy like you," baited Harry.

The man clenched his fists but quietly stood his ground, glaring back at the man with the knife. He waited and watched for the opportunity, but nothing so far.

"Not West Russian? Ah, now I know. We, the Breetish Scouts, as you call us, used to laugh at your kind. So, what is a Pallarusian thug doing here with a Brit carrying this pointy

East European stick?"

The big man's lips twitched in surprise, wondering how this man knew. But he stayed still. He was warned about him.

Harry waved the knife in Barys' face, goading him to try to make a move on him. He swapped the knife back and forth.

Barys' eyes were fixed on the knife, waiting for Harry to make a mistake. He missed Harry's right-hand hammer blow into the side of the head where Jess had struck him. He staggered back and screamed. "I tell you nothing. You cannot kill me. I know too much about you, Harry Logan, and your preetty leettel friend, Jessica Lloyd, and her brother Thomas. You need to know what I know. But, I say nothing."

"Thank you. You've told me some of what I needed to know. And you're right, I'm wasting my time on you." Then, to Jess, Harry asked, "anything you want to say to this gentleman?"

She walked up to Barys and pointed the gun at him, at close range, but not too close. She stood silently, glowering at him.

"You might want to answer my questions," warned Harry. "Honest, she's not nice like me,"

Barys laughed at Jess. "Leetel girl, with the leetel pussy. Give me the gun, and I promise, next time I have you, I'll be gentle."

"Harry, are you sure?" queried Jess.

"Think of all those men and times. He's yours if you need it."

Barys wondered what they were talking about. He then saw such a hatred growing in Jess' eyes he'd never seen before.

"Seriously, this is your last chance to tell me everything."

Barys spat on the ground and glared at Jess. He made a leering, licking gesture. "Leetel pussy, you don't have the balls."

She shot him between the legs. "True, now neither do you. Your raping days are over."

Barys couldn't believe what had happened, what she'd done. He screamed in pain and angst, then covered his damaged bits with his hands.

"Speak, your last chance!"

Barys screamed out, "Fuck you, bitch, and you Logan!"

"No, it's you that's fucked." Jess shot again through his hands, just to make sure.

Barys roared in pain and sank to his knees, while trying, with broken hands, to clutch what was left of any manhood down there.

She remembered, safety on. Then she screamed obscenities at her ex-assailant as she repeatedly pistol-whipped his head. She hit out, not only at him but at those who'd abused her over the years.

Barys was evil. From what they'd said to her, this wasn't the first time he'd done this. Unfortunately for him, he was in the wrong place with the wrong woman.

She only stopped when he stopped moving. He was breathing, at least for now.

Jess spat at the fallen man, "final lesson, they don't walk away, according to the Oracle," she nodded to Harry and sidled over to him, still eying the fallen man.

Harry raised his eyebrows at her to see what response she might give him.

Trembling from the adrenaline rush and the realisation of what she'd done, she handed over the weapon.

Harry immediately shot Barys in the centre of his

forehead. He needed to do that for her. To kill in cold blood was the final barrier. He'd crossed it long ago and hoped Jess would never have to. Because she was emotionally in a bad place he didn't know if what he'd enabled her to do was the right thing. But he felt she needed closure from Barys and the others.

He gave the gun back to Jess.

Their attention now turned to Colin. She sauntered over to him and raised the gun, but not too high.

He raised his hands. Fear showed in every tremble and every orifice. The front of his trousers became very wet.

"Talk," ordered Harry. "Who are you? Who sent you and why? Or do I let the woman play with you?"

Colin quivered in terror as she stared at him with that same look of loathing. He thought of what she'd done to Barys. He was keen to talk but could only gurgle.

"That wasn't bright, father," she continued the charade of him as her father while pointing to Colin's damaged voice box.

"Oops," commented Harry, "musta misjudged the strike."

Jess shook her head in mock chiding.

Harry noticed the light return to Jess' eyes.

He turned his attention back to Colin.

Colin held up one hand and slowly put his hand in his jacket pocket. He pulled out a pen and a piece of paper.

Harry nodded to go ahead.

Colin showed what he had written. "Friend is Barys Novok. I am Colin Farmer, ATS. My boss, Colonel Gerard Armstrong, ordered us to take her. He told Barys to do whatever he wanted before he killed her. Honest, I wasn't going to do anything!"

Harry looked at him aghast. After what he'd seen, this

man was equally complicit. However, instead of challenging him, he went with the flow and asked, "where's your boss?"

"Here," he wrote.

"Shit!"

Jess looked at him, wondering what was worse than what had happened here.

Harry held his finger to his lips and called the house.

When Tom answered, he light-heartedly announced, "Tom, almost finished at the shop. Anything else we need?"

"Someone wants to talk with you," said Tom, his voice faltering as if in pain. "Sorry, but…"

Another voice came on the phone, "Ex-Sergeant Harry Logan, so nice to hear from you. Please come on home. Tom awaits. Your little lady friend, Jess, is already in safe hands. We like to cover both angles."

Harry played along. "If anything happens to Tom or Jess…"

He was interrupted. "Anything that happens to Tom and Jess will be down to you." The man on the other end cut the line.

Now Jess understood.

"You don't deserve to live, but you will if you reply with the truth. What is the confirmation of success that Armstrong is expecting from you."

Colin wrote down, "SecureApp message, already sent."

"Who's your boss?"

"The Colonel is UK Station Operations Director of ATS."

"What's this about?"

"He's a job he needs you to do."

"What job?"

Colin wrote again. "I don't know, neither of us do.

We're just deniable muscle for whatever he's up to."

"Who's he with?"

"Dunno, honest. But when he hired us, he was with Paddy, one of his closest from all accounts. That's all I know."

"I'm going to lock you away for one month with provisions. If we survive, we will let you out. You will come to no further harm from us."

Jess delivered a challenging look.

"Jess, please trust me. I've given my word. We may need more information from him. We need him alive for whatever information we might need. He needs to know that his compliance will give him his way out."

Jess angled her head in reluctant agreement. She couldn't admit it, but what she'd just done now disgusted her. It wasn't because of what she did, it was the uncontrollable anger that overtook and drove her. Harry was right. Her demons had been unleashed on Barys. She had now been the abuser, and that had brought about a change in her. Her anger wasn't cured. The weight of her earlier abuses hadn't gone.

After her extreme retaliation to the attempted vicious rape, things now seemed more in perspective. Maybe what she'd done wasn't the way forward, although, at the time, it felt good! And that also worried her.

Back to Colin, Harry continued. "If we fail and die, you will rot there. So, you'd better be right."

Harry took Jess to one side. "Whatever's going on, the man on the phone assumed his two men had succeeded in picking you up. That gives us a potential edge to get Tom free from them."

Harry addressed Colin. "Show me your phone and the secure app you're using."

Colin wrote on the paper, "you promised you'd not kill me."

"Yes, and we'll keep that promise. Now show me."

Colin extracted his mobile and opened the App. Harry saw the last message from Colin's boss. "Nice work. Enjoy her, remember, no body, no repercussions."

Harry knew what that meant. Once they'd finished with her, she'd be buried deep somewhere. However, he needed this man's help and as insurance. Tom needed to be rescued.

"Who has the car keys."

Colin fished them out of his pocket and threw them to Harry.

"Stay with our friend here," Harry asked Jess. "I need to get their disabled car, un-disabled."

The parting words from Harry to Colin were, "I'd not rile her. She doesn't like you."

After Harry changed the spare in the SUV, he found a gate into the woods a couple of hundred metres down the road. He drove the car down the track, level with where he left Jess and the two men. He turned the car around and returned to Jess.

"Right, got a job for you before your holiday accommodation," Harry announced to Colin. "Car's over there. Get Barys there and dump him in the boot. When all this is done you'll be free to head back to the sewer where you're from."

Colin did as asked. While Barys was big, Colin clearly worked out and managed to drag the man to the car and get him loaded into the back. He pulled over the tonneau cover to conceal the dead man.

Harry tied up Colin, fully disabling any movement, and put him in the back of their estate car on top of several bin bags. The man was bleeding, albeit not at dangerous levels, assuming his wounds were soon treated.

11. PREPARATIONS

They dropped off Colin in their dilapidated cottage's secure bunker. As well as food and water, there was an army field medical kit with sutures and painkillers.

Harry placed the still-tied man face down on the floor. "This is going to hurt you more than me." At that, he rapidly cleaned, then stitched the wounds that the writhing man couldn't reach himself. "I'm sure you can sort the rest."

Job done. "Right Colin, make yourself at home. There's books to keep you company, enjoy. No one comes here, so no one will hear you gurgling," he grinned. He didn't like this man, but should what he had said turn out to be true, a deal was a deal.

"There's a camera up there and one outside. We'll be watching. There's ventilation that we can close off at any time should you feel the need to break our deal. Are we clear?"

Colin nodded in agreement, not that he had any choice.

Then they left Colin secure, safe, and monitored for one month.

The SUV and the dead body needed to disappear, and he knew how. His runs and reconnaissance had given him a good knowledge of the area. Harry, driving their car, led Jess in the SUV along the narrow road that skirted the western side of the loch. He stopped at an outcrop, which people used as a viewing spot over the loch, hills, and mountains in the distance. The outcrop ended in a vertical rocky overhang over the loch. Below them was deep brackish loch water. Harry couldn't see the bottom but knew this loch well. It would be at least 20 metres feet there and dark enough for their purposes.

After cleaning the SUV of their presence, Harry drove it over the edge. The cleaned gun was back in Barys' holster. Hopefully, it would remain undisturbed until this was finished; whatever 'this' was.

Harry took Jess to one side. "Take this." Harry handed the thick envelope to Jess. "You've got your way. You're Oakleigh as you wanted. How's about Oakleigh Woods? Even I can remember that."

"That'll do. But what happens now?"

"First, let's get you a mobile. Shuggie stocks them." In the meantime, he needed a plan.

After Jess was mobiled up, Harry followed up her question. "Can you find a B&B or hotel in Auchtershiel or the area? Stay there, and when I know the lay of the land and get the chance, I'll ring you. OK?"

"And if they kill you when you go to the house?"

"They won't. Otherwise, this would have played out differently."

"Why don't we go back together?" she challenged, worried about him returning alone. "We've the firepower. We can rescue him."

"I've thought about that. I played the angles, how this could play out. We don't have surprise on our side. I expect this man will have planned for any attempt to free Tom. Holding Tom, they have the edge. As a minimum, he'd be killed. I cannot let anything happen to you or Tom."

He saw her about to push back, so he added, "saying that, if I see a way through this when I get there, we can re-group. That OK? If you don't hear from me, stay clear."

Jess nodded. Everything seemed to be happening in a blur. But she accepted Harry's orders. It was the only certainty that she had for the moment.

He lightened the mood and suggested a covering story. "You've left home. There was a fight." He pointed to her bruised lips and face. "Any ideas?"

A smile twitched on her lips.

Harry suggested, "how's about you fought with your parents? They're old-fashioned. You're keeping to cash since you didn't want them to find you until you'd gotten your head sorted."

"Sounds OK, but I'll think about it and work on a flashier version."

"Not too flashy, and try to bring in as much of your life as possible. It'll make the story more plausible since your reality will be in there."

Jess had an almighty urge to hug Harry; it might be the last time she saw him. "Harry, what's going on?"

"You know some of my history with ATS and are aware of my earlier life. From what our friend said, I expect ATS to have something lined up for me that needs me alive, for the moment at least. Whatever it is, I'll get Tom out alive. If it's what I suspect, I need you outside the game. You need to be my support and my eyes and ears."

He'd a reputation as a killer, and ATS knew it. So, the job almost certainly required a deniable expert hitman outside their organisation.

He dropped Jess at a bus stop for Auchtershiel. The bus was due in fifteen minutes, assuming it was on time.

"I'm scared."

"You don't have that luxury. This is what you've been training for."

"Not for me, for you, and Tom. I love you, Harry."

"And I love you, my daughter, Oakleigh Woods." He gave her a smacker of a kiss on her forehead.

At that, he drove back toward Taigh Locha. As she watched Harry drive away, her thoughts drifted back to when they were still safe and happy at the Taigh. She smiled, remembering the conversation that brought about her new, Oakleigh, alias.

After their usual post-training sessions, they were taking breakfast in the large welcoming kitchen, discussing their getaway status before their first arrivals appeared. She remembered Tom going through their new identities with them. He'd already built each of them a social media following.

Their existing, 6-month-old, new identities, Barrie, Tessa, and Ronald, would cease next month on 'D2-Day'. D2 was their internal code for the forthcoming second departure day, when they would run for a second time, leaving no trace.

She remembered how she couldn't resist winding them up. This time, she also had an agenda. "Why do I have to be a Tina! Do I look like a Tina?" she challenged the new name she would soon take on. "What's wrong with something from the 21st century," she pushed back. "I wanted Alaiya, perhaps Oakleigh. They're more me."

She thought back to Harry's pleading response. "Jess, we've already had this discussion. Come on, not again. We agreed all this two months ago when Tom started on our new personas and identities."

"But it's not fair I'm always over-ruled by you two, all the time."

She remembered Harry trying the logical approach. "You were born twenty years ago. It wouldn't read right having a modern name. Sorry."

Jess folded her arms and stared at them. "I'm always

side-lined because I'm a woman, or the youngest, or both. It's not fair. I seem to be the outsider." She gave her well-rehearsed frown, supported by her quavering sad bottom lip that always weakened Harry's resolve.

It had taken years of self-determination for Tom to overcome that lip, and she saw him smiling knowingly. She'd had Harry beat.

'Harry's a lot to learn.'

She knew Harry had resolved to be firm on this point. He had to get his way. Their new identities couldn't attract attention. But she had him pinned on her emotional ropes. So, to appease the pet lip that would haunt him the rest of the day, he attempted a conciliatory approach. "OK. Next time, you pick everyone's names from the years Tom and I were born or whatever our personas would be then. We'll abide by your decisions as long as they're appropriate."

"Deal," she agreed. She held out her hand. "You two, shake on it!"

Harry smiled and accepted the handshake.

Tom was less than enthusiastic but capitulated. "Jess, please be nice with mine."

"Always," she laughed, with an overt undertone that made Tom cringe.

She remembered that look Tom gave her. She loved teasing him and knew he also enjoyed the banter with her in some perverse way. He would dread what was to come in a few months with their new names. He knew her of old.

"You're a cunning madam," she remembered him mumbling.

"Always," she whispered back to him, grinning from ear to ear.

Her thoughts returned to the present.

The car, with Harry inside, had almost disappeared. She

had to challenge his last goodbye. "But I'm not your daughter! I'm a grown woman. And, Mr Harry Logan, I do love you so much. Please come back to us, to me."

12. JOB OFFER

An hour after his call with Gerard Armstrong or whoever was on the phone, Harry arrived back at the Taigh. A large black SUV, the same model as Jess' abductors, was parked outside. Two heavies waited for him at the front door to his house. The two gorillas looked similar to Barys and Colin, your usual steroid-and-protein-supplement-gobbling, weight-pumping, nil-for-brains, grunt-for-hire. But he'd need to check.

One pointed to his upper arm. "Hand it over. By the strap, slowly."

Harry undid the arm straps and handed over his running knife and sheath. They could see from the running attire he still wore that he wasn't hiding additional weapons. However, they carefully checked him out in any case.

"In." One stepped to the side, allowing Harry to follow the other inside. They escorted him into his own house.

A man sat on the settee with Tom. Like his two escorts, he'd a pronounced bulge under his arm; certainly a gun. Harry could see that these men regularly trained and assumed all were most capable in a brawl and willing to do whatever was required; for the right price.

Another sat in Harry's preferred armchair. He assumed this man was Colonel Gerard Armstrong. The man looked up at Harry when he entered. If he expected Harry to acknowledge or even address him, he was about to be disappointed.

Harry ignored the man in the armchair. "OK, Ron?"

Tom nodded in the affirmative, but he wasn't. He'd cuts to his face and lips, possibly a broken nose, and the makings of a black eye. The real swelling and bruising would materialise in due course.

From what he could see on Tom, Harry knew there'd be other injuries, but his friend was brave.

All Tom could say was, "I think the bastards have got Jess. They know who you are, who we all are."

Harry saw that saying those words hurt Tom. He glowered at the man sitting in his chair who was responsible.

The man decided it was time to take centre stage. "Yes, we know all about you, Jess, and this little fella here, Tom. As I said, Jess is in safe hands. I've a job for you. We'll hold Tom here as insurance. As long as he behaves, he'll also remain unhurt. This all assumes that the little bit of work I have for you goes the right way."

Harry glared back at the man sitting in his chair. "Who did that to Tom?" There was no point pretending he was Ron.

"Silly boy didn't answer my questions, but he reluctantly gave, of course, after a bit of encouragement from my colleague." He imperceptibly, or so he thought, glanced at the culprit. "Anyway, we're all here now, and all's good. He'll heal, and he will remember."

The man stood up from Harry's chair, walked over to the tall glass-fronted drinks cabinet, and poured himself a whisky. "You do indulge yourself, a nice choice. However, I prefer the more peaty Islay malts." He never offered Harry a drink of his own whisky.

• Harry gauged his opponent, the boss. He was tall, around six feet. And yes, he was the same man Harry saw on the hill with the poachers and most likely the one asking about them at the Forge.

'Obviously ex-military, Rupert-class, smart, smug, educated, and full of shit. Late 50s?'

The man sat down and savoured his, or rather Harry's, whisky.

He then started. "You are starting a new job as a care assistant in a very special care home run by our esteemed Home Office. You've already been vetted and got all the paperwork. Everything's set up…" He stopped when Harry turned his back to him.

Harry went to the drinks cabinet and took his time to pour himself a large one.

Harry mimicked the man's posh, Etonian-type accent over his shoulder, "you come into my house, beat up my staff, sit in my chair, and pour yourself my favourite malt. And to make matters worse, you didn't pour me one. How rude! I would say ungentlemanly. Positively unbecoming, sir."

One of Harry's escorts planted his hand on Harry's shoulder. In a similar accent to that of Barys, Jess' de-balled attacker, he commanded, "you don't turn your back on Colonel Armstrong like that." He then placed his hand on Harry's shoulder, intending to spin around and physically admonish the man who'd dare insult his boss.

Harry expected the move. That's incorrect. He'd hoped for that move from the man who he knew had beaten Tom. The man's reflection in the glass of the drinks cabinet had visibly announced his approach. Harry whipped around, grabbed the offending wrist, and twisted the man's arm into an extended arm-lock. Harry continued the movement, forcing the man to be bent double.

The speed of Harry's move took the man by surprise.

The bent-over man cursed in Pallarusian, adding a couple of expletives Harry recognised as Russian.

"Don't tolerate bad language in my house." Harry kicked him in the face, wrenched and broke, or maybe merely dislocated the man's shoulder. He threw the Pallarusian man away, where he landed like a sack of potatoes at Armstrong's feet.

"Tsk, tsk. You should have warned your man not to touch the goods," commented Harry.

There were three clicks. The man next to Tom had his gun pointed at Tom. The other two pointed their guns at Harry.

The face of the man Harry now knew to be Colonel Gerard Armstrong beamed into a grin. He then laughed. "Excellent, Harry. You haven't lost your touch. That now useless lump of meat was one of the better ones."

Armstrong snapped at his men, "I warned you lot about him." He kicked the man on the floor in front of him away. "Get out! Into the back of the car. You're no use to anyone in here."

The injured man got up one-handedly. He was no longer the arrogant beater of a weaker man. Avoiding Harry, he left the room.

Harry poured himself the interrupted whisky, then sat in the other armchair, facing his opponent because that's who Armstrong was.

The whisky retaliation incident had three objectives. Harry needed to know the people he was dealing with; success. He hoped to reduce the odds; success.

Finally, he hoped to rile his opponents into giving up information. The man confirmed his opponent's name, also success.

He always tried to avoid emotions in circumstances like these. However, he was pissed at the unnecessary abuse of Tom. So, striking out felt good. He achieved an unexpected fourth objective; even better.

"So, Armstrong," teased Harry, using the man's name without title to gauge response. "Why the use of Eastern European goons? Can't afford to pay minimum wage?"

Armstrong eyed Harry but said nothing to the taunt.

So, Harry continued. "As you were saying before we were so rudely interrupted by your Ukrainian goon."

"Not Ukranian!" spat the other heavy who'd come in with Harry.

'Ah, so I was right, another Pallarusian. So what's the angle here?'

The one with the gun pointed at Tom twitched his lips in amusement but kept his counsel.

Harry considered the reaction from the one sitting next to Tom.

'Now you're a different beast, aren't you? Methinks proper ex-military and most likely, retained staff. Wonder if you're Paddy?'

The colonel glared at his entourage who'd been so useful to Harry in gaining those snippets of information.

So far, Harry had managed a few pieces in the puzzle; it was a start.

Armstrong forced a smile. "Finished playing games?"

Harry merely smirked in satisfaction.

"OK, Logan. Pay attention. You've got a reputation as an exceptional killer. That's the job. The name of the hit is Fedor Kotova."

"I'm not in that game anymore, so piss off. If you want someone killed, do it yourself! Why drag me into your cesspit?"

"I'll tolerate your insubordination once, without repercussions. Let me explain. You will do this, or Jess and Tom will die, then so will you. Why ask you? That's easy.

You're good at this, and you're deniable if you screw up. And, having worked for the authorities, your involvement will get enough questions asked for us to avoid the limelight."

There was nothing Harry could say at this point. This man currently held all the cards.

Armstrong continued. "We believe he will try to kill a man called Jacob Collins, an ex-agent of His Majesty's Spooks. He's a resident in a special care home run by His Majesty's Home Office. If Kotova appears, you are to immediately kill him. No arguments, no questions, no complications. Simple. When he's dead, Jess and Tom will be released."

"What if he doesn't appear?"

"He will. We know him of old."

"How do I know Jess is OK?"

"You'll have to trust me. No way am I going to let you speak with her and pass codes back and forth or whatever you'll have up your sleeve. You're a cunning operator, Logan, but I'm not stupid. Her guards are under orders that any non-agreed communication from me, and she's dead. There'll be no further communication until the job's completed. They'll get a one-word release or kill command. Got it!"

Armstrong studied Harry and internally grinned.

'Probably already dead, or wishes she was by now,'

However, he kept his poker face straight. He knew the reputation of the pair now enjoying Jess. They were the ideal dogs for that job, wholly without scruples.

Armstrong pointed to a file on the coffee table. "It's all in there. New ID, pass, CV, qualifications, pictures of target, burner phone, etc. You leave in thirty minutes. I suggest you get packed to start your new caring career."

Harry would have loved to tell Tom that Jess was safe. However, there was no way to do so safely. All he could say to Tom was, "remember what I told you." What Harry meant was to remember your training and play to your strengths.

He packed and was off within 30 minutes.

****

Through the window, Armstrong watched Harry leave. He lied to Tom over his shoulder, "if he's successful, you and Jess get out of this alive." It wasn't to make Tom feel better, he didn't give a hoot. He'd done his research and knew how much Tom cared for his sister. So, her being visibly at risk if things didn't go to plan would keep Tom in check.

Armstrong addressed the heavy who guarded Tom, "look after my little friend. I'm off."

"Jury, with me," ordered Armstrong to the other able-bodied heavy.

The two walked to the front door and out of earshot of those in the living room. "I need the little man unharmed for just now. Logan knows where he is and might set up for someone to check on him. However, once Logan's done the job, kill Tom. No witnesses. Do it without involving Paddy. He's not good with killing non-combatants. If he interferes, kill him as well."

13. POOR LITTLE GIRL

Jess sat at the back of the single-decker bus as it traversed the narrow roads. The bus was old and slow, with many stops before her destination. A couple of hours after Harry dropped her, Jess saw a sign announcing they had entered Auchtershiel, pop. 374. A few minutes later, it stopped in the centre of this grand conurbation. It was lunchtime already, and she was hungry.

Jess, aka Tessa, and now Oakleigh, checked out her destination on her newly purchased mobile. Her old one was still at home.

The MapsApp announced that the small town had two shops, one hotel, several craft shops, two pubs, a church, and the always mandatory estate agent-cum-lawyer. The two shops between them encompassed the other requirements of a thriving community, including a post office, butcher, fishmonger, and off-licence. She was surprised there were no charity shops. Then it dawned on her. In a small, integrated community like this, with everyone knowing everything about each other, there'd be no need for a second-hand intermediary.

She made a beeline for the Auchtershiel Hotel, her first choice of accommodation from the reviews she'd seen. It sat on the corner of Castle Street and the High Street. She could find no castle, but its street, if at one time it had one, had the bulk of the shops and businesses. The High Street housed the official businesses, such as the solicitor.

The hotel's main door took her directly into the bar. It

took her aback. She assumed a run-down establishment similar to the Forge. She didn't expect a pleasant, clean bar with comfortable wooden chairs surrounding sturdy tables. An elegant fireplace held an open log fire that roared away to itself at the far end. The bar stools weren't stools. They were comfortably upholstered high chairs for the discerning drinker.

'Now, this'll do me nicely.'

"Can I have a room for two nights?" she asked the middle-aged woman behind the bar.

"Sorry, dear, Easter's around the corner, and we're fully booked into May."

"In that case, can I have the menu and a glass of red wine, a Merlot if you have it?"

A man came over from one of the tables and hovered, clearly waiting to be served.

The phone rang. The woman picked it up and announced into the cup of the old phone, "Auchtershiel Hotel, can I help you?"

The ping of a timer emanated from the kitchen, followed by a panicky man's voice. "Nessie! I've got meh hands in dough, table two's steak pehs 'r' done an' need pulled oot afore they're burnt. Can you serve 'em?"

Jess had been long enough in Scotland to pick up the local slang-cum-dialect. She knew that the man in the kitchen was busy rolling dough and table two's steak pies were about to be cremated unless the woman dropped everything and took them out of the oven.

"Chick, ev got meh hands full wi' a' these folk here!" shouted Nessie back to where the man's voice had come.

Jess couldn't help giggling at Nessie's response to the man in the kitchen, that she was rather busy."

Nessie apologetically smiled and shrugged at Jess,

signifying she'd have to wait. The woman was stressed, and it showed as she hunted for a pen to use on the pad in her hand.

Jess' impish sense of humour came to the fore and delivered a quiet chuckle-ette.

'This is going to be fun.'

Jess went through the doorway at the end of the bar from where Chick had earlier shouted for help. It opened into the kitchen. She grinned at the red-faced man who was trying to deal with the preparation and delivery of multiple food orders. Seeing a clean apron, she put it on after scrubbing her hands. She'd trained for this eventuality at the Taigh but without real guests to practice on. So, today, it would all be put into practice.

After extracting the pies from the oven, hands on hips, she looked at the man, who gawped back at her. He didn't know her, but he did know he needed help. Assuming Nessie had hired her, he gestured to where the accompaniments were. With two full plates of food in her hand, Jess walked to the front of the bar and shouted, but not too loudly, "who are the two steak pies?"

Two hands rose from one of the tables, and she deposited the scrumptious-smelling offering. "Do you have everything you need?"

The couple nodded a yes.

She went back behind the bar and pulled a pint of 'heavy' for the still hovering man. Jess motioned to the man that the barmaid would take the money later when she was ready.

"Nessie!" came another agitated shout from the kitchen behind the bar.

Nessie, still on the phone, looked at Jess in bewilderment as she sallied past her to deal with the stress-head in the kitchen. It went on like this for the next hour or so. Jess loved it. She'd had a ball. Her earlier life on the street taught her all about people. In this role, she could positively interact with people, chatting, serving, and appeasing the clientele.

For a short while, what had happened earlier was pushed to the back of her mind while she dealt with the ongoing mini-emergencies.

A couple got a little stressed while waiting for their bill, and the man expressed his frustration a little too aggressively. In response, Jess displayed her ever-successful little-girl-in-peril look and manner. The woman chastised her husband for his cruelty to the "pair wee lassie who's just dae'in' her best fir ye'.

When others in the bar also glowered at him, the man wished the ground could swallow him. In the meantime, all this had given Nessie sufficient time to compile and present their bill.

Jess offered the lady her hand and said, "thank you." To the man, she beamed, "please do come again. Ever so sorry for the delay. It was lovely to meet you both."

He melted like butter in her hands. "Yer a wee stotter ye are."

Jess knew that expression meant she was beautiful, or lovely, or super, even all three. She giggled at his compliment. "Thank you, kind sir."

After the lunchtime rush ended, the only guests left in the bar were a couple of regulars finishing their pints. Or perhaps this was them settled for the afternoon?

Nessie reached out and grabbed both of Jess' cheeks and excitedly shook her in a genuine display of appreciation. "Yer a wee doll, a life-saver. Whit possessed ye tae help. Mind you, it was appreciated. You did us a favour there."

Jess laughed and, at the same time, winced at Nessie's

physical display of appreciation. Her face still hurt from the Barys' slap and Colin's punch.

Coming out of the kitchen, Chick saw Jess' discomfort. "Nessie, ya numpty, can ye no' see the wee lassie's face's sair?"

"Oh meh goad." She'd just realised the bruising and the unintentional pain she'd inflicted on Jess. "Who did that tae ye?"

"I'd rather not talk about it. I've left all that behind for the moment. I've sorta escaped to find time to think about what's next."

Agnes put the cup of her hand under Jess' chin and while inspecting the bruising, gently asked, "boyfriend?"

"No, no, don't have one. It's awkward, embarrassing, I'd rather not say." Jess collected herself and changed the subject. "Anyway, I've enjoyed myself today. It's taken my mind off 'stuff'. I need to head off and find a room for a while."

"No, you'll no dae that. Firstly, you join us for our usual late lunch. And you can have the wine you never got. Then together, we'll help you sort out that accommodation. It's the least we could do."

Jess capitulated. Having a couple of locals on-side would be useful to help her get settled.

Nessie introduced herself and her husband, "I'm Agnes Macpherson and a'body calls me Nessie. That lump ower there is Charles, Chick to his friends."

"I'm Oakleigh Woods." Jess held out her hand, and they shook.

Charles Macpherson retrieved a dish from the kitchen. "Shepherd's pie, unless yer wan o' they veggie, or vegan sort?"

"No, no. I mean yes, that'd be wonderful!" Jess was

hungry when she arrived. And now the adrenaline had sufficiently died for her stomach to remind her that she was famished.

Agnes, a natural inquisitor, was not one to miss an opportunity. She saw a challenge to help out this 'sweet little thing'. So, over lunch, she verbally prodded Jess from various angles to get her story.

Jess, ever the windup merchant, toyed with Agnes unashamedly and eventually capitulated. She'd by now rehearsed the developed story in her head. As Harry had suggested, there were also similarities to her real story, which helped round it off.

"It's not complex. My mother threw out my father and my brother when I was young and refused him access to me. She accused him of beating her and got a restraining order. In reality, she was the abuser of us all, but I was too young to realise. Eventually, I was taken away from her and brought up by my grandparents. I don't want to say anymore. Sorry, but I'm so ashamed of myself and what I am and what I did to them, to everyone."

Jess let that hang as she took a couple of mouthfuls of food. She'd also played the story about the poor father and referenced her brother in case they appeared, which she prayed they would, soon.

It was too much for Agnes to bear. "Lassie, I know yer a good ain. You can tell us."

"I can't." Her eyes welled up. Jess was an expert at the sob story.

It was too much for Agnes. She had to know. "Come on lass, in yer ain time."

"You'll not like me when I tell you, no one will."

"I'll be the judge o' that."

"My grandparents are very religious, very traditional, they're well known in their church. I'm sorry, it's awful."

She stopped eating and cried. "I hurt them so badly."

"What could you have done to them that was so bad? Are you pregnant?"

"No, no. It's worse. A lot worse. They found out what I did. I couldn't help myself. They were devastated when they found out from one of their friends at church, and then they challenged me."

"What about?" Agnes was now getting desperate.

"They found out I was…"

"What darling? What did they find out that was so bad." Agnes took her hand and offered this young woman her most caring smile.

"I was seen kissing another woman, a woman in their church. I'm gay, a lesbian. Grandad flipped. He hit me, did this," pointing to the developing bruising on her face, "when I admitted it was true. I could never lie to them."

"That all?" queried Charles.

"Grandma was in tears. Granddad then started shouting that now everyone would know. They threw me out of the house. He shouted I was like my mother. They're good Christian people. They're from that generation who don't understand. I thought they loved me and would. I was wrong."

"Is that it? Is that all?" Agnes gawped.

Then Charles interrupted proceedings with a hearty laugh. "Listen, ma wee puppet. Nowadays, a'body's gay. We're the only heterosexuals in the village."

"But not in their village, or so they'd like to believe. My crime's enough for them. My life there is ruined. So, I've gotten as far away from Surrey as I can. I need to think. I heard my dad's up here somewhere. So, once my head's straight, I'm going to find him. He's a good man, and I miss him. I worry about him."

And that was true about Harry. Her worries and thoughts helped her bring out the wells of tears.

Agnes stood up, walked behind Jess, and hugged her. "It's nothing. We are wit we are. As lang as we're good, that a' that matters. And, I know yer good."

Agnes looked toward Charles. "She wis looking fir accommodation when she came in. Looks like she's no' got a job."

Jess shook her head in agreement that she was currently unemployed. "I've got money for a room. And if you know anyone looking for someone, I'd take anything."

Charles picked up on his wife's look and enthusiastically nodded in the affirmative.

"We'll gi' ye a job," Agnes announced. "Startin' two hours ago. And there's also accommodation fir ye. Not magic, but a clean room wi' ensuite."

"I'll take it." At that, Jess stood up and hugged Agnes and Charles.

Jess felt ashamed for the lies to this lovely, hard-working, and caring couple. However, she was safe for the short term, at least. And no matter what, she would help them as much as she could in return for their kindness.

14. CHEDWORTH MANOR

During the drive down, the whole situation played around Harry's head. He'd had history with ATS, and it wasn't pleasant. In truth, they weren't pleasant. ATS was arrogant, and this heavy-handed approach was typical of it. Harry knew the likes of Colonel Gerard Armstrong from his time in the army. Once the job had finished, Armstrong would not let anyone walk away.

Stopping off at a motorways services rest area en route, Harry did some basic internet research on Fedor Kotova. Using Kotova's picture he'd been given by Armstrong, Harry found him in the 2009 Lepsk University yearbook. Kotova, the ex-army major, by then had turned lecturer in political and strategic sciences.

Officially, he was a wanted Pallarus terrorist. For most, he was the leader of the opposition, challenging the authoritarian government's rule. He was regularly arrested. The charges, typically sedition and promoting anti-Pallarusian propaganda, were concocted to block his activities. However, he was too visible to be held for too long.

He was dangerous to be around. Those who associated with him, his political party, and his beliefs had an extremely high mortality rate from accidents and deaths from 'natural' causes.

Harry also searched Colonel Gerard Armstrong, his new non-paying employer. This man kept a low personal profile. The open-source information on him was limited to his position as Operational Director of Albatross Tactical Security, UK Division. He and ATS, with its list of reputable directors, including MPs, and a list of A1-rated customers, promoted themselves in the public eye as respectable.

'Bollocks! If only they knew.'

****

After an overnight stay in a motorway services, Harry was early for his 9 am start at Chedworth Manor, his new place of employment. For the last few hundred metres, he followed an eight-foot-plus stone wall that he knew to be the boundary to his new job. The wall curved away as far as he could see. His MapApp showed that Chedworth Manor was on the other side of that wall, encompassing about 2000 acres, approximately three square miles. It sat in the centre of that plot, overlooking the landscape at all points of the compass.

Harry pulled up at the main entrance and got out. He was no longer bespectacled, nor did he now have grey tinges in his hair. He'd shaved off his stubble this morning. What stood at the gatehouse was the original Harry Logan. The ID that Armstrong somehow procured showed the image of the genuine Harry Logan because that's what ATS had on file.

A security guard exited the gatehouse on the LHS of the entrance and checked his ID. On the opposite side was a dark-windowed 2nd Gatehouse, after which continued the eight feet wall. While the security guards from the innocuous gatehouse thoroughly checked his car, others escorted him to the opposite discreet gatehouse. There, armed guards thoroughly searched and scanned him.

Once satisfied and having received confirmation on the

108

radio, one of the LHS security men climbed into the passenger seat of his car. Now the formalities were over, and this new employee checked out as one of the wider team, the guard could drop his stern face. "Welcome to the Manor. I'll direct you to the car park." They weren't allowing him to roam around himself, for the moment at least.

Another security man in a golf buggy followed Harry's car plus his passenger the several hundred metres up a hill between luscious gardens and lawns to the car park. "Lovely place," Harry commented to break the ice. "I think I'll like it here." It was a prompt to elicit feedback from this man.

"Yep, it's a dream job. Been a rough few years on my last tours. When I was de-commissioned, they offered me this job. The team's professional and relaxed. Yes, I think you'll like it as well."

So, this one was ex-services, which was what Harry expected.

After parking in a semi-secluded car park at the side and toward the back of the building, his 'guide' escorted him toward his new place of work. During their walk to the house, Harry noticed that they passed through multi-levels of covert security.

Last night, Harry had browsed his new place of employment. It was registered as a simple residential care home. There was no reference to it being in any special; that was telling in itself.

From what he'd read in the file about the place where he now worked, as well as the highly redacted profile of Jacob Collins, he assumed all the residents were ex-special services and related government employees. This place was more than just a residential care home.

Suffering from whatever mental illnesses each resident

had, all needed to be kept safe. A normal residential care unit wasn't going to cut it. It wasn't only from outsiders that they needed protection. Some residents were at risk to themselves, and worse, from what they knew and might say, of which he could only guess.

Harry stopped about 100m away from the main building's entrance to take in the majesty of its construction and its location. It was an old, possibly pre-Victorian mansion, built in the days when the landed gentry had money to spend on lavish construction. This property had the look of one of those buildings in historical TV dramatisations or old films of Victorian private schools.

He turned round to take in the view from the front. The rolling green landscape ended in the Malvern Hills, several miles distant.

'And interestingly, we're close to the watchful eyes of GCHQ. So, we've got tighter security than meets the eye.'

Behind him, and also behind Chedworth Manor from where he looked, almost five miles as the crow flies, was Cheltenham, the home of GCHQ. And everyone knows about CGHQ.

His guide piped up, interrupting his thoughts, "sorry mate, we need to get going. They'll be waiting for you, and I've to get back."

Harry smiled and nodded for the man to lead the way. Later, after he'd more information, Harry would deal with his thoughts and the issues Armstrong raised. Right now, he had to concentrate on the job at hand.

A beige-jacketed male employee, possibly an orderly, met them at the entrance of the building and took over from the guard. He escorted Harry into the building through the large, ornate, covered entrance housing a wide-open, massive double door. They entered a large vestibule with large double doors that opened into what was once a hall and now served as the reception area.

A grey-haired, immaculately dark-grey-suited, elegant woman, probably in her late 50s, sat behind the beautifully carved large desk that served as a reception. She stood up, leaned over the desk, and shook Harry's hand formally yet warmly. "Good morning Mr Fox. Welcome to the manor."

And, yes, Arthur Fox was another pseudonym for Harry Logan. This was to be his employment pseudonym at Chedworth Manor.

"Thanks, I'm Arthur." He thought his offer of informality would soften her demeanour.

He was wrong. She smiled, "Mr Fox it is then." She stuck to pleasant formality.

She picked up a phone. "Could you please tell Doctor Barclay our new orderly has arrived." Then to Harry, "he's on the way down." She pointed to several comfortable chairs and coffee tables. "Please, make yourself comfortable in the waiting area. He'll be down soon."

At that, she ignored him and went back to the paperwork and computer screen his arrival had interrupted.

The orderly sidled away to wait by the main entrance, remaining ever watchful.

Fifteen minutes later, Harry caught sight of a sprightly middle-aged man in a lab coat taking two steps at a time down the wide stairway. In Harry's eyes, middle-aged meant late 50s to early 60s.

The man looked at the receptionist, who smiled in Harry's direction. He strode over to Harry. "I'm Doctor Barclay. You must be Arthur Fox. Welcome, welcome. So glad to have you on board." The doctor shook hands warmly with Harry. "We always seem short of staff here. It's so difficult to find people with the right qualifications and background."

Harry was immediately intrigued by which of his

qualifications made him suitable for this position. Instead of asking, he responded, "thank you, sir."

"You're not in the forces now, and I'm not an officer. Doctor Barclay is fine. Where are your bags?"

"Still in the car." The car park was at least 300m away from the building. He didn't know if that was a security measure or just aesthetics.

"Good, good. Let's have a wander around the place, and I can explain your duties as we go. You can collect your bags later."

At that, the doctor showed Harry around and introduced him to other staff members. From their responses, Harry had a growing feeling of an outwardly friendly environment.

He also felt an undercurrent of something from the doctor, which he could only describe as uncomfortable, perhaps even tense. Perhaps the doctor could sense his unease. In any case, he gave some unexpected background. "I'm only the Chief of Psychiatry here. I struggle to properly help my patients because of the security blocks on their files. Without clearance to have full access to their history and background, I'm limited in the treatment I can offer some of our patients. And that frustrates the hell out of me."

Harry was shocked to hear this doctor talking like this, and it showed. The doctor was giving of himself and, in so doing, was drawing him into his issues. It was a tried interview technique, which always worked; well, mostly.

Doctor Adams elaborated. "I don't know why or what traumas our residents have experienced. No one tells me anything outside of what is bland and clinically useless; Official Secrets Act and all that bollocks. I'm only their doctor after all! My clearance is limited. Shit, you've probably got higher clearance than me."

Harry stuttered, "I, I'm not sure about that…" He was rarely speechless, but as well as being surprised, he had to act like an innocent new employee.

"Yeh, yeh, I know. Don't worry. I'm not going to delve further. Whatever the case, and without giving anything away, these are my patients, and I need you to help me with them. By the way, this is my standard pep-talk to all newbies here."

"Of course, Dr Barclay."

The file Gerard Armstrong gave to Harry explained the hierarchy of the establishment. Doctor Barclay was a well-renowned clinical psychiatrist who'd written extensively about covert operative traumas, PTSD, and other related subjects. Most of his research was widely published. However, some of it only circulated to a few in the 'trade'.

He was the Chief Medical Officer of this establishment and was operationally in charge. He worked under the unit's non-medical director. She was what one would call the behind-the-scenes boss. There was little information about this woman. According to Armstrong's file on her, she was a high-level spook.

Dr Barclay knew the boss had access to the heavily redacted files that could help him treat his patients more effectively. So, it was an understandable frustration and reaction for a medical professional. Unfortunately, he sometimes blurted out his feelings to the most unlikely people, in this case, Harry. "Sorry to dump on you like that. I've just come from a, let's call it a meeting, where I sounded off about the lack of information on my patients' background. As usual, I was stone-walled. What to do, eh? Just gotta grin and bear it."

Dr Barclay explained in layman's terms what Harry had already surmised. "Our patients all suffer various forms of debilitating mental illnesses. Everyone says they're kept here for their safety. This is bollocks! They're kept here for

113

national security. I can tell you now that most, if not all, my patients know state secrets. In their current states, none here could be trusted outside."

After the doctor had finished sounding off to Harry about the patients and his limited knowledge of some of them, he explained Harry's role there. "The orderlies, of which you are now one, are what we call "attendants". You are primarily employed as a first line of defence. We need to prevent my patients from harming themselves and those around them, as well as protect them from external forces. I know you are all trained in hand-to-hand combat. Here it can only be Hand-To-Hand, without the Combat bit. This is what I call H2H Defence or H2HD; always using minimal force." He grinned at Harry. "We in the medical trade love our acronyms."

The doctor explained that many of the manor's patients had been highly trained in combat. Managing them meant that the attendants needed high skills in close combat training.

"However, I have an added agenda, or role, for you and every one of our attendants. I need you to also help the medical staff by interacting, when possible, with the residents. Your support also helps our medical staff deliver their care roles with minimal fuss."

"I see you as part of the extended medical team. While you're not a trained medical professional, you've been around, as have all the attendants. I believe you can empathise with what our patients have been through. So, be natural with the residents, but not too close. Use the medical staff to guide you. Any medical concerns about any resident, my door's always open. Got it?"

He eyed Harry intently. "Don't forget, but for the grace of god, you could be here as one of them. The mental and physical traumas that many of them have experienced could have happened to any of you. I don't know the details of your background, just what's not redacted. So, I can be almost certain it's similar to them. Our residents are your people. They deserve your respect and compassion for what they've done and gone through."

Harry was beginning to like this man. He focused on one thing, patient care. As well as a good man, from all accounts, he was also an excellent clinician.

Harry noticed that all medical personnel wore white lab coats. Attendant personnel, like Harry, were dressed in beige tunics, grey trousers, and black shoes. The only casually attired people were what the doctor referred to as the residents.

Medical and social care staff delivered the care side of things. Attendants were the as-needed backup support. Harry noticed the attendants hovered in the background while the residents enjoyed their walks. He often saw them sit or walk with the residents for short periods. Some residents acknowledged their presence and even welcomed it. Others gave no outward reaction.

In the distance, he also noticed what he took as security personnel, who were also in beige tops. He wondered if they avoided the overt colours of blue and black uniforms reminiscent of prison-type establishments.

Doctor Barclay called over to a tall, well-built attendant. "Pato, this is your new man, Arthur Fox. Arthur, Pato Dante."

Pato's face lightened with a genuinely welcoming smile. He took Harry's hand and shook it enthusiastically. "Welcome my friend. We've been expecting you. Glad you're here."

"Pato, can you take it from here? Show Harry the ropes, his room. Give him the Nelly's elbow treatment." Harry knew this phrase referenced the colloquial British phrase, *'learning at Nellie's elbow'*. In other words, Pato would be

115

Harry's hands-on guide.

"I'll catch up with you both later." At that, the doctor answered a call on his mobile and wandered off.

Pato gave Harry a heavy pat on his back and said, "let me introduce you to some of our gentlemen." He took Harry on a walk around the grounds close to the manor.

"While Dr Barclay was showing me around, I noticed different sexes among the medical personnel and attendants, which is what I'd expect. But, I also see some casually dressed women. Does this mean we've female patients? Sorry, I meant residents."

"Yes, this is a mixed community, but men outnumber the women by more than 5:1. It's the nature of the security community in which they worked. We look after the men, and there are female attendants for the lady residents."

"We've got a medical staff plus attendant to resident ratio of 1:1. Attendants are in the minority. We don't get actively involved with the care of the residents. However, informal chatting and generic bonding with them is encouraged."

"Before we go any further, let's get you sorted into your room billet. I'm sure you'll want to unpack and sort your stuff. Your uniform's already waiting for you in your room."

Harry raised his eyebrows.

"Bet you didn't expect them to know and have it all ready for you. It's all in your file. They'll have gotten it right, don't you worry."

That was not the concern that Harry had. He wondered if ATS' information on his clothes sizes was still correct. As he was later to find out, his training regime had pretty much kept him in optimal shape and size.

After retrieving his bags, Harry followed Pato to his room on the 1st floor. It was small, simple, yet comfortable.

In that space, he had the essentials one would have in a city hotel where space was at a premium; a wardrobe, double bed, TV, chair and desk, shower-cum-toilet, etc.

"The attendants are split into four teams of four for the men. On each floor, there are two wings. There are, on average, twenty residents on each floor in each wing. We are their first port of call. The on-duty medical and social staff are based downstairs. We can buzz them from any of the alarm points on the floors and the rooms."

"For privacy, we have our small rooms. However, each group of attendants shares a communal room, if we want a little space to stretch out. It's all here. For me, it's a home from home."

Harry remarked, "nice." And it was. The large room contained two settees, two armchairs, a dart board, a basic kitchen with fridge/freezer, washing machine, kettle, and other basics.

"You asked earlier about the female residents and attendants. They are in the annexe; definitely out of bounds."

"We use the manor's laundry services, but we do our own ironing," he added while opening a cupboard door containing simple cleaning items. Like you, we're all ex-military here, so that's not a problem. Can't think of anything else."

As an afterthought, "oh, and by the way, no booze is allowed on the premises and while on duty. There's a decent pub in the village you can use on your days off and downtime. That's it. Any questions."

Pato looked at his watch. "Oops, almost nosh time, 1223. We stagger eating between the different groups of attendants. We're on 1230-1300. Get changed, come on."

Harry, in his new uniform, followed Pato bouncing down every second stair, and entered a large communal dining room.

Harry noticed that the only staff members sitting with the residents were the medical and social care staff. The attendants who were eating had their table near the entrance but discreetly set back, half hidden by a partial partition. It was obvious that they were backup if anything kicked off in here.

The physically and mentally able residents queued and helped themselves to the buffet. The on-duty attendants served and looked after the other residents. "Once we're done eating, we'll help with the food. In the warmer weather, those residents who struggle with the basics get their food delivered to them on the patio."

Harry looked around. It was well organised, almost regimented. All flowed efficiently and simply.

Once they'd eaten and done their share of helping with the meals, Pato continued his tour of the premises.

"We might be security here, but no one carries. The biggest issues we face are from the residents. Most of them are highly trained ex-spooks and ex-military, and all are potentially dangerous. Under no circumstances do we use lethal force on them."

"Dr Barclay already told me that. So, clear and understood."

"We have an arms strong room if needed, but that's in case of trouble from outside. It has never been opened in anger, to my knowledge. I'll show you around it in a couple of days once you've settled. There's a range we can use at the local Barracks down the road. You've been vetted already for it. There's a rota if you're interested."

"That'll be handy thanks."

As they patrolled the grounds, Harry noticed the CCTV cameras. Some were very discreet. "So, where are the CCTV operations?"

"Just a few cameras around, as you can see." Pato was a bit hesitant in his response. "Don't know much about them, but most likely managed by the gatehouse team."

Harry could have played dumb, but he wanted to test this man. "The gatehouse must be a Tardis or something." Harry smiled at his guide innocently.

"Eh? Dunno what you mean."

"I've counted 24 cameras so far and we've not fully gone around the property. I'm assuming others are on the boundaries. There are infrared beams strategically placed. There's a sophisticated security alarm system. The gatehouse must be massive!"

Pato capitulated. "Understood. I asked the same question when I arrived. It's hush-hush, and no one talks about it. All I know is that it works."

Pato chuckled at Harry. "Let's walk a little further. I'll point out the main points of interest, and you can tell me how many more cameras you can identify."

15. MATCHING

The doctor caught up with the two attendants and their surreptitious camera count. "Hello Arthur, OK so far?"

"Yes, sir."

"Follow me." He led Pato and Harry to the large patio. One man, wrapped in a thick blanket, sat in a wicker chair on the large patio several metres away from them and out of earshot. It was cold outside at this time of the morning, not that it would warm up much in the afternoon at this time of the year. It seemed most unusual to be sitting out there alone. All the others outside the building were moving around.

Dr Barclay whispered about that resident, "If OK with you, let me introduce you to Simon. Your predecessor often sat with him, and while he doesn't show it, I think he misses him. It's not a test, so please don't worry. But if you don't mind, I want to gauge your interaction with him. Let's see how you both get on. I like to marry up my teams, so please don't worry if it doesn't work out."

As they approached the man, the doctor explained that Simon Ford had suffered from a severe head injury. "He should have died. There's a lot of brain damage."

He waved over at the seated man as they approached.

Although directly facing them, Simon gave no acknowledgement of their approach.

"He can have angry episodes that dissipate as quickly as they come, so watch out for that."

When they reached him, Dr Barclay made the introduction. "Hello, Simon, this is Arthur."

"A pleasure to meet you. What do I call you?" asked Harry. He wasn't too sure of the procedure, but it seemed a safe bet to allow Simon to determine how he should be addressed.

"It's OK, Arthur, you can call him Simon," interjected Pato.

Then to Simon, Pato added, "that's your name isn't it?"

"Yes, I'm Simon."

Harry noticed another medical member of staff hovering in the peripheries.

"I'm new here," opened Harry. "They thought you might be able to help me with the ropes here."

"OK. I'll keep an eye on Arthur for you," responded Simon without looking at them. "You are dismissed."

"Arthur, if you're OK here, we'll leave you both to chat and we'll swing back shortly."

Harry acknowledged he was OK by sitting in the chair next to Simon. After the two left, Simon quietly replied to Harry's first question. "You can call me Major Ford or Major. Wait, let me think. Yes, that's right. What's your rank?"

"Sergeant."

"Ah. Enlisted. Call me sir. When they are around, Simon is fine. And Pato's a patronising twat."

Harry looked at Simon, bewildered.

Simon stared ahead, not batting an eye.

"They're scared of me. Worried I'll say something and let the cat out of the bag. Then all shit'll be let loose."

After those words, Simon remained quiet for some time. Still staring forward as if Harry wasn't there, he spouted,

"I'm not stupid, you know. I know this is a ploy, and I'm not where you said I was. I'm not saying anything. I know nothing. You're only getting my rank and serial number."

"Yes, sir."

Harry had seen similar behaviour, the erratic and the normal interspersed with each other. Being out of his depth, he said nothing. There was nothing to say. One of his mantras was that if there was nothing to say, say nothing. So, together, they stared across the fields.

This inaction also gave him time to survey the gardens, the distant high-walled perimeter wall. Even with all this formal training, there were certain security aspects he'd never have identified. However, a certain Molly Bloodworth's guidance and expertise had opened his mind to further security aspects of the manor he'd never have been aware of. Whoever put this lot together was good, perhaps as good as Molly.

After 30 minutes of silence, Harry noticed Pato returning.

With a head gesture, Pato signalled for Harry to come over.

"Gotta go now, sir."

"Good man, watch your back."

At that, Harry left and joined Pato and observed the medic walk away.

Pato saw Harry noticing the medic leaving. "You're new. They're just making sure you're covered. You never know what they'll do." Pato referred to the residents. "No one does."

Harry twitched a smile of understanding.

"Simon's not much of a conversationalist is he?" observed Pato.

Harry filled in most of their exchange, which was not a

lot. He left out the "Pato's a twat" part.

Pato again signalled with a jerk of the head for Harry to walk with him. "All of us are allocated residents to pay special attention to. The doctor watched you and your interaction with Simon. He'd like you to keep Simon as one of your 'specials'. Just do as you did there during our slow times. It doesn't show, but he's been downbeat since the guy you replaced left. You'll get others in due course. That OK?"

"Of course. It was actually pleasant sitting there, looking out over the countryside." Harry gazed into the distance. "It's so peaceful here."

"Yep, we all need some peace in our lives." Looking at the distant hills, Pato sighed. "Don't know about your background, don't want to know, we're mostly private here. But, for many of us, this is a bit of a secure haven." Then he chuckled, "if the bosses only knew they were paying us for this peace and tranquility."

He turned to face Harry. "Many of us have the same pained look about you. Caring for these people and being their friend is important to me. It's my work and my therapy, my way to manage my issues."

Harry didn't know what to make of this man. However, he was beginning to like him.

Pato changed the subject. "It's getting late. We need to head back. Good news. We're not on the night shift. See you in our common room," and he headed off.

Harry introduced himself when he entered the communal room alone. "Hi, I'm Arthur Fox. Seems we're on the same team."

The two additional members of the four-man team he was part of jumped up to welcome him.

"Hi, I'm Russ," said the smaller of the two men, shaking hands with Harry.

"I'm Krish," added the other equally enthusiastically.

They made introductory small talk.

Pato arrived soon after with some teabags. "Fancy a cuppa you lot?"

"Thanks, but nah, pretty knackered. I'm off to kip." Harry (aka Arthur Fox) replied. "What time do we need to be ready in the morning?"

"Breakfast is at 0630. Then we're on duty from 0700. OK?"

"Looking forward to my first full day on the job. It's a bit nerve-racking though."

"I know," Pato sympathised. "How's about we knock on your door at 0615? We can all head down together, platoon-handed?"

The others responded with "that works," and "perfect."

"Cool, goodnight all." Harry left the three of them to their devices. He had work to do.

16. UNCLE JACK

After their 0630 breakfast the following morning, and from 0700 Harry was gainfully employed over the residents' breakfast time. He helped the medical and care staff bring down the residents, pushing wheelchairs or supporting them walking. The attendants also brought food to seated residents, even up to their rooms, and then picked up the remnants.

Harry enjoyed the freedom from always looking over his shoulder, his ever-watchful morning runs, and regular monitoring of comings and goings in the area. Here was as safe an environment as he could have.

But he wasn't free. That element of relaxation was overshadowed by worrying about how to get Tom out of Armstrong's clutches. At least Jess was safe, for now at least. How long that would last depended on her wits and his training. Then there was the longer term. Assuming they survived, what was next for the three of them?

During breakfast, he'd identified Jacob Collins, his target's target, in the dining room having breakfast. Harry scanned the room as usual, as was his job. During his overview, he watched Jacob have breakfast, reminding Harry of a mouse. It wasn't Jacob's actual eating. He ate and drank slowly and methodically. It was Jacob's eyes. They darted back and forth, watching everything and everyone.

He caught Harry watching him. He looked away, surveyed the surroundings, then back at his food, and yet again at Harry. He watched Harry like a prey would watch its stalker; eating and glancing, watching and waiting.

Pato didn't miss the interaction with Jacob. He came over to Harry and said, "looks like Uncle Jack's clocked you."

"Eh?"

"His name is Jacob Collins, but everyone calls him Uncle Jack. This one frustrates Dr Barclay the most. Upstairs won't share the slightest hint about Jacob's background, so the good doctor's hands are tied, as he says. And Jacob's a strange one."

"I'm afraid most of the residents here seem strange to me. Oops, I suspect what I said might be out of order. Sorry."

"Don't worry. We're just the hired muscle here, and we're allowed our own opinions. No WOKE stuff between us mate." Pato quietly chuckled. "However, I suggest you keep those observations to yourself or at least between ourselves. The medical and social care folks are twitchy about comments like that. They live in a world of medical and social care dictionaries and terminology rules. The rest of us normal people have to walk on eggshells around them with what we say. So, best to say nothing."

"So, what's the issue with Mr Collins then? Why is it him in particular that frustrates the good doctor?"

"Between you and I, seems there's even less on the system about him that Dr Barclay can get a hold of. And, as I'm sure he's told you, without proper background, his treatment is a bit hit and miss."

Harry noticed one of the medical staff was having difficulty with a spat between two of the residents. He looked to Pato while motioning in their direction.

"Nicely picked up Harry. Let's mosey on over, as they say in the worst westerns."

Jacob relaxed now Harry and Pato ignored him while attending to the other residents. However, every so often, he'd glance over to his erstwhile potential adversary, Harry.

They'd only taken a few steps when whatever had kicked off subsided as quickly as it started. "It's almost always the way, but we have to stay alert. And you picked this up before me. You're learning fast."

While he had Pato's attention, Harry asked, "so, why's he called Uncle Jack?"

"Who?" Then he remembered their conversation a few moments ago. "Ah, yes, Uncle Jack. That's all down to his nephew and niece; they call him that. They've been coming here since he arrived. So it's sorta stuck. Over time, it just seemed to stick, and that's how we refer to him. They are the only visitors he gets. No, that's wrong. There's another one, a woman, comes once or twice a year. She just sits and talks to him, then leaves. Very strange."

"Come to think of it, it's Saturday, and at least one of them will be here today. They're a lovely couple of kids, well, not really kids, fully grown up now. They rarely miss a visit and tend to arrive mid-morning. They live quite far away from here in a small town called Shawbury Heath, near Shrewsbury. They're still in the family home after their parents died. I remember the place coz a couple of times I escorted Jacob there. The guy you replaced used to go with him for the weekend when they weren't working. As I said, Jacob's a special character, so a bit of special treatment for him. I think it's more to do with Dr Barclay trying his best with the poor blighter."

"When they visit, he seems less tense, more alert, sorta sharper. As I said, he's a strange one."

With the breakfast session over, it was just a matter of helping the medical and social staff with the residents. The catering and cleaning staff dealt with the rest.

Mid-morning arrived, as did the first visitors. All were vetted, even close family and friends. True to what Pato said, Jacob did have two visitors, a young woman and a young man, the former a little older.

Harry watched Jacob's eyes brighten at the arrival of his two visitors. His eyes were still watchful but now more confident. His glances around were less of a nervous prey but more of a parent watching out for its offspring. He saw Harry looking over. Harry noticed the eyes seemed now to project a warning.

'Most strange indeed.'

The young woman hugged Jacob long and hard. Their relationship was clearly deep. She was in her mid to late 20s, with a figure fuller than slim. Her short, dark hair didn't hide her features. She was naturally pretty, without overt effort. Her softness and kindness to her uncle warmed Harry to her.

The younger sibling, the nephew, was tall-ish, possibly six feet, and reasonably well built. He'd the sort of physique that comes from active sport rather than down at the gym. Like his sister, he had attractive features, actually quite handsome. He greeted his uncle warmly but with the formality of youth that avoid over-affectionate displays.

Harry and Pato occupied themselves at opposite ends of the lounge, supporting the caring staff as required but ever watchful. The management seemed to have the balance of their duties right. This was a care establishment after all.

The attendants could have been tasked to just stand and watch. However, that would have been uncomfortable for the residents, and boredom would drop the attendants' guard.

Harry had just finished helping one of the nurses with a resident and was getting to his feet to stand back when the niece came over to him. She kissed him on the cheek.

"Smile damn you!" she hissed. "We're the best of friends, OK!" she grinned at him as she spoke. "It's for Jacob Collins' benefit."

Harry did as requested and smiled back as best he could under the most surprising and unusual of circumstances.

"For some reason, Uncle Jack doesn't trust you. He thinks you're here to kill him. I've told him you're the father of a friend of mine. Hence the informality. OK?"

"OK, but referring to me as your friend's brother would have been better," he grinned, feigning hurt at the reference to his age being more than he'd like from her.

"Father fits the storyline better, sorry. I'm Natalie. Call me Nat. My brother, sitting with our uncle, is Michael, and you can call him Michael. Come over. Say hello, but don't stay. Got it?"

Harry looked to Pato, who, equally bemused, could only shrug his shoulders. It seemed this was OK.

Then back to Natalie, "I think so." In reality, Harry was as confused as hell but went with the flow.

"What's your name?"

"Arthur, Arthur Fox."

Following close in her footsteps heading back toward Jacob, he couldn't stop himself from admiring the view. Now, on closer inspection, his initial impression was right. She was quite cute, more than cute, and not so much of the fuller figure than he thought. It was her choice of dress that didn't do her any favours. And no way was he going to say that.

Natalie took Harry by his hand when they'd reached Jacob. She introduced Harry. "Uncle Jack, this is Arthur. He's the dad of a friend of mine, Joanne. You don't know her."

"How do you do, sir."

Jacob gave Harry a complete once-over look and said nothing.

"Uncle Jack, say hello. He's here to look after you. You can trust him."

Jacob accused Harry with, "you're new."

"Yes, sir."

"Why are you here?"

"I was offered a job here."

"But, why here?"

"I've had enough of fighting. I just want to help now. This seemed to be a good way to start." There was a lot of truth in Harry's response, and it showed.

Jacob saw the sincerity. "Nice to meet you. Call me Jack."

"Thank you, but I think when I'm on duty, I need to call you sir. I hope that doesn't offend you?"

"Heavens no!" At last, Jacob relaxed. His earlier cautious look was replaced with a relaxed twitch of the lips as a partial grin.

"You can at least call him Mr Collins," interjected Natalie, who'd forgotten that she didn't give Harry her uncle's full name.

"OK," agreed Harry yet again to Natalie. "As a relation of Nat's, anything you need, let me know. She's also family to me. I hope you don't mind, but I'm needed over there." Harry pointed to a nurse trying to placate a distraught resident.

Sometime later, when Harry was free, Natalie caught up with him. "Thanks for that. He's been a little on edge since an attendant he was close to left. He doesn't like change."

Harry laughed. "I'm a softie for a peck on the cheek from a pretty woman."

"In that case," Natalie kissed him again on the cheek, then headed back to her uncle.

Harry watched her leave.

'Now, was that kiss for Uncle Jack's benefit or mine?'

She glanced back toward Harry as she headed away. She had an agenda. Uncle Jack didn't have anyone there with whom he interacted. She remembered him being such an outward character, full of stories, jokes, and fun. She hoped to get this man on-side and, in so doing, might get a little more attention paid to her uncle. Also, if she would but admit it, she quite liked this quiet, yet somewhat forward, flirty attendant. He'd nice, kind eyes, with a certain softness about him. Then there was that guarded look that intrigued her. All in all, he was quite attractive in an understated and gnarly way.

Doctor Barclay approached Harry while he hovered around in the background of a nurse settling one of her patients. "What was that all about?"

"Not really too sure. I had to pretend I was a relation to a close friend of hers. It seems Mr Collins was a bit stressed about me being here and new. I understand I might have replaced someone who used to interact with him."

"Ah, yes, Uncle Jack. Yep, he doesn't do change very well. He needs consistency. Whatever you or they (he referred to the niece and nephew) did or said seems to have worked. He's perked up now and seems OK with you."

"It was his niece who set it all up. I just went with the flow. If I might say, I think she has a bit of an agenda that I might interact with him. Apparently, I'm a close friend's dad."

. "Good. Since she's set the scene for you with him, would you mind adding him to Simon? Just sit and talk with him every so often. Let's see if he'll engage with you. I'm sure, or rather I suspect he's had some extremely bad

131

trauma. Unfortunately, I can't get to the bottom of it. Information on him is almost all fully redacted. Sadly, I'm working in the dark with him. Jack is a special concern of mine. I've seen you with the patients. You're a natural, gentle, and caring man. Can't imagine you as normal front-line forces as the other attendants here. Anyway, no one here cares what you've done in the past. In my establishment, you can be you. No judgements. Got it!"

"Of course, sir, I mean Doctor Barclay."

"Good man. Keep me posted."

At that, the doctor carried on with his rounds.

When the niece and nephew made to leave, Natalie waved over to Harry. He smiled and returned the gesture and pretence.

Around noon, during a quiet spell before lunch, Pato came over to Harry. "You've made an impression with the boss. Nice one. You're already getting the hang of this lark."

"I thought Dr Barclay was only the head doctor here, not the actual boss?"

"As far as anyone's concerned, he's the boss. That's all you need to know." Pato's response wasn't aggressive, merely matter-of-fact.

"Cool. I understand. Thanks. In that case, good to hear I'm OK with the main man."

17. CATCHING UP

Harry was desperate to contact Jess. However, Chedworth Manor didn't give him sufficient privacy to have that first call should things not be well for her. The place was an uncertainty. He didn't know what surveillance equipment the security staff might use in addition to what he was aware of. After all, this establishment was an offshoot of the Spooks.

He could hardly hide his elation and definitely couldn't show it. Three days after he arrived, Harry had his first afternoon off.

'Result. What a relief!'

He'd been overdue calling Jess and been worried about how she was doing. He knew she was resourceful and would be fine, but the uncertainty niggled at him. While he wasn't her real father or uncle, or whatever their relationship was, he was responsible for his two 'kids', as he referred to them.

The four teams of male attendants worked two shifts on and one shift off during the two daytime six-hour periods. Nights were one attendant team shift on duty, supported by the actual security team, which helped minimize the strain. The other three attendant groups slept. All were ex-military, so there were no late nights watching TV or whatever they were interested in. They took sleep where they could get it; life here was on duty when around.

Rotas were arranged differently in the female annex, and occasionally, male attendants supported them as necessary.

Their days off were when their individual time-outs coincided. 'Bulldog' Matthews managed this complex rota, and any requests for changes had to go through her.

"The Bulldog cannot be bribed," warned Pato. "However, returning with flowers, chocolates, or a decent prosecco can put you in her good books. Conversations are easier when she's taken with you."

So, on his first afternoon off, he left the manor to do his own thing. Tewksbury seemed a good enough location to explore. In his rear-view mirror, he noticed a not-so-inconspicuous medium-sized saloon car following him, with two large men in the front seat. Technically, they did a good job of keeping back, a minimum of two cars in between, and always positioned in the blank spot most cars had. However, they let themselves down with the personnel. If the following vehicle held only one man or the passenger was smaller than the one in there, perhaps elderly or a woman, it would have been less conspicuous.

Harry was well-versed in this game, so he immediately noticed them. He'd have picked them out anyway since he expected to be followed. For now, he was content to know where they were and what they looked like.

He parked up and entered a well-known coffee chain. They didn't get out and follow him in. That'd just be too obvious. So, sitting in the back of the café, he partook of a coffee and muffin. From the shadows inside, he observed his entourage without being seen.

He called Jess. "Hi, Oakleigh?"

"Hello, Unc!" she blurted. "You got my message. Thanks for calling back." It was obvious, in the way she talked, that she was in an area where others could overhear. So, knowing the cunning 'niece' Jess was, he went with the flow.

"Everything OK?"

"Fantastic, now at least. Everything's going great here. I'm really happy to settle here for a while. Thanks for checking up."

She paused for effect. "Yeh, I know you're worried, but I'm a big girl now."

In other words, she was in control of whatever situation she was in.

"I've gotten a temporary job here. They're a lovely couple who own the hotel and are short-staffed. I'm working as a receptionist-cum-chambermaid-cum-kitchen help."

She paused again as if listening. "Yes, I know Grandma was angry at me and worried that I'd gone. Please tell her I'm safe and keeping a low profile to get my head straight. I don't know if Granddad's sorry for hitting me because he found out I'm gay."

She paused again in the pretence she was listening, and also to let that part of the story settle in Harry's head. "Thanks for offering to deal with him. And yes, I'd be happy to come with you to help, in any way I can, even at short notice."

She again paused for a few seconds. Before Harry could fill in the gap, she followed up. "And when you do talk to my dad again, I'd be happy to come to live with the two of them."

She was good. Harry was proud of her. In addition to reassuring him she was safe, she'd given him all the information he needed, her availability to help him, and her background rationale story. It was such a relief. He didn't need to get her away from where she was. She was ready to follow what he suggested were the next steps. Anyone listening would think there was nothing untoward happening.

Arthur Fox (Harry) and Oakleigh Woods (Jess) chatted

back and forth, and he explained what was going on with him. He didn't realise until this call that she'd been worried sick about him, as much as he was about her. He felt guilty about not calling earlier, but there was nothing he could have done. In hindsight, their call had been so innocuous he could have called earlier. On the other hand, the call could have gone the other way, and that wouldn't have worked at all.

On this first call, they couldn't talk about the elephant in the room, Tom. On their next call, they'd go into more detail. At least now, Harry could reassure her that Tom was safe for the moment, and he'd a plan to ensure he stayed that way.

They agreed to talk every day or two, and now he could call her from the Manor.

****

Harry made another call. "Good afternoon Armstrong. Thanks for the references. The job's going well. I think I'm going to like it here. It's a nice, caring place. I've already met a couple of the residents. I can't give names or anything, but one guy, in particular, seemed to respond to me. I think I can do well there."

The colonel also kept up the pretence. One never knows who might be listening in. "Good to hear from you. Please keep in touch and let me know how you're doing. Oh, and by the way, a couple of your friends, Tessa and Ron, have been asking about you. They were wondering when you'll be able to get back for a pint. They asked while you were there if you could sort out their health insurance or something like that."

"Tell them that work's tough and busy. I'll deal with that matter as soon as I can. By the way, speaking of health, how're you doing? Heard one of your rottweilers damaged its front leg in a fight with a more powerful animal. That sort of thing could happen to any of them. And, at your age, worse things could happen, so please be careful."

"Thanks, Arthur," responded Armstrong without missing a beat. "I'll be sure to warn them."

"Do you have Ron's and Tessa's numbers? I'd love to call them to confirm they're both good."

"Sorry, I've lost their contact details with this new phone. Once everything's sorted, I'll be happy to release everything." The emphasis was on the out-of-context word, 'release'.

Harry wasn't happy that he couldn't talk with Tom to see how he was. On the other hand, Armstrong's over-cautious approach, keeping the siblings away from everything, played to Harry's advantage. But he had to be seen to be pushing. As long as Armstrong's paranoia continued, he'd not learn that Jess was free and one of his goons was at the bottom of a loch, the other one, caged.

"Seems to be a problem with your CCTV cameras." the colonel commented. "But don't worry, I'll get them sorted."

Harry knew that Armstrong would immediately disable the internal CCTV cameras. This act gave him a further edge over Harry and increased the tension.

Harry now took his opportunity to ensure Tom was still alive. "Oh, and by the way, Armstrong, we have six guests coming tomorrow, a previous booking. Please ensure your goons stay out of the way so Tom can look after them."

"Cancel them now!" snapped Armstrong.

"Sorry, too late, they're coming, end of! All that stress made me forget they were coming. Also, their presence is my way of confirming all's good there. If you refuse them, I'll know that both your aces are jokers. Without your leverage, I'll be popping over for a visit."

"If you're playing a game with me, there will be consequences."

"You can check the booking. They made it weeks ago. I couldn't have cancelled. It would have been unfair and ungentlemanly. Not the sort of thing you would want to be party to, eh."

"OK." Armstrong knew that Harry had played him and backed him into a corner.

"Oh, and while I remember," continued Harry in the same vein, "other guests are arriving after them. It's the start of spring and all that. I love checking guests' social media posts. It's such a handy way of monitoring their happiness and satisfaction. If there's anything out of the ordinary, I know I'll need to close down here and deal with the issues. You know I always sort out problems."

Armstrong knew he had to keep Tom alive, for the short term anyway, so it wasn't going to be an issue. He'd have to call Paddy and Jury to explain about the bookings. However, he didn't take well to being threatened by an insignificant little shit like Logan. "If anything goes wrong with the job, it'll be the other way round."

Harry didn't want to get into a macho pissing contest, not at this point anyway. So, he quietly sighed with relief that Armstrong bought the deal and merely said, "good, we've a deal, and that's settled."

After the call finished, he texted Jess that Tom was still fine and would be staying that way. He also asked her to monitor the BnB's social media pages for customer feedback. He explained that this was their way of checking all was going well there.

So far, so good. But this was only the first skirmish in what was yet to come.

****

Harry sat back and read his paper.

"Do you mind if I ask a question?" A thirties-something woman had just sat at the next table. Harry had seen her enter and order, as he'd noticed all the others coming and going. He'd watched her from the corner of his eye come over from the serving counter with a coffee in her hand to where she now sat.

Harry recognised her from when she'd come to the Manor a couple of days previously, the same day as the Natalie kiss incident. She was also there yesterday. Both times, she'd visited Simon. He noticed that there wasn't much going on between them. Simon rarely talked, occasionally uttering a word or two to Harry, rarely in context. Saying that, perhaps this was Simon's context. She and Simon sat in almost silence for the duration of her visits.

"How can I help?"

"Have I seen you at the manor? I'm Simon Ford's niece. I'm doing work nearby over the next few days, and I'm sure I've seen you there?"

Harry was initially a bit hesitant about confirming where he worked. However, for this woman to visit, she'd have been vetted. So, confirming shouldn't be an issue. He knew it'd be OK to talk with her in general terms about Simon but to avoid discussing anything about the manor."

"Yes, that's right. I saw you there with Simon. With a smile of combined sympathy and levity, Harry added, "he's not the greatest conversationalist, is he?"

"You're right, he doesn't say a lot, but he mentioned you. I think he likes you. Do you mind if I join you, or are you waiting for someone?"

"Of course." Harry automatically stood up and pulled out a chair for her. It was an ingrained behaviour, dating back to his upbringing.

She looked at him in surprise. "Thank you." No one's ever done this for me for a long time."

"Sorry, I blame my parents."

"No, no, it was a lovely gesture. My grandfather always used to do this for my grandmother until the day she died."

"Now, you make me feel very old."

"Oops, now it's my turn to be sorry. I didn't mean... I mean, I wasn't implying you were old-fashioned or anything like that." She continued to stammer. "It's just that... the thing is... well, no one seems to do it these days."

Harry laughed, the first time he'd done so in days. It wasn't just the woman stammering, which was funny enough. He'd just heard that Jess was fine. He'd set it up for an indirect validation that Tom was still alive and needed to be in good fettle for the visitors. The humour and the stress relief had just been the release he needed.

He noticed she was upset that he was laughing, which she took to be at her. "I've embarrassed myself. I shouldn't have imposed. I'll leave now. Sorry." She made to stand up.

"No, please don't." Harry reached out and gently touched her upper arm. "I'd love you to stay. It's me who should be sorry. I shouldn't have laughed like that without any explanation." It was now Harry who was now uncomfortable.

She hesitated.

"I've just received some excellent news about the health of my son who I've been worried about. All that was just a release of joy, and you helped. I do apologise if I upset you."

She sat down again and grinned back at him.

"Can we start again? My name is Arthur Fox. Perhaps you know that?"

"Hi Arthur, I'm Helen Welsh. Simon's a cousin from my mother's side."

They shook hands formally.

There was something about her that was pleasantly compelling. Then the answer came to him. While Helen didn't look much like his ex-fiancee, she had many of her mannerisms and a similar dress sense. As the afternoon progressed with more coffee, he realised Helen's conversation was far more interesting. She was tall and elegantly dressed in a dark pin-strip dress that reached below her knees. The short slit up the side was long enough to show enough of a bit of thigh to be attractive but not obvious.

While not beautiful, she was damned sexy; her jacket caressed her curves in all the right places, or so he thought. Her jet-black hair was tied up into a bun, highlighting her long neck and almost blemish-free, lightly tanned skin.

Harry had to control himself. He was almost leering. It didn't seem to bother her. He assumed she got this reaction everywhere she went. When she looked at him, it was as if a beautiful hawk was hovering over her prey.

Now she'd settled, Harry noticed she had the confident look of a salesperson, perhaps an estate agent. He asked her what she did for a living. Instead of the mundane response of a salesperson, she replied, "I flog tractors."

Harry laughed again at her response.

This time, she joined in. "It's true, it's what I do."

"I've never met a tractor-flogger before. How'd you land a job like that? Please forgive me if this might seem somewhat sexist, but it's not the sort of job I'd expect a woman to make a career out of." Harry had to add, "I hope I haven't offended."

"You haven't. It's just that I've been in agriculture all my life. I'm from farming stock and know how it all works.

And yes, it's a man's world. But if you look like this," she gestured to herself, "the old buggers open the door to me."

Harry looked her up and down. "Yep, I get what you mean."

Again, they both laughed.

While his response was outwardly a joke, he meant it. He could see that she spent a lot of time, and probably money, on that look; it paid off. He was rarely gob-smacked by the appearance of many women, but today, he was.

"And once the doors open, and their guard's down, they get the real me."

"And what's the real you?"

"I'm the one who doesn't stand on ceremony or take any of their bullshit. I work harder and look after my customers better than my counterparts and my competition. They respect that. So, I do very well out of this business."

He hadn't enjoyed such pleasant female company in such a long time. Jess was lovely and female, but she was under his care; it was different.

After a couple of hours chatting, she regretfully announced, "unfortunately, I've a meeting I can't get out from, as much as I'd really love to."

And that brought Harry's pleasant afternoon to an end. She did, however, take his number, promising to call him when she was next in the area.

His mind made a play on the girl-in-every-port expression.

'A boy in every farmstead.'

She kissed him on the cheek as she stood up to go.

He internally and smugly grinned.

'I like this place. Two pulls in a week,'

Harry and his one-car following convoy drove back to

142

the Manor. Would she make contact as she promised? While he'd love to see her again, he hoped he'd be long gone by then.

Remembering Pato's earlier advice, he stopped off at a specialist confectionary to buy a decent box of definitely non-bribery chocolates.

After entering the Manor, he made a beeline for the Bulldog. "Sorry, I couldn't resist it when I drove past. I hope you don't mind. You've been so helpful and patient with me during my first few days here. Could you please take these? It'd make me feel a lot better."

The formal demeanour, the Bulldog's armour, slid off her body. She reddened, smiled, and graciously accepted the gift offered to her without any hint of an agenda.

At least for now.

18. TAKE YOUR MEDICINE

The security part of his new job was easy; it was second nature to the likes of Harry. It's what he'd been trained for in his many years of peace-keeping while on active service in the army. Oh, and yes, we shouldn't forget his subsequent less-defensive role as a humble pen-pusher.

The biggest challenge newbies faced when entering this role was balancing how best to support the care staff with the residents when things get fraught. Harry had grown up with medically trained missionary parents, a vet, and a doctor. Working with them and helping people in the field now showed its benefit. That time, long ago, was a life that took him across continents while his parents plied their medical and caring trade. That background, built up throughout his formative years, helped him ease into his new role. He experienced less stress and internal conflict than most of his compatriots, many of whom only knew how to fight to survive.

In summary, he took to his new role like a duck to water. However, even here, there were times when his skills were tested.

It was the day after his check-ins with Jess and Armstrong and his meeting with Helen (however that might end). Harry was in his usual post-lunch wandering around and monitoring routine. He talked with anyone who might return the gesture or just said hello while watching the post-breakfast pills being dispensed.

The regular drug rounds were the most challenging

times of the day. After all, who likes taking their pills? Harry was warned from the start by Pato to pay particular attention when residents took their medication.

As the medical staff trolled through the residents on this morning's drug dispensing, Harry caught sight of a resident refusing medication. This wasn't unusual in itself. Harry knew how to read people, a natural talent that had saved his life in combat scenarios. In this relaxed environment, something in the man's disposition piqued Harry's attention. The male nurse gently talked him into taking the pills. The man shook his head defiantly.

Harry's protection radar peaked when he recognised how the resident glared at the nurse. So, he sidled out of the resident's line of sight, then nonchalantly made his way toward the pair.

From his seated position, the resident leaned forward and screamed at the nurse, "you're not testing your drugs on me!"

"Charlie, you know this is your usual medication, and you know how it helps you feel better." The nurse reassuringly smiled and leaned in. "Don't you want to feel better?"

"No! No more pills. Who are you? I don't know you!"

Harry was too far away to prevent the resident strike out with a sharp, left roundhouse punch to the nurse's face. Although delivered from a seated position, the blow from a highly trained and large-framed man sent the nurse backward. Blood spattered across the stunned nurse's face.

The resident leapt to his feet to deliver a vicious follow-up punch, but it never got executed. Harry had by then reached the pair from behind and right of the violent man. He locked and disabled the attacking arm before it could do any further damage.

Harry spun the resident round to face him and let him

go, smiling, hands up in a gesture of compliance.

With the resident's attention now on Harry, the nurse managed to pull back out of harm's way.

The resident smiled in return. Harry recognised that smile and waited.

Even out of shape, the resident's straight kick to Harry's groin was well-executed and fast. Harry's cross-fist downward block took the momentum from the kick as he pushed it to one side, out of danger. The resident was sufficiently off balance to prevent him from delivering the automatic follow-up he'd been trained to execute.

Harry again took up his complaint stance, pleasantly smiling, with his hands openly displayed to the man opposite him. The man feinted with his right, then again with his left, playing with Harry, his victim. He struck out at Harry again, which Harry blocked. The resident spun low and upward. Now close in, he delivered an elbow strike, followed by a roundhouse punch with the other fist. His strikes were accurate and hard, designed to offer maximum damage to his opponent.

Unfortunately for the man, Harry was his opponent. He anticipated the moves, weaving away when he could and blocking the more cunning ones. Nothing got through. The resident realised his efforts were futile. He grinned, but this time with a full facial expression. He also put his hands up. Was he still playing with Harry?

Another nurse came to assist and finish giving the resident his medicine. However, that nurse's arrival was met with the palm of Harry's hand to the front of his face.

The resident had waited for any opportunity for Harry to be off-guard. Seeing Harry's attention was now on the new nurse, he launched a combination of kicks, knee, fist, elbow strikes, and head-butts.

Harry was ready. He parried some strikes and danced

away from other attacks.

After that third flurry of strikes ended, Harry again took up his smiling, open-gestured stance, confident and ready.

And Harry's attacker knew it. He stood up straight and chuckled. At last, he realised the futility of his attacks. The resident calmly sat down again; it was over. The whole incident lasted less than a few minutes. Pato and another attendant, having dashed over, panting from their exertions, arrived and blurted out, "got ourselves out of breath for nothing." Pato chuckled. "Nice one fella."

"Is the nurse OK?" queried Harry. "Sorry I took so long to get here."

"Better than he would have been had it not been for you. He's a new hire. Hopefully, that'll be a lesson for him."

"Is it often like this? Or was this an exception?"

"I've been here for three years. Things do flare up. There's often no rhyme nor reason, but I'm no medic. For me, there's always something new to learn," Pato replied. "I expect he knew it was a new nurse and tried to retaliate for whatever's in his head."

Harry surveyed the people around and could see that most had ignored the incident, or it had gone over their heads. He couldn't tell. He was neither medic nor psychiatric trained. For some reason, he felt compelled to glance toward Jacob Collins. His sixth sense was correct. Uncle Jack seemed to give him a twitch of recognition and seemingly a nod of understanding. Or was it respect or both or his imagination?

Pato added, "when things kicked off like that, you did great reacting professionally, keeping your emotions out, and staying calm. By the time we got here to support you, it was almost like nothing had happened. Keep up the good work, and we'll all be fine."

After that extreme incident, which Harry single-handedly defused, Pato mostly left him to his own devices. Every so often, Pato did pop up to see how he was doing, but that was all.

As well as the attendants, Harry was also gaining the trust and respect of the medical staff. Such was their comfort with him, Dr Barclay had allocated a couple of other more needy residents for him to accompany on quiet times. These added residents enabled him to stay in contact with and oversee Jacob Collins without drawing particular attention. It was perfect for his principal agenda. A couple of times a day, he'd also sit with Jacob.

When Harry came over to keep Jacob company, more and more, he was starting to get a glance of recognition when he sat in the next chair, although not always. On good days, Jacob would sometimes read a newspaper and ignore Harry. Other times, he would sit, stare out and around, and ignore Harry. But that was all. After the initial recognition, there was rarely any discussion or further interaction.

When others had visitors, Jacob's furtive glances would exacerbate. There was one thing that gave Harry a certain feeling of satisfaction. When in the same room as Jacob, even when not nearby, Jack's furtive glances seemed to reduce. He wasn't the only one who noticed the behavioral change.

Later that afternoon, Harry had managed to take a few moments out to enjoy a cup of tea at the back of the lounge. It was all quiet on the Western Front, as they say. Dr Barclay noticed him there, came over, and sat by him. "Saw the report after the incident this morning. Are you OK? You took a helluva beating from Charlie."

"Luckily, nothing landed, and all pretty much OK."

"I saw the video. There was no luck there. But if you want to stick with the luck story, all good by me."

Harry shrugged and added, "saying that, I think I'll be

heading for a mosaic of bruises to my arms and legs." He had to add words of reassurance, "a lot less than I've had before, so I'll heal."

The doctor's eyebrows raised. "You've had worse? Of course, you're ex-military."

"Much worse, and I'm still here," Harry smiled. He remembered back to the beating that almost killed him.

The doctor looked over to another of the attendants standing at the far end of the room. "The last incident like this morning, David over there, lost two front teeth." He nodded to another, "Eric suffered a fractured clavicle over a month ago. And your man was bigger and faster from what I could see."

"How's Bill?" Asked Harry of the nurse who'd been hit.

"I checked him out myself. Broken nose. Possible broken jaw. Sent him off for an X-ray. Your man hurt him."

"Sorry, I was too slow."

"Don't knock yourself, young man. The camera footage also showed you catching the pre-incident. You stalked the potential situation without fuss, and you were definitely not slow."

The doctor looked over to Jacob Collins. "You mightn't notice it, but since that incident, Jacob's calmer when you're around. He's picked up on you and in a positive way. Keep up the good work with him. Simon and a few of the others you've been allocated are already responding in their own small ways to your presence. It's only been a few days, and you've already made your mark here."

At that, Dr Barclay stood up and carried on with whatever he was doing.

19. ACCESS?

Harry began to wonder if all this had been a waste of time. He'd seen no evidence of unauthorised people coming in. The attendants had access to powerful field binoculars, and he'd seen no evidence of anyone near the boundaries or on the grounds.

When the opportunity arose, he'd surreptitiously checked the grounds for evidence of intrusion.

"You're always on alert, aren't you?" asked Pato one evening in their social room while off-duty.

"Can't help it, it's the training."

"It's fine, not having a pop at you. If you're OK to check on things, so are we."

The other two nodded in agreement.

Pato added. "Just want to reassure you that it's all good. You don't need to worry. Whatever security they have around here, it works. There's never been anyone, or anything at all, coming in who's not been vetted in triplicate."

Harry kept his thoughts to himself.
'Yet, here I am.'

Russ piped up. "When I got here, I used to worry how it all works, but I could never find out. No one gives. They told me to back off. So, I accept it now. Whatever security they're deploying, they're doing it right."

"I was thinking just that," responded Harry. "I've not seen badgers, rabbits, foxes, and the like in the grounds. I know the perimeter seven to eight feet stone wall is a big barrier, but some animals could scale it, and there are none. There's no other visible boundary. Not knowing with what, or how, they secure this place means we don't know what gaps there might be."

"But it works," reassured Pato, "so relax."

Krish agreed with Russ. "We all started off checking things out when we first arrived. So, we know where you're coming from. It's a part of our training, it's ingrained. Over time, we've all come to conclude that it's all good."

Then it occurred to Harry. That was the whole idea. Make the security invisible so no one would know how to break it. On the other hand, someone must know because they put it in place and were managing it; somehow. And that's the risk if the defenders don't know. The security there is only as good as its secrecy.

"OK if I stick on the news?" asked Pato to the three.

"Go for it."

And they relaxed this evening. They weren't on that night's rota to take turns patrolling the house.

Harry watched TV, but his mind was elsewhere.

'How can anyone get access to the premises? How would I?'

The most obvious solution was the most worrying. Harry was there with a false identity and papers. His job gave him access to a highly secure location that held residents with potentially sensitive information bubbling around their minds. He knew ATS was well-connected, and that's how he got the job here.

The real question troubling him was, how well connected was this Mr Fedor Kotova? Could he pull the same stunt?

During his downtime, Harry had further researched what he could on this man. He had to admire his dress sense though. In every picture, Kotova was what one would call dapper, always immaculately dressed, sporting his signature cravat behind an open-necked shirt.

The open-source information on Fedor Kotova was limited. What was there was all at an overview level. However, with Jess' help and that of the highly biased, pro-Pallarusian government and anti-Kotova biased file, he was able to extract some good background to this man from the various, sometimes unrelated sites.

Kotova was intelligent, military-trained, resourceful, and a cunning operator. There was quite a bit about his earlier academic career before he turned to politics.

Kotova considered himself a Pallarusian patriot, a democrat who believed in democracy for all. To the Pallarus government, he was a rebel leader, terrorist, criminal, murderer, freedom fighter, and political nuisance. The opinions on him were as wide as they were varied. As usual, they depended on the writers' perspectives and the political agendas they served.

Kotova was a staunch campaigner against the then-incumbent president and had been arrested and jailed several times for sedition. With rapidly growing followers, he was seen as a strong presidential contender for the next election, assuming it wasn't rigged; which it always was. As it was, he was imprisoned before the election and let out a year later. Many of his more outspoken followers disappeared before and during his imprisonment, never to be seen again.

It outwardly appeared that the beatings, imprisonment, and loss of friends, relations, and followers had taken its toll. Some assumed he felt responsible for the disappearances of his close friends and supporters, which was more likely their deaths. Whatever the real reason, his anti-government activities stopped. Many thought Kotova was a broken man, a spent force, too scared to fight on.

If these suggestions were correct, then why would he be after Jacob? If this man still had anger against those who'd wronged him, he was almost certainly not broken. So, Harry pushed those ideas to the bottom of the pile.

Reading between the lines of the information Harry gleaned, Harry concluded that, to protect his people and cause, Kotova changed his strategy to lead an underground anti-government resistance.

The story about him went quiet in the autumn of 2012 while on holiday abroad in the Middle East. Kotova disappeared without a trace.

Rumours abounded about him being in hiding. Some sources suggested he'd been captured and held by the Egyptians or the Israelis. The open-source information was very vague and conflicting.

It was like he ceased to exist.

What intrigued Harry the most was where Kotova had been until now. What had he been doing for more than a decade of silence? If the man was bent on killing Jacob Collins, he was almost certainly angry, and active. Also, with all of the resources at ATS' disposal, why couldn't it track him down? If this man was a skilled 'ghost', he was potentially dangerous.

Harry went to bed, but his mind was too active to sleep. He just lay on top of his bed, hands behind his head, thinking and mulling over his underhand job, the one to kill Fedor Kotova.

And how was he going to save Tom? Because of Harry, Tom was in this life and this mess. The small, kind, and gentle man, who, with his sister, had saved his life, was in grave danger. Then there was Jess. He was so close to having lost her. He shuddered at the thought of what might have happened.

'It's all down to me!'

Harry couldn't allow himself to focus on the what-ifs. He dragged his thoughts back to what he could control, provision for. How could anyone get access to these premises? So, he thought about how he'd approach the task. Fedor Kotova had two choices for access, breaking in and authorised.

If he attacked from outside in, he'd need insider help. He'd also need to know how to bypass security. Not even the attendants had that knowledge. That meant connections in high places. The downside of this possibility was obtaining this information. Then there would be the challenge about how to execute the kill. Harry surmised that this direct approach was the least likely, as well as being the most risky.

But he could be wrong.

Parkie, his old colonel, told him once, "when you've niggling dilemmas, worry about mitigating what you can control. You can only make contingencies against what might happen that are under your control or visibility. That's your focus."

It was a lesson that helped him many times. So, Harry couldn't control how Kotova might get access. He could only mitigate against the possibilities.

He put to one side the unauthorised access. He couldn't know how this might happen.

The best way to get in would be by some form of approval. Deliveries and the like wouldn't give Kotova ready access to the residents. So, while still a possibility, it was unlikely.

Coming in as an employee would be difficult but not impossible. If ATS could get Harry access, it was a possibility that others also could. If that were the case, in what guise would the attack occur? If he came in as internal staff, he'd be visible, running the risk of Jacob recognising him.

Arriving openly as a visitor seemed the simplest and least risky approach. However, it had its risks. What if Jacob challenged him? That would put Jacob at risk. So, Harry knew he had to hang around during visiting times, should that, the most likely, situation happen.

Whatever the case, Kotova would need skilled help. Identities and paperwork weren't easy but not impossible. While here, his passport could bear scrutiny. But, how did he get into the country? Then there were the agencies after him that the man needed to avoid.

Harry had a potential but dangerous ace up his sleeve. He could reach out to his ex-controller. Her organisation should be able to get information on Kotova's travel plans. They could help him fill the gaps in his knowledge about his adversaries, Kotova and Armstrong. They might even offer help. On the other side, if this was political, they might block this operation, putting Tom at risk.

The other downside about contacting his ex-controller was that Harry would again be back in their grasp and back into the life from which he'd run. Even worse, it would mean giving in to them. He couldn't bear to hear that woman's self-satisfied voice. Then a vision came into his mind of her smirking on the phone, knowing he'd lost, as she knew he would.

He mentally slapped himself. This was not a time to behave emotionally.

'But, I'm only human!'

There was another reason why approaching his ex-masters would put Tom in danger. If Armstrong and Co became aware, they'd immediately kill Tom. So, for now, non-emotional Harry kept that ace up his sleeve.

He focussed on how he would deal with the possibilities of Kotova turning up. He was a planner. He went through the options and the counter-responses until they were clear in his mind.

Having everything planned out in his head, he felt like he was now in a modicum of control. Only then could he eventually sleep.

20. GAME ON

Harry awoke next morning to mental clarity. He always found it amazing how the human brain could juggle issues that swam around it during the night and then have them ordered for when we awoke. Now the options were clearer, he could now plan for the various scenarios and related contingencies. It always gave him a sense of comfort when he'd a plan.

Over the next two days, Harry eliminated Kotova as an internal employee. He took every opportunity to scrutinise, obviously surreptitiously, cleaners, kitchen, gardeners, maintenance, laundry, and many others that worked there. He was surprised at how many invisible support staff an establishment like this ran. His task was made easier by Kotova being well-built and over six feet. And there weren't many in that category among support staff.

On the third day, after his bedside mulling, his fears materialised. It was worse than he'd imagined! Fedor Kotova was indeed a sharp and smooth operator.

After breakfast, Harry sat with Jacob Collins, as he regularly did. This time, Harry had an agenda. It was Saturday, the second Saturday of Harry's employment there. He needed to meet Michael and Natalie and talk with them. They always arrived at the same time because routine was good for Jacob.

His sitting with Jacob was well-timed. Michael and Natalie arrived just before 10 am. Harry innocently stood up when they arrived. "Sorry, I was just passing time with

Mr Collins."

Michael took Harry's hand, and they shook. This time there was no kiss on the cheek from Natalie, but a cursory friendly hand on his upper arm.

"Anything you need? How's about some tea, coffee?" offered Harry.

"That'd be nice. Let me come and help," offered Natalie.

Sauntering to the drinks counter, Harry felt he needed to explain why he was with Jacob when they arrived. "I hope you don't mind, but after that last introduction, Dr Barclay noticed a change in your uncle when I was around. He asked that I sit with him sometimes. I'm afraid you caught me today."

"No, no. Thank you, it's kind of you." She was pleased her sub-agenda had played out.

"I could say, happy to help, but it was a request from the boss, so I couldn't refuse. But in all seriousness, my time with him is also cathartic for me."

Natalie pondered Harry pouring the tea, wondering why relaxation time with Jacob helped him. Instead, she said, "black for me and white for Mikie, no sugars for both of us."

"Doesn't Mr Collins have any friends or colleagues? He only ever gets visits from you. I'm not trained, but surely other friendly company at different times would be helpful. Aren't there any ex-colleagues, old friends, school chums, or the like? Sorry if I'm talking out of turn and you've already been down that route."

"Not at all, and I'm so pleased you're interested in him. He needs that in here." She briefly touched his hand as a sign of gratitude.

"There's no other family nearby since our father died and mother moved away to live and look after Nanna. They live very far away. If truth be told, my mother's not interested in coming anyway. As well as the issue of leaving Nanna and staying over, she never really liked Uncle Jack. We never knew why. She and my father never talked about it."

"Uncle Jack spent a lot of time travelling overseas all the time we knew him, but he loved to visit us all when he was in the UK. There seemed to be a truce between them since we loved his visits. As well as the usual gifts, he always had bedtime stories to tell us. We couldn't wait to hear about the next one."

She added. "Oh, there is one woman who very occasionally visits. I remember her from back then. She's an ex-colleague's wife and, I think, an old friend of his. Sadly, she hasn't kept in touch since her husband died. That's about it."

She looked over at her uncle and sighed. Then she lightened up. "Now, what a coincidence you asking this. A friend of Uncle Jack's from his consular time in Pallarus came to our door looking for him. He was in Birmingham at a conference and thought he might pop over to catch up. He's not seen or heard of him in over a decade. We helped him through all the vetting loopholes to help get him into here. It wasn't easy, especially since he's from Eastern Europe. He's such a lovely gentleman."

A smart, clean-cut, well-built man walked in with an attendant who pointed out Jacob sitting with Michael and Natalie standing with Harry. The arrival came over to where they poured tea. "Can I help?" he offered in a strong accent.

Harry knew this to be a Pallarusian accent since this man was Fedor Kotova. Kotova had aged well in the decade or so. He was no longer the dark-haired, slim political-academic. Who now stood in front of Harry was someone who enjoyed the gym, with what could be called distinguished greying hair. Although in his 50s, he was still a handsome man.

Harry stepped back to let the man take over the tea-pouring duties; he was only an attendant after all.

The man picked up the tray and walked with Natalie back to where Jacob and Michael sat.

Harry watched them depart, amazed at this man's calm behaviour, like everything was normal.

'You're a cool, calculated customer, my friend!'

Harry also caught what appeared to be an initial moment of recognition in Jacob's eyes when Fedor first appeared, which he quickly erased. By Fedor's almost indistinct reaction, Harry saw he noticed it was well. Jacob offered no further sign of recognition as Kotova approached Jacob and Michael.

Harry went over to the foursome. "Good morning, sir," Harry addressed Fedor, "can I get you a cup of tea or coffee as well?"

"Sorry, I should have introduced our special visitor for Uncle Jack. I was most rude."

"This is Arthur Fox, an attendant who'd been looking after Uncle Jack."

Then, to Harry, she said, "this is Leanid Kozlov. He worked with Uncle Jack in Pallarus."

"Nice to meet you." Kotova didn't stand up and looked at Harry questioningly. Then he remembered the question. "Black coffee, please, and two sugars."

"Coming right up, sir."

Harry took his time attending to Leanid Koslov's (aka Fedor Kotova) coffee while discreetly observing Kotova and how Jacob reacted to the man. Harry carefully brought the coffee over, watching the group's dynamics.

It was outwardly normal between the four of them.

Harry had spent time watching and learning Jacob's slight changes in demeanour. When Natalie and Michael visited, there was a palpable lightening of Jacob's disposition. Today, he was imperceptibly more tense and internalised.

Consciously or unconsciously, Jacob had adversely reacted to the man's presence.

'What's going on in your head, Jacob?'

"Excuse me, sir." Harry interrupted their conversation and handed the coffee to the foreign visitor. He left the foursome to it. Hanging around would be too obvious, sadly. He'd burning questions he'd like to ask this man, but knew this was not the time or the place. On the other hand, the man had played his cards. His plan around this option, which had been mulling in his brain last night, started to gain arms and legs.

During his duties with other residents, Harry again entered the lounge. He noticed Jacob was still guarded but seemed to relax when he imperceptively glanced up at Harry. There was something else. Was that a pleading look?

Fedor noticed it as well. He glanced up and saw it was Harry who had caused the imperceptible ease in Jacob.

There was nothing else Harry could do. Jacob was safe, for the moment at least. Kotova wouldn't be armed. With skilled attendants a few moments away, he couldn't do any harm.

It was time for Harry to play an ace.

No! Not Dragon-Lady, as he nicknamed his ex-controller.

Harry had a more suitable card up his sleeve, his Ace of Diamonds.

21. ACE OF DIAMONDS

Later that morning, after Kotova had left with Natalie and Michael, Harry called his Ace of Diamonds.

"Hi, Uncle Arthur. You checking up again? And before you ask, yes, I've been checking, and that expensive bottle of wine is still safely locked away in that wine cellar."

"Ah, that's good, it's potentially valuable, you know."

"Don't worry, it's improving with age. It'll be fine," reassured Jess

"Thanks, Oakleigh." He wasn't worried about the rapist in the slightest. He could rot in hell for all he cared. He worried about Jess. He still wasn't sure what she was capable of. He couldn't let her take that next step of killing someone in cold blood. He bore the mental scars and the nightmares that resurfaced every so often. No way did he want that added burden on her.

"By the way, how's our friends' new BnB doing?" he added.

"It's doing great guns, according to social media. Everything's positive, and reviews are also good."

From her coded references to the security of their captive and the safety of Tom, he knew Jess was in company. He maintained the cover. "I've got great news. I've found your father, and he's excited to see you. I know you've been dying to see him again."

"Can you talk privately?"

There was a noise of a closing door. Jess said, "we're

good now."

Harry explained what he needed her to do.

****

After final orders, Jess, at last, raised the courage to tell Agnes and Charles she had to leave.

"My uncle's found my dad and spoken with him. I'm so happy. He's excited and desperate to meet me. After all these years, maybe..." Jess paused, leaving the words in the air for dramatic effect.

"You go darlin', and you let us know how ye are. There's always a place for ye here."

And that's what Jess wanted to hear. She liked this couple. And for a few days, she'd had fun. Also, this was a place of refuge, should anything go south, as they say, and where she was about to go.

That night, Jess packed. There wasn't that much.

The next morning, she wrapped her arms around Agnes and squeezed hard. "I'll miss you and him," she nodded in Charles' direction. He loped over and joined the group hug.

"If all's well with my dad, I'd love you to meet him." She didn't know if that would be possible and in what guise it might be. But she owed this lovely couple at least that closure to her story.

"We're not going anywhere, luv."

22. NEW FRIENDS

That evening, Jess ordered a drink at the bar and sat alone at a table toward the back of the pub. This location was perfect for her needs.

A not-so-young man came over to where she sat. With both hands on the table, he leaned in and leered down at her. "Hi, there. This seat free?" He pulled out a chair and made to sit down. Jess looked younger than her twenty years, and this forty-something had an inappropriate agenda.

She looked around the pub. It was less than half full. "Won't you be better with one of the empty tables?"

"Nope, this is the best table in the pub coz you're sitting here." He leaned in, looking at her to see how well he was doing. And she was definitely worth the look. Was she biting to his charm?

"I'd prefer it if you didn't." She looked around nervously, her voice not so confident now.

Yep, he wasn't doing very well.

"You waiting for someone?"

"No, yes, I just want to be alone." Then thinking about the situation, she added, "that is until he comes."

"Well, little lady, you're wait's over. I'm here until then. Name's Gordon. What's yours darlin'?"

Jess responded nervously, and now a little louder to be overheard, "please go away."

"Better I keep you company. This is a rough pub.

Loadsa' dodgy people here," he winked at her. He made to take hold of her hand, but a man came in between and picked up her hand instead.

On her other side, a young woman said, "sorry, didn't see you come in, we're early and didn't expect you here already. Got a table over there," she nodded over to a nearby table. The female arrival looked at the man and said to Jess, "you never mentioned you'd be bringing a 'friend'." The 'friend' was said with some emphasis and not hiding her sarcasm.

Jess, now more confident, stared the man down. "No, he's just leaving."

"Yeh, all good, just keeping the lady company till you arrived. See ya." At that, the bothering man shrugged his shoulders to no one in particular as he strode out of the pub.

He returned to his taxi, parked around the corner. He was in two minds at heading back to his taxiing patch in Shrewsbury, about 10 miles away, or for a pint. Popping into his local won out.

Did he have a story to tell? He doubted his mates would believe him.

The young woman took Jess to where they sat..

****

After Harry's call that she was about to see her father, Jess left early the following morning in a taxi to Shiel Bridge, some fifteen miles away. From there, she took another all the way to Shawbury Heath, where the siblings lived. It dropped her off in the village centre. From there, she walked to the small business hotel she'd booked for two nights. It also had a good reputation for food. Despite her diminutive size, she could eat almost anything she wanted without putting on weight.

The previous evening, after packing, she searched online and found the address of the brother and sister; Harry had given her their names.

After checking in, she walked to, then down the street where Michael and Natalie lived. Theirs was a Georgian semi, set in a pleasant, quiet tree-lined avenue. All the houses had large, well-manicured front gardens, signifying a more expensive part of the town.

'Nice area!'

As Jess walked down the road on the opposite side to where the siblings lived, she caught them exiting the house. It was now 7 pm.

They walked in the opposite direction to her, on the other side of the road. She suspected they were heading towards the town centre from where she'd just come. She followed them while staying on her side of the road. They popped into a pub, the only pub there.

'Result!'

Jess grinned at the plan she'd just hatched in her head. She could have a devilish sense of humour, and now she was about to have some fun.

And that brought thoughts of Tom and how she often wound him up and vice versa. She always got the better of him, and he was always good with that. She missed and worried about him up there, alone with those two thugs.

Jess had to compartmentalise Tom for the time being. She'd a job to do and needed to focus. Her convoluted plan required her to pick up a taxi to take her to Shrewsbury train station. From there, she immediately took a Shrewsbury-based taxi back to Shawbury Heath and its village night spot, the local pub. A local, Shawbury Heath, taxi wouldn't work for what she needed to do.

Hers was a strange request. After some negotiation and

confirmation of no trouble for him, the taxi driver agreed. She made sure he rehearsed his role before the next stage. The bemused taxi driver followed her into the pub. All he had to do was to be outwardly annoying and try to chat her up for a few minutes. He was out of practice on the chatting up lark, having been happily married for almost 15 years; hence the rehearsals.

This lark would be one of his best-earning evenings for a while. After leaving Jess in the pub and now in his taxi heading back, he grinned at the thought of that pretty, strange young woman. At the same time, he patted his somewhat bulging shirt pocket, brought about by the £500 Jess had given him.

****

Jess brought her drink and sat down with her 'saviours'. "Thank you. I was supposed to meet my bestie, but she ducked out at the last minute. I thought, what the hell. I'll have a drink before I head back to my hotel, the only hotel here. Can I at least buy you a drink?"

Michael jumped in, "no, no, please let me."

"Absolutely not. You helped me. It's the least I can do. Anyway, my glass is still full, and your glasses are nearly empty. So that means you'll have to go to the bar and buy for you and your wife or girlfriend while also trying to get a stranger, with a full glass, drunk. And that's going to get worrying for the innocent barman." She chuckled at her obscure logic.

Natalie responded, "My brother's only a mere man, and they're all so easily confused." Then, to her brother, "you can buy her a drink later."

Having taken their orders, Jess picked up their glasses, stood up, and ambled over to the bar.

"She's a pretty one isn't she?" Natalie nudged her brother, who was busy watching Jess' back, engrossed in the view.

Jess was no longer the emaciated, unkempt urchin living on the street that Harry met. She was the elfin-like beauty she always meant to be. Nowadays, in her new safe life, she never felt the need to hide her looks.

Michael looked back at his sister. "Mmm, she's OK, I suppose."

"Bollocks, she's a cracker. It's good to see some life in those eyes. You've been moping around for weeks since Tanya dumped you for being a boring old fart of 23 years."

"Shush, she's coming back over," chided her brother.

"I hope I'm not intruding on your evening out."

"Not at all. You're a lifesaver," responded Natalie. "I'm trying to entertain my miserable brother here, who's recently been dumped by his girlfriend." Right from the off, Natalie wanted to reinforce they were brother and sister.

"Stupid woman! Lucky me, glad she dumped you," Jess glanced at Michael, who reddened. "Sorry, I didn't mean how that came out. Can I start again?"

Michael nodded uncertainly, and Natalie grinned.

"What I meant to say is," Jess restarted, "if you weren't here with your sister after your break-up, I'm not sure who'd have come to my rescue."

"Then isn't it a great thing that twat dumped my brother." She lifted her glass. "Cheers." And they all clunked glasses.

Jess held out her hand to Natalie. "I'm Oakleigh, and again, thank you." She whispered loudly in Natalie's ear, "and, I'm also single."

Michael's face reddened further on overhearing Jess' whisper.

"I've been locked away in a male-dominated monastery for the past six months without seeing a friendly soul."

They looked at her questioningly.

"If you ply me with drinks, I'll spill."

They clinked glasses again.

Natalie picked up the conversation. "This is my brother Michael, and I'm Nat, or Natalie if you want to be boring."

Michael held out his hand. "My friends call me Mikie."

"A pleasure to meet you Mikie." She took his hand and shook it gently.

Jess explained she had come over to visit her best friend and combine some sightseeing. "I don't like her husband. So when I visit, I normally stay in a B&B. Nothing sinister, I suppose he's OK. It's just that he's just an arrogant misogynistic twat. They've got two spoiled kids, whom I adore, but in small doses. Anyway, it's an upheaval for them when I visit, so deep down, my friend's happy with the arrangement."

Michael had to know. "Right, we're intrigued. What's with the monastery thing?"

Jess laughed. "Ah, that was the teaser to make sure you did buy me that drink." She held out her empty glass, which he eagerly took away to be refilled.

"He's nice," offered Jess. And he was.

On his return with three replenished gasses, she delivered as promised. "I run a B&B with my father and brother. To cut a long story short, we've been renovating over winter, hence the being-locked-away-for-the-last-6-months thing. This is me getting away from the noise and mess. I've sawdust and dust in all my clothes. It's a nightmare." Jess further embellished the story; she was good at that. Her giving of her story, or at least her version of the truth, opened the way for them to give of

169

themselves. It always worked.

And in response, Natalie and Michael explained about their lives and work. With a bit of nudging and delving into what they did in their spare time, visiting Uncle Jack also came up. Their one drink turned into many. The three of them had a great evening together, and it was pleasant to be flirting with someone at last. For the last few days, she was gay and had to maintain that pretence no matter the temptation, of which there wasn't a lot in that place.

As the evening came to a close, Natalie, now full of alcoholic friendship, said to Oakleigh (aka Jess), "we're meeting a friend of my uncle's for breakfast tomorrow. Would you like to join us?"

"Please do," said Michael rather enthusiastically. He was equally keen to spend more time with Jess, although his agenda was more toward the lustful side of friendship. And you couldn't blame him. He also had a great time despite being downhearted from being recently dumped.

The following day was Bank Holiday Monday, so they were all free.

23. MEETING

In addition to the hotel where Jess stayed, a couple of cafes did breakfast in the village, plus the pub.

"I prefer the Church View Café," commented Natalie the night before. "Its food is better quality than the fried-to-within-an-inch-of-its-life stuff that the greasy spoon around the corner offers."

"And, it does do a great all-day breakfast," added Michael.

The following day, the three were early and already seated at a table. They didn't want to have their guest arrive before them and feel uncomfortable awaiting their arrival.

Jess, deep in thought, looked outside the café window without focusing on anything. She thought back to Agnes and Charlie and felt guilty about her lies to them. She did try to justify that she'd gotten them out of a hole when she'd arrived, but that was little help.

Even worse were the times she'd enjoyed herself with them, and then a reality check always seemed to hit her, destroying that mood. All the time she was free, Tom was alone and at risk. Her brother, who'd always been there for her, now had his life in her and Harry's hands.

She had the utmost faith in Harry and knew he was building a plan to extract him. However, circumstances could change as they so often did. No planning could predict people's behaviour.

Noticing Jess' contemplative look in the corner of her eye, Natalie glanced back at her, but by then, Jess' façade was back in place. She didn't have time to ask Jess if she was OK. For, at that moment, Fedor Kotova entered cautiously. It wasn't a nervous caution, but more of a wondering, 'where are they?' look.

He was smart, wearing a sports jacket, grey trousers, a plain shirt, and not forgetting his signature cravat.

Spotting the group, Kotova strode over. He and Natalie exchanged one of those, we're-good-friends-but-not-that-close, air kisses. He then shook Michael's hand warmly and vigorously.

Jess watched the man. He was charming, eloquent, still handsome, and a particularly powerful-looking tall man in his 50s.

When introduced to Jess, he stared, collected his thoughts, then took her left hand and kissed it gently, while his eyes never left her. "Good morning, my dear. My word, what lovely skin you have!"

Staring back at him, she couldn't help but give an inner shudder. He made her feel uncomfortable, but she smiled politely. Then she realised that it wasn't him. She recognised similar behaviours from men in her earlier life. From them, it was a smarmy precursor to what she'd like to have wiped from her mind. His, albeit innocent, behaviour bought it all back in streaming, sickly technicolour.

In his case, it didn't seem a put-on display. Or was it a well-rehearsed show? Jess knew why he was here. It annoyed her that he was deceiving this couple for his murderous intent. Her two new friends were nice people. However, she was well rehearsed at playing along and put up a smiling jovial barrier not even he could see through.

The three younger ones knew each other from the evening before, at least based on the Oakleigh persona. When they all talked, it was clear that Fedor was the man of the moment. He was the new person to the group, and they were keen to learn more from this man. The siblings were especially keen to learn more about Jacob's past. So was Jess, but she had a wholly different agenda, and it wasn't polite interest.

"I'm an academic, and my boring university life is uninteresting." He explained how he met Jacob Collins at a university event in Lepsk. According to Fedor, Jacob had been invited as a consulate official to the launch of a new relationship with a UK University, and they became friends.

"When was this?" asked Jess.

"Ah, that would be during the early 2000s. We were friends for almost a decade, then lost touch with each other."

"Uncle Jack, sorry, I mean Uncle Jacob, had been abroad. He returned ill in the early 2010s. But no one tells us what happened to him. It's awful! We're so fond of him. Do you have any idea what might have happened?" Natalie took this opportunity to see what this man might know.

Jess saw the hint of a frown and Fedor's eyes became a little guarded. He still smiled as he spoke. "Yes, such a shame to see him like that."

"Do you know what was going on in his life then?" Natalie followed up. "We didn't see him for over a year, and no one seemed to know where he was or why he'd changed. He was going to come home to live with us, but he was such a changed man. He started talking about things. I think his consular employers became anxious, although they never explained why they were concerned. The doctors and the civil service were worried about him being a risk to us and himself. Their doctor recommended psychiatric help, and they found him a place for ex-foreign office officials, where you saw him a few days ago."

"It's all so sad," responded Fedor.

Jess could see that he truly meant those words.

"Before I came here, I never realised what he had become. I thought he'd just retired, and now I find he's in this institution and the shadow of that crazy fool he once was."

"But I thought you knew? And, by the way, we don't call it an institution these days. He's in what we call a Residential Home."

Fedor's smile momentarily disappeared, "ah, understood, sorry."

Natalie patted him on the arm. "It's OK. I was only explaining for information, not as a complaint."

With a smile of appreciation, Kotova continued, "I was aware of him having an episode, but I never realised it was so bad. He was taken back to the UK without notifying his friends or work colleagues. It left us all uncertain about what was happening with him, and no one would explain."

Jess leaned forward and was about to ask the burning question in her head when Fedor beat her to it.

"We were good friends but not 'besties', as I believe you young people call your best friends here." He'd recovered his composure and was now grinning.

Under his outwardly jovial expression, Jess could see the man had a lingering guarded demeanour. In her years living rough and dealing with people, she'd learned to read them well. To survive, she had to; if what she went through at that time was surviving.

"It seems a strange relationship, an academic and someone from the consulate. What on earth did you both have in common?" queried Jess.

"As I said, we were not best friends, more like acquaintances."

Jess put on her most innocent of looks and chuckled at him in a girly teasing manner. "I think you are hiding something, Mr Leanid Kozlov?"

"Excuse me, young lady?" His question was also a challenge. His earlier hint of annoyance, or was it discomfort, changed to one of barely guarded anger. He frowned at Jess for a moment, his eyes darkening.

Jess had innocently baited him. If he was indeed innocent, he wouldn't react in the negative way he did. She got what she needed. To keep the mood relaxed, she kept up the innocent-silly-me expression and followed up with, "I was thinking, it's a long way to visit someone who was only an acquaintance over a decade ago. I think you liked him, and you are a caring man."

There was a pregnant silence between them, which Jess again filled. "Actually, sorry, it's none of my business, but strange all the same." Her bright inoffensive smile never left her.

Fedor quickly snapped out of having been taken aback. "Very perceptive, Miss Woods. I think perhaps Charles and Natalie might explain the nature of where he is living. That's the reason why I can say no more."

Jess admired how he handled the challenge. She saw Natalie looking at him, also questioning his lack of an answer.

Picking up on the dynamics, Fedor lightened the mood. "However, if there is anything I could do to help him, let me know. I'd love to spend more time with him. Perhaps recounting our time in Lepsk together might trigger some memories."

"If you could, that'd be wonderful. But aren't you going back this week?" asked Michael, not picking up on the dynamics between Fedor and the two women.

"I'm planning to leave on the Sunday flight. I need to be home the day before work on Monday morning. I have some prep to catch up on."

"I love your suggestion, and I'd try anything to help

175

Uncle Jack," responded Natalie with genuine appreciation. Her earlier querying expression and discomfort had somewhat subsided but not completely gone. She had been left with a feeling she couldn't put into words, not here anyway.

"I have a great idea," added Michael. "Why don't you visit on Saturday? We can arrange for Uncle Jack to come and stay over. He's due us a visit anyway. Natalie, what do you think?"

Natalie hesitated. The offer had been made. It would be difficult to back out. "Yes, of course," she responded. Then putting her suspicious thoughts to one side about this genuinely caring friend of her uncle, "good idea, I'll contact Dr Barclay and set it up for him to visit."

To Fedor's obvious relief, the subject turned from about him to Jacob.

From then on, it was the usual small talk, during which Fedor continued to be evasive about his past, current life, and the work he had to get back to.

****

"Harry," opened Jess on their planned call for her to debrief him about the Fedor breakfast meeting. Harry was almost as desperate to know what was said at that meeting as Jess was to tell him.

"I queried him about what you asked. He alleges they were only acquaintances and was very evasive on the topic. There was also a hint of his involvement in your sort of covert shit, which he then evaded. I think they were close, closer than he'd admit."

"Thanks, that ties in with what I know and gleaned.

Jess left the best till the last. "And there's more. Michael

176

and Natalie plan to bring Jacob Collins home this weekend to stay Saturday night."

"Yeah, I heard they do this about once per month."

"But your target, Fedor Kotova, the man who's planning to kill that patient of yours, is invited!"

"Shit!"

24. PLEASURE, NOT WORK

The following days after Fedor's visit to Jacob passed without further incident. Even better, Jacob became more comfortable in the presence of Harry. He even started to talk snippets about current affairs while reading his paper. However, he clammed up about anything personal or from the past. Harry soon realised these were no-go areas and steered clear of all historical references.

Overall, his objective of building a rapport with Jacob was going well. He enjoyed his work here and began to relax. And with that came his concern. It would have been so easy to drop his guard.

It wasn't only Jess who'd recently enjoyed a new-found personal life to feel guilty about. Harry had stayed in contact with Helen Welsh and had been messaging each other over those days.

It felt good to be interacting with someone of the opposite sex and an attractive one at that. He enjoyed their back-and-forth flirting, looking forward to their online exchanges. Harry hadn't experienced that level of interaction since having been dumped by his fiancée, but that's a different story.

Harry was part of a team with defined duties and availability on standby, even when not on shift. The advantage of this structure was that he knew well in advance when he could take time off. Bulldog Matthews was also a planner.

When Helen Welsh had meetings in the Cheltenham

area the same Wednesday he had an evening and night off, he knew it wasn't a coincidence. He suspected she'd arranged her meetings accordingly when he explained about his shift pattern.

She called him. "I'm going to be alone and friendless, not far from you after my meetings on Wednesday."

Would you believe it! Harry hesitated in his response to this woman who'd effectively asked him out on a date. He'd never been good at this dating stuff; he still wasn't. "Yes. Oh. Mmm. I'm also off. Do you, would you…"

She saved him. "Yes, I'd love to catch up with you for a drink, dinner, or whatever's in that head of yours on Wednesday evening."

"Ahem, OK then. Is a quick drink before you head home in order?" She'd earlier told him she moved from London to the outskirts of Bristol to be close to her sales patch.

"A long drink would be better."

He could imagine her grinning at him on the telephone, at his earlier discomfort.

Harry knew mixing work and pleasure was complex and potentially dangerous. However, he knew how to compartmentalise to minimise risk. This relationship was not going anywhere, and she was a pleasant distraction. After the worry over the past couple of weeks about Jess and Tom, he needed some time out. He told himself it was only a drink with pleasant, non-involved company; it would do him good to relax. He'd not been on a self-instigated date for almost a decade; his ex-fiancée had been the last.

The pub he chose was quite noisy, actually obtrusively so. "Sorry," he shouted in her ear. "I don't know too much about the pubs around here. The reviews were great."

"This pub is a great lunchtime venue, but it's horrible in the evening with the band playing," she shouted back at him. "I expect all those reviews were from the likes of those." She nodded in the direction of the sub-twenty-somethings standing 8-deep by the bar, gyrating to whatever the beat was supposed to be.

Harry tried not to show how downcast he felt as he admitted, "my first attempt to impress hasn't been good so far, has it?"

"Can Helen of Troy rescue Odysseus this time?" offered Helen with a sly grin.

Harry wasn't sure if she had the correct historical context, but he didn't care. "Please, anything!"

"As I said, I know this area. Thank god you didn't book this knowingly. Otherwise, it'd have been only a quick drink. My eardrums can only take so much. What's about a quiet-ish dinner?"

"I don't know where would work." Harry was at a loss. "As I said, I'm new around here."

"You said Asian food is your favourite. Thai OK?"

"Absolutely."

"Perfect. I've already booked."

Harry studied her. She was some woman indeed.

They downed their drinks and left post-haste.

He now realised why she was so good at her job. She was direct, organised, articulate, and had a fantastic sense of humour. And she didn't take any prisoners. She'd already pre-booked a taxi for 30 minutes after they were due to meet. Whatever was happening, she was leaving then and going for a Thai.

She called the taxi company and asked if they could have their taxi a little early. The taxi dispatcher advised her they couldn't come early. Then the bomb fell. "We're very busy tonight," added the dispatcher. "We can get you a car in one hour."

Harry had nightmarish visions of having to re-enter the pub and hang around.

Helen was having none of this. She wasn't having her evening spoiled by the woman on the other end of the line. With a grimace, she retorted, "you know I've already booked it to come in fifteen minutes."

"Things change. There have been issues with drivers and traffic. One hour is the best I can do."

Helen's grimace changed to an expression of contempt as she calmly and slowly spoke into the phone. "I want my taxi as agreed. I'll wait until the time I've booked it for."

"Your taxi will be with you in one hour. Would you like it or not?"

The dispatcher never expected the response Helen delivered. "Do you know your office is one thousand yards from where I now stand? I'm walking toward you now. If no taxi picks me and my boyfriend up before I reach you, I suggest you leave work early."

"You can't threaten me!"

"I'm walking." Helen hung up and waited.

A few minutes later, a taxi came into view doing double the 30mph speed limit and stopped abruptly alongside them. The portly, angry driver got out and stormed round the car to where she stood.

Harry stepped in front of Helen, who stood her ground, mockingly, hands on hips.

The driver shouted and pointed at her, "you cannot abuse my staff like that!"

"Uncle Bob, tell Cheryl she's an arse. Just because you're screwing her, it doesn't mean she can piss all over me. The taxi was booked. You know the games she plays."

The driver glared at Helen, then capitulated and opened the door for her. "In!"

181

He held out his hand to Harry, "I'm Robert, Bob, the meat between two bickering women."

Harry gawped at what was going on. He recovered. "Arthur Fox. I'm not sure what I am at the moment?"

"You joining her?"

Harry offered him an expression of bewilderment but followed Helen inside the car.

Looking into the rearview mirror, Robert, the frustrated uncle and dispatcher boyfriend, asked, "where?"

"Bow Thai."

"Bowtie?" Harry asked.

"Bow, as in bend over, and T-H-A-I," she spelled out the last word.

"Ah, cute, very cliché." Harry commented. It was typical of these places to play on words.

"Nice place?" he added.

"Better than your choice," she mocked him while giving him a kiss on the cheek. "It's quiet, the food's good and some say it's romantic."

'Was that a glint in her eye?'

****

The food at the Bow Thai was excellent, and that evening, so was the sex. After the initial practice session, as she called it, Harry was compelled to perform again. From her post-coital demeanour, he measured up to expectations.

She'd pre-booked a room on her company account since it was too late to drive home from a business meeting.

****

Harry was up before dawn. He kissed a drowsy Helen. "Have to be back at the Manor before 6 am to be ready for duty by 7 am." Although sorely tempted, no cajoling from the enticing, half-asleep, barely-clad woman on the bed could make him stay for the next round.

"Can I…"

"You'd bloody better, and I can't wait."

His smile never left him during his almost-skip to where he'd left his car last night.

'I so love separating business from pleasure.'

25. FOILED PLAN - FORTUNATELY

It didn't take a genius to work out that Jacob's forthcoming overnight away would be the perfect opportunity for Fedor to kill him. Even worse, Michael's and Natalie's invitation laid out that opportunity on the proverbial platter. It didn't matter that they didn't know. The ideal opportunity had presented itself to Fedor, which was almost certainly what he'd angled for in the first place.

Jess was also going to be around. With her relationship with Natalie and Michael, she might even be able to keep an eye on what was happening, perhaps even popping in for a visit-cum-cuppa. However, there'd be little she could do against this man who'd most likely not be alone; he wasn't stupid.

The bottom line was that somehow, Harry needed to be on hand in Shawbury Heath if something kicked off. He started to work on a plan for Jess to visit the house while Fedor was around. He'd make sure he was close by, one way or another. She'd be able to give a signal if the worst was about to happen. It wasn't a good plan, full of holes, and they'd have to adjust on the fly.

If things did kick off, there was always the risk that Fedor could die. Fedor being alive ensured the kill request set by Armstrong was still in motion. A dead Fedor meant that Armstrong would have no further use for Tom.

Harry requested at the first opportunity he had, once he knew his course of action, "Pato, I'm really sorry, I need a big favour. Can I have this coming Saturday off? It's a family thing, a problem with my father." He could have said the usual funeral, wedding, etc., but that would have raised questions that could put him on the spot. It was better to be something personally important yet uninterestingly vague.

Pato grinned, "yeh, yeh, been there, but you owe me and the guys the next time we're in a hole."

"Mega thanks. You guys are a life-saver, or whoever I'm changing shift with."

Pato added. "You need to confirm with Dr Barclay though. Tell him I'm OK and we're good to cover you. Let's see what he says. And if he's OK, don't forget to tell the Bulldog or the fires of hell will descend upon us all."

"Will do, appreciated."

When Harry got some time with the doctor, his response was not what Harry expected at all. "Ah, that's a shame," replied Dr Barclay.

Harry frowned, wondering what was going on.

The doctor added. "You seem to be getting on so well with Jacob I was going to ask you to accompany him on his visit to see his niece and nephew this weekend."

Harry couldn't believe his luck. That's incorrect, his bad luck now. He'd screwed himself by being too quick off the mark with this request for leave. After all his hard work and patience with Jacob, which had paid off, he'd screwed himself up.

How could he get back into the escorting thing? He decided his response would be an expected normal reaction in this case.

"Dr Barclay, I hope I don't appear defensive, but sir, there's no way I'm going to let someone else take Mr Collins. He's comfortable with me in a way he isn't with anyone else. I've worked so hard with him. I don't want to go backward with him. I even think he trusts me." Harry thought about what he'd said. "Well, as much as I expect he trusts anyone here. I even got him talking yesterday, well, a few words anyway. But it's a start."

Harry became stern. "My personal stuff can wait. I'll bribe my teenage niece with a nice dress. She loves her clothes, and for once, she can support me with this problem. And I'll blame my boss, that's you." Harry chuckled. "Don't worry, she'll not come looking for you."

Dr Barclay also joined in the humour. "Bribery and corruption always works with youngsters. I've got my own."

"So, I'll take Mr Collins, if that's still OK."

"Good man!" Dr Barclay patted Harry on the shoulder. "You're right. I've been watching him, and my medical staff think you've been great for him. That's why you were our first choice to go with him overnight. I don't know why, but whatever charms you've been distributing around the residents allocated to you, they seem to be working particularly well on him. And you're right. Even after the short time you've been here, he trusts you more than the rest of us, including me."

"I'll set it up for you then. Or rather, I'll inform Mrs Matthews, and she'll arrange everything. Better you pop down to see her, just to keep her sweet."

As Harry made to leave, the doctor called him back. "Oh, Arthur, you're probably not aware, but we also need to do a routine security assessment on the location and occupants the day before the resident arrives. Although they've had him many times before we still need to go through the process. According to your records, you've done this before. However, our processes may be different from what you're used to. So, how do you fancy accompanying Pato on Friday, and he'll show you the ropes for that part of the check-up?"

As an afterthought, the doctor added, "they also do an

electronic surveillance check on the premises and surrounding area the day before, the same Friday. So, if you're there at the same time, you can see how they operate as well. Although, I expect there's nothing too much new for you there."

The doctor threw in a parting shot when he saw Harry's eyebrows furrow a little. "I know, it's excessively bureaucratic, but I suppose we at least need to protect ourselves on these visits, if not him. Could you imagine the questions asked if we didn't and something went wrong?"

Walking down the corridor from the doctor's office, Harry mulled over what the doctor had said.

'So, I've done this before, have I indeed? So, Armstrong, it seems there's more in my file about my new persona than was in the briefing document you gave me. What on earth's that about?'

Harry later learned from Pato that for these weekend visits, or even this overnight one for Jacob, the family and other occupants of the house would have been pre-vetted for this activity. They'd also have been instructed how to handle their visitor, who to contact for help or guidance, and what medication was required and when. Where the resident stayed would be pre-inspected.

Jacob had visited Natalie and Michael on many occasions, so the process was more relaxed for them. However, bureaucracy demanded that on every visit, they had to go through the same ropes again. Circumstances change without notice, and people forget. So, the checking process had to be followed every time, although not to the same level as the initial one(s).

26. PREPARATIONS

It surprised Harry that Pato didn't want to drive since the mileage payments were generous. So, Harry drove in his car.

The car, with two large occupants, had again followed them. If Pato had clocked them, he didn't say anything. It stayed with them until they reached the siblings' house, parking a couple of hundred metres past the house.

So, it was late afternoon when Pato and Harry arrived at the Shawbury Heath house. Pato had things to finish at the manor before they could head off.

Pato was leading the session, and Harry's role was to be the observer, to learn the process.

Natalie opened the door to Pato's knock. They shook hands like long-lost friends. She beamed a smile at Harry, who she just noticed standing in the big man's shadow. They also shook hands, albeit less enthusiastically than the earlier greetings. From both sides, it felt more appropriate. After all, this was a more formal occasion.

She welcomed them both in. "I'll let you get on with whatever you're doing. I'll be in the kitchen with Michael if you need either of us." As an after-thought, she quietly advised, "oh, and your little friend's arrived. Such a strange bloke, never says anything, always does whatever it is he does."

When he and Pato entered the living room, Harry noticed a small, bespectacled man sweeping the house for bugs; not the creepy-crawly ones, but the hi-tech eavesdropping type.

Pato lightheartedly made the introductions. "Derek, this is Harry. Harry, Derek, our pet bug exterminator."

It was met with a deadpan response. "Hello, Mr Fox. I know who you are. It is in my file here." The man's methodical response was curt but not rude, but formal to the point of being bureaucratic.

"So, you're here to learn the pre-visit process. So let's start with the most important part, what I'm doing here. I'm not a bug exterminator or anyone's pet. I am here to sweep for listening devices and other covert snooping in or around the house. We can't have Mr Collins accidentally blurting out something sensitive, can we? And, if he does, we don't want others outside the household to overhear."

Harry controlled the laughter that was bubbling inside him. The thought of Jacob blurting out anything or dropping something into his eloquent conversation was, at worst, hilarious.

The small man surprised him with some unexpected humour, or was that sarcasm? "By the way, good luck learning anything from Mr Dante," he mumbled to himself, but loud enough for others to hear.

Pato chuckled and patted the bug-man on the back. "Let's leave Derek to his stuff, shall we."

Harry also suspected this man's visit would be a reason to check bugs they'd earlier planted. If some information popped out, the authorities would be the ones who should hear. If Jacob might drop something, it would be here, where he was more at ease.

Harry felt the need to check his assumption. "I'm here tomorrow when there is the most risk. How's about I borrow a portable scanner in case someone has planted anything between now and then?"

"No need," Derek responded hastily. This time he looked up. "It's all good."

From the small man's response, Harry suspected the family was monitored when Jacob was over, and the small man knew more than he was letting on. On the other hand, Harry assumed Pato was none-the-wiser about what was happening there. He was here to go through the process as required and as instructed.

Pato added, "Harry, if at one time Uncle Jack had any government secrets, they're long gone. So, no risk of disclosures from him."

Harry turned to Pato. "From what I've seen of him, you're probably right."

Then Pato added, "you may well wonder what you and I doing here with Derek. But that's the job, eh Derek?"

No response. Derek busily ignored him.

Pato winked and grinned back at Harry; they'd annoyed Derek enough. "Let's chat with Mr and Miss Collins at the back."

Pato knocked on the doorframe of the open kitchen door. "Are you OK to have the review now?"

"Knock yourself out," sighed Michael over his shoulder. He turned around to face them, knife in wet hands. They'd interrupted him preparing vegetables at the sink.

Pato picked up on Michael's mood, annoyance, perhaps frustration. He waved several stapled sheets of paper. "It's the usual checklist and boxes to tick. Gotta go through this, sorry."

"That's OK," piped up Natalie. "We know you're only doing your job."

"OK, shoot," joined Michael, his mood a little lighter.

Pato got Harry to ask the questions and guided Harry through filling in the responses. All was well except for the answer to the question about Jacob having contact with anyone else.

"No one else," Michael interjected, a little quicker than he should have. His response dragged a glare from his sister, but she said nothing. Michael got in his response before Natalie could raise a flag with a yes.

"Next on the list is the house tour. Harry's new here, and I need to spend a bit more time than usual showing him around the house, especially where Jacob's sleeping. Do you want to accompany us?"

"We trust you. No peeping into my sock drawers though," joked Michael.

"Of course not sir," Pato chuckled.

Harry was more than happy with this next part of the process. He needed to know the lay of the land should the worst happen. And based on tomorrow's meeting with Fedor Kotova, that 'worst' was, most likely, going to happen.

While the two visitors were upstairs, Natalie challenged Michael. "What was that all about?"

"What?"

"You know what I mean. You lied about Mr Kozlov visiting."

"You know what they're like. It'd be more bureaucracy and time-wasting bollocks. They might even stop Uncle Jack coming. I like Mr Kozlov. And I think he'd be good for him."

"You'll call them first thing tomorrow, got it!"

"Yes, boss."

While Pato and Harry were upstairs, they heard the door close and realised that Derek had left.

Once finished upstairs, Pato took Harry around the grounds and explained the key points that Harry needed to look out for.

Harry said nothing but picked up on several additional

points of interest that Pato hadn't noticed.

Entering the house by the back door and then into the kitchen, Pato announced, "we're done here. Harry will see you tomorrow morning with Jacob. Any questions?"

"Yes," replied Natalie. "It's after 6 pm. You're going to get caught in rush hour traffic. Why not stay for dinner again? Michael's cooking up a dish for a dish who's shortly joining us." She grinned at her private joke to a reddening Michael. "As you know, he's a great cook. He'll need company while he struggles to chat her up."

Michael dug his sister in the ribs. Then, to Pato and Harry, he added, "sorry about being a bit grumpy earlier. I was just keen to finish off preparing the food. And yes, we do have a visitor. And, she's more a friend of Natalie's."

"In that case, we can't refuse," offered Pato on behalf of Harry. "I've not had decent home-cooked food in weeks."

"That's settled." Natalie opened a rather nice bottle of red Burgundy.

And that was why Pato had taken his time to leave and was happy for Harry to drive. He'd done this before and around this time.

'You bugger. You knew there'd be an offer to stay if we were late.'

****

Thirty minutes later, there was a knock on the door. Michael was still up to his neck in food preparation, so Natalie answered the door to Jess, all hoodied-up. Once inside and behind closed doors, Jess pulled down her hoodie mumbling, "it's cold outside." She followed Natalie into the kitchen, who motioned her to sit down. Jess ignored the others sitting around the large table and gave

192

Michael a peck on the cheek. "Thank you for the invite."

The simultaneous glance at Harry confirmed that that display of affection for Mikie was for Harry's benefit.

Turning to the other two visitors, she remarked, "ah, didn't notice you had company, sorry."

From their previous evening's catch-up, Harry knew Jess would be coming. Jess didn't know he'd been invited to stay until a short while ago; mobile messaging can be so discreet these days. He warned her he'd been followed, and she needed to take precautions in case she was recognised; hence the hoodie.

Natalie introduced her three guests to each other.

While introducing Harry, Jess didn't fail to notice Natalie's hand touching Harry's upper arm. They shared an almost imperceptible glance, which Jess picked up on.

Harry saw the glint in Jess' eye as she picked up on that little bit of shared affection. He inwardly groaned at what he suspected was about to descend. Jess could be a devious windup merchant.

Harry knew her feelings for him, which he could never return; or, in any way, encourage. He could never compromise on the safety of his two wards, his 'kids' as he referred to them.

Relationship dynamics needed to be maintained for their safety and he tried to avoid all illicit thoughts about her. In his mind, she was still vulnerable and far too young. And there was the large age gap. He was her influencer and her mentor. They gave him power over her, which he could never abuse. He loved her too much; as a guardian, of course.

Natalie piped up, "how's about we leave Mister Chef to his ministrations? Otherwise, he'll end up grumpy again."

"Good. Go." Michael waved them off. "Almost done, gimmie ten to finish off."

Natalie took their guests into the large dining room she'd set for the five of them. Once she dealt with her guests' drinks, she disappeared. Shortly afterward, she reappeared with Michael and five starters. They all sat down and hit-chatted, as a group like this does.

Little did they know that Jess had that agenda carried on from earlier. Jess asked Pato and Harry what they did for a living.

"We're both residential care assistants," replied Pato vaguely. "And you?"

"I own a small hotel with my father and brother."

"Ah, I remember you saying you were imprisoned there with them all through winter without seeing a soul," joked Michael.

"Bang on. I'm the brains of the operation. But, I'm misogynistically out-voted because I'm a mere woman."

Harry looked up and chuckled but carried on eating. It'd be safer that way.

"You find that amusing?" challenged Jess.

"No, no. Sorry." He still had a grin on his face. "It's just déjà vu. I have a young daughter who'd say exactly the same about me."

"You're married?" interrupted Natalie. Her intrigue showed.

"No, young, free, and single. I was engaged, the closest I ever got to marriage. However, that ended badly for me."

"So, how come you have a daughter? Tell more."

"I acquired her by accident, sorta stumbled onto her and her brother." He couldn't resist a smidgen of a tease-cum-verbal-poke-back in return.

"Oh, I'd like to know more." Jess leaned in and stared Harry out.

"Not much to say. It's a long story and for another time.

194

She's supposed to be with her Uncle Barrie and keeping out of trouble. She's a pest that one. She's always winding people up," he added with a smirk.

"She sounds fun girl," commented Jess.

"She can be." Then he gently added, "and I do love her."

Now Jess laughed. "Good response." To Natalie, she said about Harry, "I like him. If only he was thirty years younger."

Natalie defended Harry, "he's not that old." To Harry, she added, "you're not that old, are you?"

"No, not at all." He joined in Jess' laughing. However, his laughter was a smidgen contrived.

The others watched the interaction.

Natalie looked at Harry and Jess in turn. She wondered how such strangers could bond so well yet hardly know each other. Looking at her young guest, it was understandable why any man could feel attracted to Oakleigh. And, if she would only admit it, she might even be a little jealous of the diminutive beauty sitting opposite her. No, that's incorrect; she was jealous. She quite liked this Arthur Fox.

Michael, usually gormless to interpersonal interactions, had also picked up on the bonding between this little beauty and that older man. And he definitely felt jealous, but about Harry.

After watching the shenanigans between Jess and Harry, Pato felt he had to come to Harry's defence. "Harry's only been with us about two weeks. He's a natural carer. The residents all seemed to have warmed to him. Even your Uncle Jack is less anxious and calmer when Harry's around. Dunno what he's got, but we're all envious."

Everyone looked at Harry, awaiting his response.

Jess had to tease Natalie, "Nat, so what do you think Harry's got? I like him. He's kinda sexy in an older man sorta way."

Natalie laughed with Jess but said nothing more.

Harry had to say something, and best to stick with the truth. "My parents were missionaries and very religious. Now, they were the real carers. They didn't do it for the money or the glory. They were just kind people. I suppose all those years with them sorta rubbed off on me."

"But your ex-forces?" challenged Pato. "What made you join up? Seems a strange career for you after your background. But, I've seen you in action, and you're a natural fighter."

"I'd been travelling all my life, and I suppose I had nowhere else to go. I was eighteen and not in a good place when they died." His disposition dropped to the floor, remembering that sad part of his life.

"With all their travelling around, I was always the outsider and bullied. Fighting became natural. My parents disapproved, of course. It seemed a good choice at the time."

He snapped out of his dysphoria. "Anyway, enough of little ol' boring me." He looked at Natalie, "sorry to dampen the mood."

Natalie watched this kind, gentle, and intelligent man talk about some of the pain in his life. "Not at all. I'd love to know more about your stories. Sounds like you've led such an interesting life."

Harry glanced back at her. He liked her, but there were stories he could never tell her, nor anyone, not even Tom or Jess.

"Next time, I'll tell you the exciting ones or make up some."

"Even now, I miss Uncle Jack's stories," Michael put in.

"I know I was young then, but I still remember some of them. All about knights of old, damsels in distress, and honour among men."

"Yes, those were good times," added a somewhat solemn Natalie.

The main course, pudding, and coffee came and were enthusiastically downed by all. Then, it was time for Pato and Harry to leave. They had the best part of a two-hour journey to make, and Harry needed to be up early for his return with Jacob.

"Thank you for paying particular attention to Uncle Jack." She kissed Harry on the cheek.

"If that's the reward I get, I'll keep doing whatever it is I'm doing."

Pato and Harry drove off. Their two-car convoy was still intact; the same car followed.

Jess stayed on with the promise from Michael to drop her off at the hotel. She noticed that sign of affection from Natalie to the man she adored but who was out of reach.

27. TORPEDOING THE CONVOY

The following morning Harry would drive Jacob to his overnight stay at the siblings' house in Shawbury Heath. After he dropped off and settled Jacob in, Harry would take a cheap, the emphasis on cheap, local B&B/Hotel to stay nearby in case he was required. He had to stay local, so he could personally check in on them at intervals during the afternoon and evening.

Harry would be still on duty, so no alcohol. However, Pato suggested a glass or two with his meal was acceptable. If he could legally drive, he was OK as far as anyone in authority was concerned. It was academic. Harry was on a mission. He had no intention of consuming alcohol in any quantity. His mind would have to be crystal clear all day and night. Harry planned that he and Jess would take shifts monitoring the house overnight.

The hotel where Jess stayed was cheap. So, that was also his choice. It would satisfy the Bulldog, who vetted everyone's expenses. He didn't have much option. It was the only one in the small town. He could have moved out of the village, but that would have defeated the purpose of him being close at hand.

Harry and Jacob set off early to have a relaxing journey. And, he had a plan that involved him taking precautions en route.

He needed Jacob's would-be killer alive and secure in his hands. It was the only leverage he'd have over Armstrong to secure Tom. All the while, he had to manage the risk to

Jacob from Fedor.

An hour or so into the journey, Harry pulled over into a secluded lay-by just after a left-hand bend in the road. The narrow cross-country side road, with its high hedgerow and trees on either side, had been built through a wood. So, as well as lateral seclusion, overhead was a green-shaded canopy. It was an ideal location to have a secluded rest stop without anyone noticing. His MapApp wasn't wrong; it was perfect.

"Excuse me Mr Collins, I think I had too much tea for breakfast. I need a comfort break. Are you OK? Do you need a pee as well?"

Jacob surveyed Harry, then a brief shake of the head conveyed no. He stared ahead.

"I'll be back in a couple of minutes. Is that OK?" He'd have to risk Jacob being alone for what he had to do.

Jacob continued to stare ahead but gave the briefest of nods.

Harry ducked into the trees. Parallel to the road and through the foliage, he headed back in the direction from whence he'd come. Silently emerging after about 100 metres, he yanked open the passenger door of the innocuous car that had again followed them. He delivered a sideways slice to the man's throat that sufficiently distracted and disabled him for his next move. He grabbed the partially immobilised man by the scruff of the neck and jerked the man sideways and forwards. Harry slammed the door shut, wedging the man's neck in the quarter-light doorframe.

It was a fast and vicious combination of moves, but he had to move fast before the driver could react.

Wrenching open the door again and still crouching low, he used the passenger's bulk to protect him should the driver be alert enough to fire a round. He wasn't. Harry pulled the gun out of the passenger's shoulder holster.

By now, the driver's gun was trying to find its target, Harry.

From his position and the passenger's bulk, Harry was limited where he could shoot. He fired several rounds, in quick succession, into the driver's legs and feet.

The man screamed in pain.

Harry shouted. "Throw your gun out over your friend, or this time, you'll be gut shot."

A small automatic landed behind Harry. Harry slowly got up, looked at the driver, and surveyed the mess he'd caused. He leaned over the immobilised passenger and pointed the gun at the man's head. "Talk and make it quick. If you don't, you'll bleed out. Answer my questions only, nothing else. Then, you're free to call for help."

"Who sent you?" He knew it would be Armstrong since it was the same pair as before, but he had to act innocent.

"The colonel's going to fu...."

Harry hit him in the face with the gun's barrel, interrupting his flow. "Only what I ask, got it!"

The man nodded.

"ID."

The man slowly pulled out a small wallet and passed it over. Inside was his ATS security pass.

"OK, Bruce Norris," Harry read his name out loud. "How are you tracking me?"

"Your phone."

That was a relief to Harry. He expected that would be the case but had to check.

Final question. "Why are you following me?"

"The colonel doesn't trust you. If you screwed up the Kotova hit, we were to do the job ourselves, and afterward, you."

It was what Harry assumed. "Call the colonel and hand it to me."

Bruce unlocked his phone, called a number, and passed it to Harry.

"Armstrong here. Norris, why are you calling? Everything OK?"

"Nope," responded Harry.

"What are you doing on this phone? What have you done to my men? Are they OK?"

"In short, your men will need roadside assistance, not the AA sort." Harry checked if the door-injured man was still breathing; he was. "So, one of your men is up to his neck in it. Bruce shot himself in the foot handling this operation, so to speak." He thought his response was a nice play on words.

"I warned you to follow my orders. Your action means that Tom will pay."

"Listen Armstrong. I didn't know who they were," lied Harry. "They could have been Kotova's men for all I knew. I couldn't have them attacking us on the open road. So, I had to take decisive action, then ask questions later. You know the ropes. This incompetence is down to you! If Tom comes to any further harm, I'll know about it."

"One year ago, I'd have killed them. Try any more games, send any more of your boys after me again, and the next time I will."

He didn't have a problem being followed earlier. However, today was different. Harry couldn't take the chance of Armstrong finding out too soon that Kotova would be with Harry and Jacob. He'd expect Harry to do the deed, but that was farthest from his mind.

"You and I are going to have a discussion after this is

over," warned Armstrong.

"Definitely, but only after Jess and Tom are safe."

"I hold the cards. Remember that. I tell you…"

Armstrong never finished speaking before Harry closed the call. Harry needed Armstrong to be angry because angry men make mistakes. He prayed he'd not over-played this 'chat' to Tom's detriment. The colonel was the type of man who needed to be in charge. Harry threatened the status quo that the man was used to. Since Armstrong wasn't at the Taigh, Harry assumed repercussions would not descend on Tom.

He knew the Armstrong type.

The sort of upper-class thug who likes the personal victimisation touch!'

Harry retrieved Bruce's gun from the kerbside and emptied it into the floor well. He then threw the gun to Bruce. "Pick it up and fire it."

"Piss off."

Harry pointed the passenger's gun at Bruce's middle. "I'm sure they warned you about me."

Bruce manually fired the empty gun.

Harry then placed the passenger's gun in the unconscious man's hand and made him empty it into the passenger seat padding.

Before he left, Harry wiped everything he'd touched. He wiped then threw Bruce's phone to him. "Think you might need an ambulance."

Harry left them to it and rushed back to his car. He didn't know what other opponents might be in the vicinity, worse still, the police. All could confuse matters. He and Jacob needed to get away from there and fast.

Harry ran back to his car. When settled, he apologised to Jacob, "sorry I took so long, sir."

Jacob ignored him.

Harry made ready to drive off. Checking the rear-view mirror, he noticed it was not exactly as he'd left it. Did he see the slightest acknowledgement in Jacob's eyes?

****

Less than a minute after Harry and Jacob left, a car pulled immediately behind that of the two injured men. The driver had heard the shots a few minutes earlier. She cautiously approached the passenger side of the car, keeping out of sight of the road. Suspecting what might have happened, the driver didn't want to be seen as involved.

Helen Welsh was right about what she expected to see. "Tut, tut, Harry," she admonished him out loud to no one there. "What a mess!"

"Please help," pleaded the driver when he saw her approach the car. It was too soon after his call to the colonel. She wouldn't have been from his team, so she must have been a passer-by. "Do you have a first aid kit?" he asked.

"Of course. First, let me take the gun from this man. Need to check if you have extra bullets. You have a gun as well?"

"Are you police?"

"Oh, my goodness no. Just a very cautious passer-by."

"I cannot help you unless you cooperate. Is that OK," she said sweetly.

"Yes, but it's empty," he winced. "Extra box of bullets in the glove compartment. Take them."

She put three bullets into the passenger's gun.

"What are you doing?" challenged the driver.

"Tidying up." She then executed the two men.

She shot the driver twice in the head. The unconscious passenger shot himself in the mouth; with a little help from her.

Helen, the now killer, put the empty gun back in the dead man's hand and surveyed her handiwork. She liked to ensure there were no loose ends and that all would look right for the authorities. Now, this crime scene was tidier. It could even be a possible suicide or a fight then suicide. Without other evidence, there was a chance the investigation would remain between the two men.

Sorted!

Helen walked back to her car while removing her latex gloves. After what she'd done, Helen grinned as her mother came into her thoughts. "Why is it that we women always have to tidy after you men," she often shouted to her father and brothers."

Getting back into her car, Helen said out loud to Harry, who wasn't there. "Look what I did for you, my darling. I expect you to be very grateful next time we meet. Even more grateful than the last time."

28. FAMILY WEEKEND

It was almost 11 am when Harry pulled up outside Natalie's and Michael's house. Jacob got out of the passenger seat before Harry could come round and help. He enthusiastically shuffled up the path as best he could.

Harry, carrying Jacob's small case, followed closely behind. Whatever happened to Jacob long ago, had not only taken its mental toll but affected his walking and coordination.

Natalie had seen them pull up and had opened the door before her uncle could use the knocker to announce his presence. She hugged him long and hard. He reciprocated in his way.

Then Natalie noticed Harry. "Hi, Mr Fox. Nice to see you again. Please come in." She took Jacob by the hand, gently led him into the lounge, sat him down, and handed Jacob today's newspaper. "This is his routine, and where he likes to sit and what he likes to read," she explained. "It hasn't changed from all the time I knew him when he used to visit. Even then, he used to insist on sitting there."

Harry grinned, "I'll remember that."

She looked at Jacob in his chair and sighed. "My mother once asked him why he had to sit there. In his usual half-joking, half-serious, half-wind-up way, he responded, "Feng Shui my dear"."

"Once I heard them argue. Or rather, my mother had a pop at him. You shit. I know what you're into, and I don't like it." She rarely swore. But something riled her. Between you and I, I think she suspected he was into something illegal, and that's why after dad died, she never saw or spoke to him again."

Harry noticed Jacob's 'happy' chair was at the back of the room. It gave the occupant a view of the doorway, and via the bay window, across the garden, and into the street outside. It would have been his choice of seat. Did this hark back to Jacob's operational days, or was it to appreciate the view or both?

Harry still didn't have a complete plan for how to deal with Fedor. Of course, he needed to ensure that Fedor didn't get a chance to kill Jacob. Whatever Jacob had done or was in the past, he was no longer that man.

Fedor looked like he could take care of himself, and there was no way he was leaving Jacob alone with Fedor. Even worse, the niece and nephew could also get hurt; they were innocents in all this. While he did have the outlines of plans for the various scenarios that might happen, this was one of those times when he knew he'd have to wing it to a certain extent. Each plan-cum-scenario depended on Fedor's approach.

He had to take control of the situation. He thought back to a couple of evenings ago with Helen when he wasn't in control. But funnily, with her, that was OK. She was assertive enough for the both of them and pulled him along on that date. Not that he was complaining; she was fun, and the sex was great. He needed that release.

However, after spending time with Natalie yesterday, he concluded that he liked her; a lot. She was just a nice person who was easy to talk to and spend time with. No way was she getting hurt in all this! And, as an afterthought, the same applied to her brother.

And what was now going to happen with Helen? She was a force to be reckoned with. And when she required that he again comply with her sexual urges, how could he, a mere mortal man, refuse?

On the other hand, there was Natalie. She was a patient's relation with all that came with it.

'But I do like her.'

Harry admonished himself for his lack of concentration. He dragged his mind back to the urgent present.

So, as far as Fedor was concerned, Harry would have to force the issue into the open. There was no alternative.

Picking up on what she'd said about Jacob, "I don't think he was into anything bad. If he was, he would not be living at the Manor under His Majesty's Government's protection. I'm sure he was and possibly is important."

"Yes, of course, you're right."

"Now, can we go through what I need to do before I head off? I'm new to this escorting process, so if I'm over-cautious, I apologise in advance. I want to get this right. So, would you mind if I asked a few follow-up questions before I leave? Sorry again. Once sorted, apart from a few check-ins every so often, I'll be off and back tomorrow morning, 9 am as planned."

"Of course."

Harry started the process. "Jacob will be staying within the grounds of this house and under continual supervision by at least one of you?"

"Yes."

"And no one else will be coming into the property during Mr Collins' stay this weekend?"

Natalie hesitated. She wasn't as good at lying as her brother. And she definitely couldn't lie to this man in front of her.

To ease the confession he expected to come, Harry added, "I noticed yesterday that you looked at each other with some uncertainty around this question. Not to put you on the spot, I didn't say anything then. I do need to re-check. Are you still OK with your response?"

"Ah," responded Natalie hesitantly. "There's has been a change." Harry was relieved that Natalie wasn't comfortable with Michael's previous answer and was coming clean; well, clean-ish.

"It's OK Nat," reassured Michael entering the room. "We've had confirmation that Mr Kozlov is visiting today. We weren't too sure yesterday, so in truth my response was correct. He's since confirmed his visit this afternoon, so I called and checked with your people this morning. They told me that since he's been fully vetted your people don't have an issue with him visiting."

"Mr Kozlov?" asked Harry. "Sorry, but I'm not aware of this change in plan. No one has mentioned anything to me." Harry acted very nervously, pretending to know nothing. In truth, he did take a call en route to confirm this visit would be OK. The Bulldog did, however, request that he be cautious.

"Yes, you met him a few days ago. He's a friend of Uncle Jack's from many years ago and was sitting with us. You brought him over a coffee. Remember?"

"Ah, yes, I do remember now. Foreign accent, right?" He remembered as innocently as possible, as one would in normal circumstances.

Both nodded.

Harry followed up with an expression of uncertainty. "Yes, he'd been vetted to attend the Manor under close supervision. It's different alone here. Could you please advise if he has been specifically approved to spend time with you here?" Harry already knew Kotova's clearance approval was at a high level.

That man is indeed connected.'

"Yes he has," interjected Michael, exhibiting annoyance

at being challenged.

"Would you mind if I called to check if this is OK?"

"Really?" Michael wasn't happy; impatience of youth and all that.

Big sister Natalie was more pragmatic. "Yes, please do."

At that, Harry stood up and made the pretence of a call from the hallway, out of earshot.

He re-entered the lounge. "That's fine. However, would you mind if I wait for Mr Kozlov to arrive? Need to make sure he's alone and all that. If everything is OK, I'll be on my way, I promise."

Harry stood at the window side of the warm hearth to avoid blocking the heat off the embers. That position gave him a clear view of the outside, and he watched for their visitor to arrive.

To break the ice, Natalie piped up, "anyone for tea or coffee? Mikie's made a cracking drizzle cake for Uncle Jack's stay."

"Yes please."

Natalie motioned Michael to follow and help her. In the kitchen, she admonished him with a, "lighten up, that man's only trying to help! All this was down to you."

Michael offered a pout of compliance. There was nothing he could say; she was right.

When they returned with the goodies, the ice had broken a little. However, as time wore on, the tension returned.

Between mouthfuls of tea and pieces of cake, Harry smiled every so often. He tried to open a conversation. "Thank you for a superb dinner yesterday."

"Our pleasure. It was a lovely evening," responded Natalie.

Michael said nothing, only rocking his head in

acknowledgement.

Apart from tea and cakes, it was a somewhat strained one-hour wait for their visitor.

Harry tried a safe question. "Jess is an interesting character. How do you know her? Her accent's not from around here."

"We, sort of, rescued her in the local pub. She was being bothered by a man, and we sort of just, well, went over to her table, pretended we knew her, and invited her to join us. We got on well together that evening, hence inviting her over again. And Michael likes her. And sometimes he can be an awkward bugger with new people."

That last sentence raised a smile from Michael.

Further efforts at conversation died a polite death.

Jacob didn't move from the armchair. He was oblivious to the tense waiting of the others. He read his newspaper, sipped his tea, and nibbled his cake.

Natalie sat by the front bay window, mostly reading her book to pass the time. She looked out to the street every so often.

Michael initially leaned against the door frame, hands in pockets. Eventually, he sat down after Natalie needed to pass him to make more tea.

****

Around noon, a blacked-out SUV pulled up on the street in front of the house's driveway. Fedor Kotova exited from the offside rear door raising Harry's concern level. He deduced that in addition to the driver, there was another man in the car. He occupied the nearside rear seat. There was no shadow in the lighter front passenger window. So, in the car were two others, a driver and Mr Rear Passenger-

Man.

Kotova grinned and waved at Natalie when he saw her at the front window. As before, he was smart, wearing a sports jacket, trousers, shirt, and, as usual, cravat.

Kotova strode up the path to the house and was met by Natalie standing at the already open door. "Good afternoon, Mr Kozlov. Please come in."

When Kotova entered the living room and saw Harry, his smile changed to a grimace. He forced the smile back in place. "Ah, the attendant, I forgot your name, sorry."

"That's OK. We're supposed to be discreetly in the background, so I succeeded."

"Indeed. And yet, here you are again?"

"I was the escort to bring Mr Collins here today." Harry also with his smile fixed in place, followed up, "I heard you were visiting and had to say hello." With a shrug, he added, "and discreetly check you out." His practiced innocent smile now beamed wide.

"Of course you did," responded Kotova, trying desperately to hide his irritation. "How am I doing so far?"

"Oh, perfectly as expected." Harry's smile was no longer forced. He was enjoying this exchange.

"So, are you leaving now?"

"Not yet, sir." He waited for a moment to gauge Fedor's reaction. Fair play to Fedor. Harry observed how the man didn't drop his guard nor his outwardly relaxed composure. Harry added. "Just a few formalities."

"With me, or Natalie and Michael."

"Sorry, but with you, sir, if that's OK?"

Natalie and Michael watched the strained banter, unsure what was going on. Jacob ignored everything. He just read the paper.

"So, what do you need from me?"

211

"All I need is to check your pass and approval document. Then I can call my bosses to confirm all's OK, which I'm sure it will be. Once we're all good, I'll be on my way."

Kotova relaxed. "Of course. It's in my car. Never thought I'd need it for this social visit. I'll ask my driver to fetch it." He called a number and said something in Pallarusian.

Harry watched a large man step out of the rear nearside passenger door. The driver followed him up the path carrying a briefcase. Harry now knew it was game on.

Harry strode to the lounge entrance and announced to Fedor, "I'll meet them at the door. In case you're not aware, they shouldn't come in, so I'll take the information from them there."

Harry watched Natalie nodding in understanding and Michael shrugging in acceptance of this interfering jobsworth.

Kotova had initially glowered in frustration. However, since his call, his face sported with a beaming smirk.

Harry smiled at Kotova. "I'll sort this quickly." Before Harry exited the room, he added, "it's the least I can do after holding things up." He closed the door behind him.

Michael and Kotova exchanged looks and shrugged; the pettiness of it all.

Natalie stood back and watched. She had been nervous about inviting Kozlov (the name she knew him by) here, and what was happening now made her feel decidedly uncomfortable. However, she couldn't back out after Michael's suggestion.

Michael felt he had to break the ice. He gestured to the closed door. "Bureaucratic nonsense!"

"He's just doing his job," defended Natalie.

"I agree with Michael," smirked Kotova. "Don't worry, my dear. As Mr Fox said, it'll be sorted in a few minutes, you'll see. Then we can get back to the task at hand?"

"What do you mean?" challenged Natalie.

There was a loud bang, and the wall between the living room and the hallway shuddered.

"What the hell!" exclaimed Michael.

Fedor put his right hand up, his palm facing the young man while he walked over to the radio. He turned the volume up sufficiently loud to prevent eavesdroppers but not so loud to upset neighbours and have them coming around complaining.

He knew the house would have been checked out in advance of Jacob's arrival. Those very same 'checkers' could have planted their own bugs; these things happen. In this case, Fedor and Harry were aligned.

"This is our house. You can't go around doing things like that without our say-so." challenged Michael.

Fedor pulled a gun and pointed it at Michael. "This is my say-so. Now, let's wait for my men to bring in Mr Fox, shall we? I hope Viktar hasn't hurt him too much."

Natalie, in shock, exclaimed, "what are you doing? You're Uncle Jack's friend! Why are you here? You can't do this!"

He waved his gun for her and Michael to be seated. She stood her ground. No way was she letting him off lightly.

Michael, surprisingly calm, took her forearm, and to calm her down, he gently spoke, "Nat, let's do as he says."

She shrugged off his arm. Her demeanour had changed to anger. "Get out of this house. You're not welcome."

"Sit," ordered Fedor, to which Natalie at last capitulated, only after Michael had almost dragged her to the settee.

At that point, Jacob chuckled.

Natalie and Michael stared at him. "Uncle Jack, you laughed. It's not funny!"

"Yes, it's funny. Fedor is funny."

"Who's Fedor?" queried Michael.

"Your Leanid is my Fedor." When he saw that Michael wasn't getting it, Jacob added, "That man," he pointed to Fedor, "is Fedor Kotova, not Leanid Kozlov."

"What the hell!" exclaimed Natalie and Michael, almost in unison.

****

Harry knew what was coming. Or rather, he knew what he'd do in their circumstances. Reaching the entrance before the men were even halfway up the path, he opened the door and held it partially ajar. He stood behind it to prevent access by the men without his agreement. He held out his hand for the documents.

The big man smiled as he approached, and Harry, equally pleasantly, returned a nod. With lightning speed, the larger of the two men lunged forward, smashing both palms of his hands against the partially open door to throw Harry back inside the hallway. Then, he'd deal with his stunned opponent.

But Harry was faster. He stepped to one side and let the door fly open to slam against the wall. The big man was off-balance and staggered forward. Harry jabbed him hard at the side of his head and neck, twice in quick succession, knocking him out. Those strikes could have been fatal, but Harry was well-versed in this technique and held back.

While helping the concussed man by stopping his head from hitting the hard floor, Harry extracted the man's shoulder gun. Yes, he could have let him fall, but the man might have hurt himself; most perverse considering what Harry had just done to him. Unlike the two following him earlier, who he knew would have had orders to kill him, Harry had no quarrel with this big man who was only doing his job.

The shocked man with the briefcase recovered his composure and stepped in after the big man. However, he wasn't quick enough to draw his weapon. Harry, who'd remained inside the house to avoid being seen by the neighbours, had the drop on him.

Fortunately, the big man's momentum had taken him almost inside the doorway before he fell. One protruding foot prevented the door from closing.

"Name!" commanded Harry.

"Yuryi," the driver responded.

"Right, Yuryi, move that leg and slowly close the front door."

"Left hand, pull out your gun, slowly."

Yuryi complied, watching Harry for any opportunity.

"Kneel down, beside your friend, and lay the gun on the floor."

"Good," acknowledged Harry, "now slide it over to me."

Once Yuryi had again complied, Harry continued his orders, "While you're down there, check his pulse and breathing."

He looked up at Harry and nodded OK.

Harry picked up his gun. "OK, Yuryi, make him comfortable and place him in the recovery position. He'll be fine like that for the next few minutes."

Once the man completed that task with the big man, Harry ordered, "now slowly get up."

Harry moved to the living room door. "Now, hold the

briefcase handle with both hands in front of you. Pretend you're a defender against a free kick, and you're covering your vitals."

Once the man complied, Harry opened the living room door and growled, "IN! Let's join your boss inside, shall we?"

Yuryi, the briefcase-man-cum-driver, carefully did as requested. It was an ungainly entrance by the man, which was what Harry had intended. The briefcase bounced off each knee with each step.

Harry followed him close behind, but not too close, holding the gun on him. He frowned when he saw Kotova holding a gun to Jacob's head.

"He'll not shoot me when he hears what I have to say," said Jacob, who'd looked up from his newspaper. "No one can shoot me. What I have is too valuable." He went back to his paper.

29. ANSWERS

Michael interrupted the proceedings. "Will someone tell me what the fuck's going on?"

Harry ignored him but instead gestured for Yuryi to stand next to Fedor. He then trained his gun on Fedor. "You pull, I pull, impasse."

Still, with the gun trained on Jacob, Kotova asked Harry, "Viktar?"

"Clumsy blighter tripped on the doorstep, having a snooze."

"I need to confirm my man Viktar is OK." He glanced at the man standing next to him for an explanation. Briefcase-man said something in Pallarusian to Fedor, who nodded in understanding and seemingly relief.

"Seems he is out but comfortable for the moment." Via a small shake of his head, he offered a gesture of appreciation to Harry for that small effort to make Viktar comfortable.

The driver continued with a short speech.

Fedor's eyebrows lifted. "Yuryi explained what happened. Only one man has ever bested Viktar, and he's here." He nodded in Jacob's direction.

"Now there's two." Natalie sneered at Kotova. It was her house, so she felt compelled to interrupt him and gloat. "I heard people in the manor talking about Arthur…" Then addressing Harry, she added, "…how you placated one of the residents. I heard people talking about you afterward.

They said you were more than just special services."

Harry couldn't be distracted by answering her. He could only put his free hand up to get her to hold off further questioning. Then, with a grimace and a forceful nod, he stated, "you owe these people an explanation.

"Jacob was correct. My real name is Fedor Kotova. Apologies for the deception." He didn't mean it. It was a useless platitude, said for effect. "A few weeks ago, I was released from prison. I spent the best part of 11 years there because I was betrayed by someone I thought was my friend." Knocking the newspaper partially from Jacob's hands, he looked directly at Jacob. "You betrayed me!"

Jacob tidied his paper and folded it up. He looked up at Kotova but said nothing.

Was it because he was experiencing the frustrations of youth, or was it that he was pissed off at guns, fighting, and threats in his house without his permission? Either way, Michael screeched, "will someone tell me what the hell is going on here? Whatever you're accusing Uncle Jack of, it's shite! He'd never hurt a fly or do anything wrong."

Now it was Natalie's turn to put her hand on his arm to calm him down.

"All in good time," Kotova continued. "Before then, I worked with the West, and we had, let's call it, a symbiotic relationship. I don't like Russia and don't trust its leadership. The West feels similarly."

"I am Pallarusian and was in conflict with its current puppet government, as was the West, albeit behind the scenes. I want my country to be free from the madman we have in power. I want the people to rule. The West wants another Western-supported buffer between Russia. They'd be happy if Pallarus could have a government close to what they call democracy in my country. My version of democracy is more of an egalitarian view, not big business sponsored like yours."

"So, our common enemies and goals were sufficiently aligned for us to work together. I wanted the tyranny in Pallarus to stop. The people and I would deal with the politics our country needed when we'd achieved our goal of free elections."

Fedor pointed to Jacob. "He was my handler. It had to be a British agent I would trust. And, in case everything failed, the US could wipe their hands of the matter and blame your lot. The West helped us acquire a small arsenal of light to medium weapons and advanced covert and drone technology in Libya. We made the financial transaction in Egypt where its history could be easily erased. We'd pick up the equipment near a small, secluded, coastal village in Libya, just over the border. Then it would have been taken by boat over the sea before being transported overland to Pallarus."

"So, you wanted to create a bloody coup," retorted Natalie. "That isn't very democratic! You're just as bad as them."

"No, you misunderstand our intentions for these weapons. The weapons and technology were for defensive and investigative purposes only. We were desperate for them. Our movement was, and still is, political. However, we needed to build evidence of the current regime's corruption and defend ourselves and our people from their covert attacks."

"It was all unofficially sanctioned at the highest levels in the so-called West. What we were doing was officially illegal, although morally right. However, as long as no one was aware, it was legal enough. So, the deal was arranged by the CIA and their puppets, SIS, what most refer to as MI6."

"After handing over twenty million dollars of our movement's hard-earned currency to the broker, the Egyptian police descended. Sir Victor Sommerville was that broker. When challenged about the money, he denied all knowledge; it all disappeared with that scumbag. Now, that once medium-to-high-ranking civil servant mixes with the most rich and powerful."

Kotova became visibly angry. "I know who he is, but he's untouchable, protected by your authorities and his people."

In visible frustration, Kotova sighed. "I found out later that Russia's External Intelligence Service was also involved in the background. You probably know them as the SVR, the erstwhile KGB. A US drone strike blew up the nearby village to mask the theft of our weapons, tech, and all our money."

"What about the village?" asked Natalie. "Were the people OK?"

Kotova became downcast. "No one talks about the atrocity that day. The strike wiped out almost everything and everyone." The sadness in his eyes welled. "The poor people not wiped out by the drone attack were subsequently murdered. Those involved made sure there were no witnesses."

"I was arrested for gun-running in Egypt but couldn't be held there since that would be outside the control of the West. They didn't want me in the hands of the Russians or the Pallarusians because you never know when I might be useful. So, I was whisked out of the country and handed over to the Israelis; for safe-keeping as you might say."

"Those powers who initially supported our independence movement decided we might de-stabilise their delicate status quo with Pallarus and its closest ally, Russia. I expect Russia applied a lot of diplomatic pressure, or more likely, in the form of un-guarded threats. And, as usual, the West capitulated."

"So, the US and Russia, with the support of the British,

put an end to the liberation of my country. They offered us up to another eleven years under that man's tyranny!"

Jacob intently watched Fedor during his monologue. Fedor looked at Jacob, tilting his head and raising his eyebrows to see if there would be the slightest reaction from him.

There was no hint of a reaction. Instead, and to the surprise of everyone, Jacob's eyes came to life. But there was no spark, just a deep sadness in them. He looked to Fedor as he spoke. "I remember something of what happened then. Yes, I was officially Fedor's British interface and handler. But to me, it was more than that. He became my friend, the most important person in my life."

Fedor pointed to Jacob. "Bah! You say you were my best friend. You were supposed to have my back. Yet you betrayed me!" The hurt and betrayal showed in Fedor's expression. "You were the only one who knew where I was and how I could be taken."

Jacob looked up at the man holding the gun. "No. I could never betray you. I don't remember much. But what I know is that I always had your back. I loved you. I still do and always will." Tears rolled down Jacob's eyes. "There was one man, my then boss. He also knew."

"Do you think I won't kill you because of those words?"

"Not because of those words, even though they are true. But you need me. I remember having a crucial key to your country's freedom; somewhere. It's what they tried to take from me for such a long time. But I never gave it up, never gave you up, no matter what they did to me."

Turning his attention primarily back to Harry, Jacob continued. "It's all a blur. I remember the SVR capturing and extracting me to Pallarus. I stayed there for what seemed forever; at that time."

Jacob shuddered with the memory. His eyes seemed to

221

come to life as he remembered. "I don't remember the details, but I remember the pain, deprivation, and degradation I felt. They interrogated, beat, and abused me for information on Fedor's network. They knew I was gay, and their brutality reflected that."

Then to Natalie and Michael, "I'm sorry you have to hear this. I'll stop now. I'll leave you to imagine the rest."

Michael and Natalie stared at Jacob, speechless. As children, they sometimes imagined he was involved in secretive work and why he was always so cagey about his travels. Their mother had gotten it so badly wrong by thinking he was a criminal. But no one ever imagined this.

Jacob continued. "After that brutality didn't work, new people took over. I think they were now Russian interrogation specialists; their accents were different. Yes, they were less physically brutal, but they were worse. I was drugged, beaten then reprieved, deprived then reprieved, over and over again. I no longer remember what happened. Time just passed in a blur. No amount of anti-interrogation training could prepare anyone for what they did to me."

Then back to Fedor. "Truly, I don't know if I said anything or gave up what I promised to hold. But if I did, it wasn't intentional. I'm only saying this now because I could never willingly betray you. But the worst thing, and what has haunted me all these years, is maybe I did. If I did, I'm so sorry. You are right to kill me. I deserve to die." The tears rolled down from his eyes towards the end of his speech.

"Eventually, the Pallarusians or Russians finished me, destroyed me. They'd wiped everything from me, left me like this. I'm sorry, the key is gone. I couldn't help it. They eventually realised this empty vessel," he gestured to himself, "to be exchanged for one of their own. It wasn't a good deal for us. I was useless to everyone, but I was thankful. Until recently, I still didn't know if all this was a

222

sham, one of their deep-fake locations to get me to give up what I no longer have."

He pleaded to Fedor. "I never knowingly said anything. I tried my best."

Fedor saw the sincerity in Jacob's tear-lined face. He now knew that his erstwhile best friend wasn't lying and had stayed true despite being physically and mentally destroyed.

Fedor put his gun away.

Jacob continued his story to everyone in the room. "I was no longer of any use to my old masters. They couldn't have me outside their control, so they placed me in that home-for-down-and-out-security-services where I try to unobtrusively survive."

Fedor interrupted. "I came here to settle a score with a man, once my best friend. I thought he betrayed me, but I could never understand why. Once I'd seen you again, I knew what people had told me about you was wrong, all lies. But I had to come here and challenge you. I needed to know the truth."

It was Natalie's turn to jump into the conversation. "But Uncle Jack, all these years, you've been withdrawn, hardly spoken. Why the change, what's happened?"

Jacob pointed to Harry and smirked. "New-Me."

"What on earth do you mean?" interjected Michael.

Back to Natalie and Michael, Jacob continued. "In the manor, under their security, I didn't know if I was really free or had been sent to Russia and inserted into their long-term scams. But when I was with you, those times I could relax a little. They couldn't replace you or get you to work for them. It became real, or was it? I was still never sure. The thing is, most of what was me is gone. There are so many gaps in my past and thinking. It's so frustrating! It's like there are faint images, but the video and sound are missing."

"Then he came," Jacob pointed to Harry. "I don't remember much, but I knew he was one of mine. The Russians don't have the ability to create the likes of us, despite what the fright-mongers might tell you."

He then looked at Harry. "When you sat with me and talked about your feelings from what you had done, I saw the hurt in your eyes. No one could replicate that. Then, seeing you in action, I realised I was truly home. And then there was the gentle and genuine care you gave people like me because you know and can empathise. That was real."

Jacob sighed and took a couple of breaths. Still looking at Harry, he continued. "I saw," he hesitated, "no, I see in you what I had once been. When you fought, actually defended yourself, it was like watching myself in the mirror."

"I knew I was safe now. For years, I didn't know where I was or what the drugs were for. And somewhere inside me, there was that damned key, a unique knowledge of how to unlock Fedor's cause, the people, everything."

He addressed Fedor. "I remembered we had a plan, but not what it was. I knew that as long as I held this information in my head you would always be safe. I was the one who could look after myself. Owning the key meant I was the target and, in so doing, your protector. When captured, I must have buried the key deep, so deep it's gone. Maybe they even took it. I no longer know. I've ruined everything. How can you rebuild without that information?"

Fedor knelt in front of his friend. He gently and firmly held Jacob's head in his hands and was about to say something…

"I think now's a good time for a break," interrupted Harry. He knew there was an announcement in the air that the siblings shouldn't hear, possibly others as well.

"Why can't he finish?" demanded Yuryi.

Fedor caught Harry's intent. "Some things between friends need to stay between friends. And more importantly, we are forgetting Viktar lying outside."

Natalie saw the opportunity she'd been waiting for. "Arthur, can we attend to that injured man out there?"

Harry put his gun away and followed Natalie and Fedor into the hallway.

After several minutes Viktar came around. Fedor and Yuryi helped him into the living room. Harry stayed in the background in case there might be repercussions from the big man.

When Viktar had sufficiently regained his senses, after a lot of fussing by Natalie, he noticed Harry.

"Sorry, my friend," apologised Harry. "I tried not to hurt you too much."

Viktar frowned at Harry while trying to collect his thoughts and listening to Fedor say some words to him in Pallarusian. Once his head cleared, his glare turned to acceptance when he remembered what had happened. "Thank you."

"He hit you and could have killed you," exclaimed Michael. "And you're OK with that!"

"But, he didn't, and he could have. For that, I am grateful. He is an honourable man."

Then, the big man took a double take of Jacob sitting in the corner. He couldn't believe what he saw. "Jacob?"

Jacob nodded.

Viktar stared at the man opposite him, once the mighty and indestructible Jacob Collins. What he now saw was a shell of his former self. The initial shock, which quickly turned to distress, engulfed Viktar's face. He couldn't take his reddening eyes off him.

Fedor picked up on the exchange and had to comment to raise the group's mood. "It was challenging times when we first met, such a long time ago. Viktar was then young and arrogant; we all were."

Viktar interjected. "I thought I was invincible. Jacob proved me wrong. We became great friends." To Jacob, he added, "I am so happy to see you, but also sad, and..." He didn't know what to say next.

"I know." Jacob smiled at the big man, releasing the hesitancy. In a lighter tone, Jacob added, "I think you can best me now, old friend."

"Never." Viktar grinned in response.

Harry asked Natalie, "could you please give us ten minutes?"

"In that case, you lot with me in the kitchen," gestured Natalie toward the doorway for Michael and Yuryi to go through. "He's not going anywhere," she gestured to Harry about Viktar, who agreed. "We can have a nice cuppa and let these men talk whatever macho bollocks men do."

Fedor also agreed to Natalie's demand. "Viktar is as much a part of the movement as am I. There is nothing he cannot know."

At that, Natalie, Michael, and Yuryi left the room for Harry, Jacob, Fedor, and Viktar to talk.

****

After they'd gone, Fedor, still kneeling by his friend, delivered a fundamental correction. "You don't have the key, you stupid man." He laughed. "You never did."

"I don't understand. I remember the conversations, getting the key and memorising it." Then hesitantly, "at

226

least I think I did?"

"I don't know when you started to believe it, but the brain has a great way of helping you with memories to protect you. They'd have killed you if you were no use. And if they knew I had the key, I'd have been in your situation."

Fedor turned to Harry. "Jacob never had the key. He insisted we make it so that everyone thinks he had it. He was desperate to keep me safe. He made himself the target, which took their focus from me. I now know he'd kept me safe over all these years. Even now, no one can know this. As far as everyone is concerned, the key is lost, buried under drugs and abuse."

Back to Jacob, he continued. "Thank you, my dearest friend. Knowing you, I believe you must have told yourself, over and over again, that you had the key. Then, during the interrogations and drugging, over the months, you grew to believe your self-created fiction. I think your mind impressed the new truth in itself. It's what I'd have done."

Fedor reassured him. "Truly, it's me who has the key. It's always been me, and now I'm out, it's unlocked the information. My people, as we speak here, are rallying behind the movement. I came here for unfinished business. Now I am angrier than ever but also joyful to see you, my friend."

Jacob breathed out a long sigh. The weight of the world seemed to slide off his shoulders. He then chuckled, "we beat them, didn't we?"

"Yes, we did, my friend. Your plan was good. They never tried to hurt me. You saved me. I don't think I could have been as strong as you."

"I thought they'd taken it," Jacob smirked. "But I never had it. The joke's on them, on everyone. You've come back and released me. Thank you."

Harry had to check. "Let me get this right. This key

227

opens the names of people, perhaps contact details?"

"It's more than that," corrected Fedor. "The key unlocks the encrypted information on political allies, bank accounts, a list of activists, you name it. It gives us everything we need to challenge those criminals running my country. While everything was compartmentalised, there had to be one master list and one way to decrypt it. It was that key to accessing the information that everyone was after."

"During my incarceration with the Israelis, I was told Jacob was in Pallarus and living a life of luxury, a hero. I never knew he pretended, then believed he had the key. I heard he stayed there for over a year until there was an exchange for a senior Russian official. They told me he was sent back to continue as a double agent, working for Russia and Pallarus. I never truly believed it because I knew the man. But when many people tell you that he is the master deceiver, you eventually begin to wonder."

"I'm so sorry Jacob. All these years, I grew to hate you." The tears rolled down Fedor Kotova's cheeks.

He put his arm around Jacob's shoulders. "You never gave up, did you? You were true to the end."

A cloud descended on Jacob. His expression became haunted and vacant as he stared into nothing. His mind inadvertently shivered, which brought him back to where he was, from where his mind had gone. "There's more I can never tell anyone about that time. I'm now weak, and if they find I am more than they think, they will find and kill me, perhaps my family, even others. But, maybe one day."

He contemplated Harry. "Maybe, if and when the time is right, you will need that information because it might save lives. For now, I must remain poor, vacant Uncle Jack."

At that, Fedor hugged Jacob hard. At the same time,

there was a knock on the door.

Harry opened the door to Natalie bearing a goodies-laden tray and Michael holding another tray with the beverages.

Seeing the two men together, Michael had to clarify something. "Uncle Jack, are you gay? Not that it matters a jot, just watching you both together. We always thought you were."

Jacob shrugged and shook his head in the affirmative; it was just a label.

Natalie shrugged. These days, no one cares. She did, however, have a burning question. "So, you both were a couple? Mr Kotova, you hide your sexuality very well. I always thought I had an excellent gaydar."

"Our friendship was only friends, the best of friends. I am what you call straight. And, if ever I'm back around, perhaps we might have dinner?" He chuckled, knowing what her answer would be.

Natalie glanced up at Harry, then back at Fedor. "No, I don't think so."

Fedor turned to Harry again. "And you Mr Attendant. You now know all about us. So, who are you really?"

Harry looked him in the eyes and knowingly grinned. "Jacob explained who I am."

"Of course. You're here to protect Jacob from me, aren't you?"

"No. Jacob was the bait. I've been sent to kill you."

Michael dropped the tray full of tea and coffee.

229

30. CONFESSION

"What the fuck!" Michael blurted out as he spun to face Harry, forgetting he was carrying the hot drinks, which he launched over the carpet.

Natalie gasped on hearing Harry's confession.

Viktar furrowed his eyebrows in disbelief.

Fedor rocked his head in understanding and took hold of Yuryi's arm to prevent him from lunging at Harry.

Jacob looked up at Harry, smiling.

Fedor addressed Harry. "And will you?"

Harry responded with, "sorry Natalie, you and Michael need to leave again, and Yuryi."

Fedor addressed the man in Pallarusian. One didn't need to know the language to understand what was said to Yuryi and to catch the angry man's curt response by being asked to leave. After a heated exchange of unintelligible words, the man capitulated, left the room, and waited outside on the front porch.

Natalie then looked at her brother and the mess on the floor and threw some napkins at him. After she and her brother had removed the worst of the fluids, she announced, "we're dismissed again. Fresh coffee and tea, methinks. Michael, you're with me. Can't bear to stand here listening to all this male bonding, and my willie is bigger than your willie nonsense. Let's let them catch up?"

Harry mouthed a thank you.

Harry had seen the ease with which Fedor hefted up

Viktar. "You're remarkably strong and fit for someone just out of prison."

"My prison was not a real prison, more like a hotel. They looked after me. Good Israeli food, exercise, TV, gym. So, I worked out. I needed to be as strong as I could. When the time came, which I knew it would, I needed to be ready."

"Yuck!" interrupted Natalie. "Enough already of this macho bollocks."

Fedor turned to Natalie. "I am very sorry for bringing all this to your door." This time, he truly was apologetic. "I hope I have not opened up too many wounds for Jacob."

Natalie pushed Michael outside the door and closed it behind him. She turned to Harry. She had to know the answer to the burning question, "will you?" She meant will he kill Fedor Kotova?

"Of course not!" replied Harry. "But I shouldn't have even said that to you. I needed to let you know that truth. I believe I can trust you. Others must believe it is my intention. It's what keeps a friend of mine alive."

He opened the door for her. But before she walked through, he added, "a game needs to be played. In that game, I'm a killer. That's all I can tell you for now."

"Are you a killer?"

Harry could only nod.

After she left, Harry asked Jacob, "who was your then-boss?"

"Colonel Gerard Armstrong."

Harry had already suspected that. He explained everything to Fedor. He still wasn't too sure how much of the conversation Jacob absorbed. However, Jacob knew how to keep his mouth shut.

After Harry finished his story and answered Fedor's

questions, he had to ask something niggling in the back of his mind. "Fedor, you mentioned a man, the broker. Where does he now play in all this?"

Fedor's face glowered as he spoke. "His name is Sir Victorious Sommerville. I don't think he plays anywhere in all this. He just disappeared at the time with the money. He currently lives a high life off the sweat of my people. One day, he will pay."

Jacob added, "I seem to remember him, I think? But I don't know in what context. I remember his lovely niece, such a lovely, kind, and sad girl." He stared at them, trying to remember, "sorry, there's nothing more."

Fedor broke the ice. "But now, as you English say, we have some other chickens to fry."

They had a further discussion on agendas and related options. Once settled, Harry suggested, "I think it's time to invite the owners of the house and your friend back in. What do you think?"

****

It was fortuitous that Natalie and Mikie had left. The conversation was less guarded, and they could analyse the situation. By the time the siblings returned, the men were relaxed and ready for that long-awaited cuppa.

Once everyone had a cup of whatever they wanted, Natalie had to ask another question that swam around her head. "Uncle Jack, those amazing bedtime stories you told us when we were young?"

Jacob looked at her and smiled. "You've signed the Official Secrets Act?"

"Yes?"

"Then we cannot talk about it in front of these people

here." He winked at her conspiratorially.

The radio still played loudly as a necessary evil. It was just after 1 pm, and it was news round-up time. Natalie was the first to notice the news flash and pick up on its significance. "Shush," she ordered everyone in the room.

The newsreader fleshed out the earlier announced headline. "Two men were found dead in a car on a C-road north of Leominster. They estimate the time of death to be around 10 am."

She addressed Harry. "That's near the route you took here. And, around the same time." Two and two made four. She looked at Harry accusingly. "Was that you?"

Up to now, all she had seen in Harry was a nice, caring man, albeit a bit useful in a scrap. He'd also all but admitted to being a killer. The look she gave him was now of disappointment. Or was that hurt?

The atmosphere in the room had now changed to sombre.

"You killed them?" asked Fedor matter-of-factly.

Harry's mind raced back to the incident, trying to rationalise what he'd now heard.

The newsreader carried on with the summary of the story. "It is believed it was a suicide pact by two gay men, married with children. They may have fought, and it looks like there was a change of heart by one of the men. One man had multiple gunshot wounds. The fatal shots were to the head. The other man, the passenger, shot himself through the mouth. Investigations are ongoing, but the police are not looking for other parties."

The newsreader carried on with the police request for the usual dashcam footage request before covering the rest of the news stories.

Natalie was embarrassed. "I'm so sorry I accused you. I just assumed after what had happened today…" She hesitated, "I don't know what to say..." she bumbled on. "I feel awful..." She paused, looking for Harry's reaction and forgiveness. "Can you forgive me for thinking the worst..."

Harry's mind was spinning. He ignored her; it wasn't intentional. He was oblivious to what she'd just said. If the truth be known, he was momentarily in shock. His thoughts raced, focussed on the fear in his mind and the safety of everyone in the house.

Harry removed his jacket and went through every crease. While not removing his chinos, he did the same. "Knife, scissors please?"

Distraught that Harry had dismissed her apology, Natalie ran out of the living room and slammed the door. At the kitchen sink, she washed the tears from her face and looked out over the back garden while drying them. She wondered why she was so upset about Harry ignoring her.

Back in the living room, Viktar passed Harry a stiletto.

Harry opened the seam and extracted a small, plastic, circular object the size of a 10p coin.

"Is it bad?" asked Fedor.

"Dunno. Could be. I need to make a call."

****

Harry went outside onto the front path. Out of earshot from those inside, he made a call. "Hello darling," Helen opened. "You left early. I vaguely remember you leaving. I was so looking forward to a post-wakeup follow-up to our previous evening's gymnastics. But you left so soon. What a wonderful night! You're wonderful."

"What have you done?"

"Ah." She paused. "I think you need to buy a girl a drink after you so wonderfully seduced me. Don't want to discuss anything on the phone. Anyone could be listening to our discussing the finer details of our intercourse."

"Where are you?"

"Not so far away, sweetie. Local pub. Thirty minutes OK?"

"Done!"

****

Harry re-entered the living room to expectant looks from the others. He noticed Natalie wasn't there. "Where's Natalie?"

"She's in the kitchen. Go to her, and be nice!" Michael's response was more of a plead than a request.

"Is there anything wrong?"

"You twat! Are you completely gormless?" her brother accused him.

Harry was unsure what the issue was. From Michael's reaction, he knew there had to be one. He found Natalie at the kitchen sink. She ignored his entrance, still staring into the garden, her back to him.

"Are you OK?"

"I'm fine!"

He recognised the words-behaviour-conflict. He'd seen it so many times. He'd done something wrong, which he didn't know what, but he should know, and if he didn't know, he was an insensitive oaf.

So, now he needed to apologise on the basis that he knew what he'd done, which he didn't. At the same time, he had to try and find out what it was, he'd done, but without asking directly.

"I can see that you're not. I know what I did was

insensitive, and I'm so sorry." That should about cover it. He assumed and cringed, very much hoping it did. Because he did like her; very much. "There's no way I'd want to hurt you, quite the opposite."

The answer came out to Harry's relief.

"I tried to apologise to you, and you blanked me. I felt horrible, wanted the ground to swallow me up."

Harry gently touched her upper arm. "I was so wrapped up in other things. God, I'm so sorry."

She spun round.

Harry expected the worst and wasn't going to defend himself. He didn't need to.

All she wanted was a long, tight hug and to know he was OK with her. The tears rolled down her eyes, making his shirt wet. She clung on, and Harry reciprocated.

'Sooner or later, she'll find out what I had to do to those men, and what'll she think of me then?'

He gently pushed her off him a little. He needed to be upfront. "I need to make a confession. I did hurt those men. But, you must please believe me, I did not kill them. It's not who I am. What I did was the only way to protect Jacob and Fedor. I had to ensure they stopped following me.

She looked up at him, "I know, I believe you. Whatever you think of yourself, I know you could never be a killer."

'I pray she never finds out the truth. I can never be honest about that time in my life.'

And he hugged her again.

****

After she'd recovered, they both re-entered the living

room, holding hands or rather, she pulled him along behind her to the amusement of those waiting there.

"About time!" blurted out Michael.

Harry's happy face became serious. "Fedor, I have to go out. Urgently. I'll be back soon."

"The killings?"

"Yes. But, it's more serious than that." Harry held out the GPS tracking device. I think I know the person responsible. But I don't know why, what they know, and what I'm up against."

He placed the tracking device in his pocket. He wasn't ready to let on he'd found the device.

"Can I help?" offered Kotova.

"Not this meeting. But I might need your help later. Could you remain here for an hour or two? Then I can explain."

Fedor chuckled in that deep voice of his. "Take care New-Me."

Harry kissed Natalie on her cheek, "see you soon."

31. DARLING LOVER

The pub wasn't that far from the house. So, rather than take the car, Harry walked. After his call with Helen Welsh, he needed space to clear his mind and organise his thoughts. He arrived 15 minutes later when the pub was toward the end of the lunchtime surge.

The pub was quiet. People would still be at home before they descended for their Saturday afternoon pint. There were a few of what looked to be farm-worker, bar-propping, barflies who were well into their first pint or second or third...it didn't matter. At the back of the almost empty bar space, he immediately saw Helen nursing what looked to be a GnT.

She'd read him and played him. She was good, very credible. He fell for her game, hook, line, and sinker. He didn't know who he was angrier at. In truth, it was himself. He'd let his guard down.

No way was he going to have an alcoholic drink with this adversary; that's who she was. Harry was coffee'd out after this morning's beverages. So, he bought and brought sparkling water to the table where Helen sat. As he made to sit down, she half stood up, leaned over, and delivered a smacker of a kiss on his lips.

"My darling lover-boy, that's a thank you for last Wednesday night."

If that kiss was meant to disarm him, it was successful, if only for a moment.

Before he could regain control of his thoughts and

speak, she kicked off their chat. "And what is it you think I have done?"

Harry fished the tracking device out of his pocket. He looked at her expectantly.

"OK?" she responded innocently, "it's a battery. And why do you want to let me see your battery?"

"Helen, please stop playing games. You know what it is. The only person who could have planted it was you. You used this to follow me."

"I was only looking after you. Thank goodness I did. You left such a mess out there. It needed a woman's touch to tidy it up."

"I left two men alive in a car," he retorted. "They're now dead. Shot in the head. Police think it's suicide, perhaps a suicide pact gone wrong."

"Isn't that good?" she retorted.

"That isn't good. It's not good at all. It's wrong."

"My darling, I was only tidying up for you. It's what I do for my special man."

Harry glared at her disbelievingly. "I'm not your special man!"

In response, and with her sexiest smile still in place, she responded, "but you are. And I need to teach you to look after yourself. What you did is not on."

"I had to disable them. What else was I supposed to do."

"I don't mean that darling. Silly you. Of course, you had to stop them. It's just that you can't leave injured bodies lying around the streets willy-nilly. It's untidy."

"They were just doing their job. They were disabled and of no harm to anyone."

The smile left her, and she was now serious. "Of course, they were of harm! Don't be so naive! They were dangerous

239

to you and our operations. People would ask questions. Those men might have said things they shouldn't. Anyway, it's all tickety-boo now."

She made to take hold of his hand, which he pulled away. "You should be thanking me. I was only helping my lover, after all."

"That was blatant murder. Were you responsible?"

"Of course. I'd do anything for you. It was the proof of my love for you." Her smile returned to those sexy lips, but it wasn't the same smile. There was something sinister in her expression.

Harry glared at this woman, who, some two days ago, he'd been intimate with. There was no longer the hint of the bubbly, outgoing person on her face. There was no remorse. She was calm and sincere in what she said. Was that psychopathic or sociopathic behaviour? He wasn't trained in that level of analysis. Whatever her condition or mental state, he knew now that she was dangerous.

"What do you want from me?" challenged Harry.

"You mean apart from another damned good rogering?"

"Yes, I mean no." Harry was emotionally on the ropes with this manipulative woman. He'd never been trained to deal with this situation, nor had any great experience with it.

Helen took the clips from her hair and let it fall, as she did that night. She repeatedly ran her fingers through her hair to straighten it out. While doing so, her demeanour changed. It softened to that of the Helen Welsh of two days ago.

"I need Fedor Kotova, and I need him alive and well. Jacob is the key to important information we need. We believe that Fedor is the key to releasing it."

"I don't know what you're talking about."

"Listen, sweetie. Let's cut the crap. I know who you are,

Mr Harry Logan. I also know that a certain Colonel Gerard Armstrong will have taken Tom and Jess hostage against the death of Kotova. Well, you're not going to kill him. I know Gerard. He is not a nice person like you and I. He'll already have killed them. I'll bet you've not had proof-of-life from him."

Harry avoided responding to that last comment. He didn't want dragged into a minefield of openness. "OK, cutting the crap as you say. You know me. So, who are you?"

"I'm just Helen, your darling Helen Welsh."

Harry could see she was teasing, no taunting him. So, he said nothing. He remembered the mantra, 'if there is nothing to say, say nothing. Let others fill the gap'.

And she did. "I work for ATS. I know you know about us, as we know all about you. However, I work for the more politically astute part of the organisation. My department ensures proper oversight of ATS' operations. Any deviance from approved activities or engagement in unapproved activities by any of our staff eventually comes to our attention. It is down to us to correct said deviance by whatever means necessary."

"And Armstrong is a deviant?"

"Yes," she now grinned. "To be 100% accurate, it's his activities that are deviating from what's approved. His deviant character is actually what makes him valuable."

"So stop him. You seem to be well equipped to do so."

"Sadly, he and his team are off-grid."

"I need to know what you know. Where were you hiding? Where did he take Jess and Tom?"

'Thank god You're playing catch-up and know nothing.'

"How did you find me?"

"Oh, that was an easy one. We have a fair idea of

Gerard's plan and just had to wait until you materialised into the picture at the Manor. We've been tracking Kotova even before he illegally arrived in the UK, with the help of his US friends. We know exactly where he's been and what he's been up to."

"I'm going to give you a little background so you understand your position in this; and ours."

"Gerard has a personal agenda and deviant business sideline. He used to work out of the ATS Lepsk office in Pallarus. We'd had enough of his deviance there, so he was banished where he couldn't do much harm; one of the trickier posts. It kept him busy. We thought he'd learned his lesson, so we brought him back last year."

"His part of our esteemed organisation and the people I represent are working for the same side. Unfortunately, we're working to different customers' agendas. He wants to kill Kotova, as required by the country, customer, he works for. However, our customer needs Kotova and Jacob alive. With them together, we believe we can extract some important information that's been sitting in Jacob's head for more than a decade. We know he's somehow been able to lock it away."

"So, what's in it for me?"

"Your freedom. Tom and Jess are dead. Once you get that into your thick skull, you can move on. He does NOT hold them over your head!"

She let that settle in his thoughts before she carried on.

"Help me, and you are free of the ATS capture-then-kill sanction. You can get back to a life of normality. Isn't that the reason you left the clutches of that non-existent organisation you worked for? We have long memories, and we can also forget. We're simple business people, and business is business. All you have to do is give both of them to me."

He pondered what she'd said.

She assumed he was considering the deal.

The good news was that she didn't know Tom was still alive from visitor feedback. He knew where Jess was. However, if truth be known, had he not have known Jess and Tom were alive and Armstrong refused to confirm it, the deal might have been attractive. But, there again, that deal would have been short-lived. He'd have hunted and killed Armstrong for the deaths of his kids. Then he'd be back to square one.

She continued. "As you are now aware, I saw Gerard's boys following you, so I just tagged on, so to speak. I know you have Jacob with you today, and you dropped him off at his niece and nephew's house. I also know that Kotova is with Jacob right now. With any luck, the two besties will be rebonding. So sweet, isn't it?"

"So, if you know all this, why don't you just storm the place and take them? Knowing ATS, you have the bodies to do that job." Harry knew the answer, but he needed her to say it and perhaps give up a little more than she should.

"Don't be silly, darling. That would be messy. With bodies and mayhem comes visibility, and we can't have that, can we? My part of the business doesn't operate like that. More importantly, we need Collins and Kotova intact, with as little stress as possible on our delicate key holder. And that's where you come in."

Harry knew now that Tom and Jess had to remain dead as far as she was concerned. If there was any hint Tom might still be alive, there was no doubt in his mind that she'd make sure he had an accident attributable to Armstrong.

And Helen definitely couldn't know about Jess being close by and alive.

"And if I don't agree, what happens then?"

"You won't refuse. Why would you? You've nothing to gain."

"Oh, and there's one more thing. Colonel Armstrong is ATS, a senior player. If anything happens to him, not sanctioned by us, all the bets are off."

Harry showed anger in his response. "If he's killed my friends, he won't walk away." This would be a normal reaction from someone in his position, so he played along.

"Yes, he can and will. It would be such a shame to include you in the body-count."

"I still don't believe you about Tom and Jess. I'll check with Armstrong later this evening when I'm next due for an update. If I don't get proof-of-life for both of them, I'll be in touch. I expect he'll need time to set up a call. So it might be a day or two."

"I'll bet you call me sooner. As I said, I know the bastard. Your two friends are casualties of circumstance. Once you're ready to deal, I'll explain how I want the handover to happen. You walk away. It's as clean as that."

Having offered her deal, she got up, kissed him on the cheek, then walked out.

Harry nursed his now flat water and thought about the non-offer he'd been given. Helen's lot didn't know about Jess being free. They didn't know about the visitors to the Taigh, which was Tom's lifeline. Harry needed to move fast. The last of the visitors, who were keeping him alive, were leaving tomorrow morning. He knew there would be no point in killing Tom so close to the deal's conclusion. But, the longer the wait, the more chance of it happening.

And another plan was growing in his mind. He smiled at the simplicity of it; well, not really that simple, but simple in principle.

32. POWER GAMES

Back in her car, Helen made a call. "Good afternoon, Sir Vic." The way she pronounced his name sounded more like 'cervix'. Yes, it was intentional and disrespectful, but that was Helen's way when speaking with him.

Sir Victorious Ambrose Sommerville, to use his full name, hated the way she shortened his name, made worse when enunciated like that. Before being knighted, he was Uncle Vic to her. Afterward, he suggested Sir Victor was appropriate for his new station and respect.

Helen, in her inimitable way, decided that Sir Vic was better. She didn't believe in all that knighting nonsense. Even worse, she knew him and his activities. Those who'd bestowed that honour would have had him dis-knighted if those activities became public. So, sometimes, she needed to wind him up.

He knew this way of addressing him was one of her foibles. However, she was too valuable and too loyal to upset matters. He'd nurtured and honed her skills and behaviour almost all her life since he'd killed her parents. Now, she was his killing machine without conscience and scruples. The downside of his careful nurturing was a smidgen of rebellion, which he reluctantly accepted as a resultant imperfection in her behaviour.

"You've now spent time with him, got to know him, as you do. What do you think? Will he kill Kotova to save those two already dead people?"

"Our friend will buy the story. He's no option. We

know what that shit, Armstrong, is like. I wouldn't have liked to have been in Jessica Lloyds shoes, with the pair of them. Those two who took her are nasty little boys."

"Barys will never learn his lesson. By the way, do you still have Barys' ear from when he chatted you up that time?"

"Don't wind me up about that. He got what he deserved. And anyway, you know I sent it back to him parcel post. Warned him the next time I see him, I'll cut his cock off. He'll never try that again with me."

She heard him laughing on the line. "And to answer your question about darling Harry. Once he hears back from the colonel that there is no proof-of-life, he'll play ball. He's not one to just kill. I think he has a plan, but I don't know what yet."

"Heli, I need to be 100% certain. I need both Jacob and Kotova alive and in our hands. We can't afford for Kotova to get away. Once he's with his people, he's lost to us. With Jacob and Kotova together, I'm sure we can persuade Jacob to give it up. After all, he's in love with him and wouldn't like to see us pull him apart. Now, if we could deliver success where the Kremlin and Lepsk experts failed, that would be a master-stroke."

"Don't worry, Sir Vic, dear. I've a plan."

"Fantastic, I trust you to deliver. Our friends in the Kremlin would pay well for that information. Then you can have your choice of job within the organisation."

"But I like my job. I'm good at it. I'll miss it."

"In that case, my dear, even better. With my brains and your skills, customers will pay top kill-dollars. You might even eventually notch up more kills than your boyfriend."

"He's not my boyfriend. He's just a mark. Mind you, Harry's a rather sexy one in a scarred, rugged sort of way. It'd be a shame to kill him, but one has to eliminate one's competition."

"Indeed, my dear. Make sure you do; when the time's right."

Then he had to remind her. "If we cannot deliver Kotova, as we've promised them, we'll have dangerous and powerful enemies after us. I'm trusting you to get him. Do you need more help?"

"Of course not, Sir Vic, we're good. And I have my lovely Harry to help me."

"Jacob is worse than dispensable, so if he cannot deliver the information, kill him. He cannot get into someone else hands. He once knew too much about certain drone strikes that could do me some harm. The US needs to remain blamed for that friendly fire and Jacob supplying the wrong information that set it off. I cannot have him waking up one day and remembering all that, and also for him killing his best friend."

"What you mean is you, not we, my darling Sir Vic. Don't drag me into that arms-cum-drug war you started. Killing is fun. Watching people suffer with the shit those people make is not. I said before, and I'm saying it again, don't ever drag me into that sewer you call your side business empire."

"Of course not, darling. I know how you feel and would never do that to you."

'One day, my dear, you will no longer be pretty and indispensable. Then it's goodbye, dearest Heli.'

At that point, he hung up.

33. THE PLAN

When Harry returned to the house, Fedor asked, "I noticed you walked. You were quicker than I expected you to be. Did you have the meeting?"

"Yes. And I have a story for you, but it's your ears only." Harry needed the utmost security. No one else could know the plan that was developing in his head. "Sorry," he apologised to Natalie and Michael.

Natalie sighed in faked frustration. "Yeh, yeh. So, Arthur, how long do you need this time?"

Harry hesitated. He'd toyed with the idea of telling her his real name. However, at this juncture, that would confuse matters too much. Instead, he responded with, "only 30 minutes, promise."

"Mikie and you two are with me in the kitchen again. Let's do some lunch for this lot."

This time, Yuryi didn't challenge Fedor about being asked to leave the room with Viktar.

Motioning to her entourage and referencing Harry, Fedor, and Jacob, she jokingly grumped, "let's leave this lot to conspire whatever they're conspiring."

Once alone with Jacob and Fedor, Harry explained what had transpired with Helen Welsh at that meeting and the organisation she worked for. He didn't talk about Sir Victor because he didn't know he was involved; then, at least.

He explained how they met, their relationship, and last Wednesday night's activities. He didn't go into the detail, obviously, but enough for them to glean how she managed to plant the bug.

Fedor responded with some advice. "I've seen how Miss Collins looks at you, and I think this is not a discussion you want to have with Miss Collins at this time. There's too much going on for her. She will not hear from me in the meantime."

They looked at Jacob.

Jacob smiled at Harry. "For the last ten years or thereabouts, I've been living to a hear-no-evil, speak-no-evil, see-no-evil philosophy. I'm not changing now. I don't want to hurt her in any way. But, there's a price you must pay."

Jacob's face then turned somber. "Arthur, or whatever your real name is, I like you. I respect you, but worse, I know you because I was you. You are playing a dangerous game. Like it or not, my niece and nephew are ill-equipped to deal with it. I want them to remain outside of whatever you're planning, and not be sucked into anything further. I know you are an honourable man. You know this cannot go anywhere. So, here's the deal. I'll not say anything because it'll be irrelevant. It will be irrelevant because you'll never see her again after this is finished."

Harry took a deep breath and grimaced. "I know. You're right, but…"

"You don't have a choice," chided Jacob. "I love them both. I can't let you hurt her. You and your life are not good for her."

Harry nodded.

Jacob wasn't letting the decision hang there. Harry's response had to be clear and decisive. He stared Harry down and waited.

"OK, Yes. You are right, I agree."

"Thank you. It's a relief."

After taking some moments to recover from Jacob's persistence, Harry explained his either Harry or Fedor-and-Jacob deal with Helen Welsh that would exclude Gerard Armstrong. He only gave the salient points. They didn't know Jess was on the loose; he had no reason to tell them. He could never trust anyone 100%. No one could know she was free.

"I know this Gerard Armstrong," commented Fedor. "I never liked him, but Jacob said he was to be trusted. That man betrayed everyone and was involved with what had happened to my best friend and me. I have a score to settle with him that cannot wait."

"In that case, I think we can do a deal," responded Harry. "We can both get what we want out of it."

"You mean another trust-the-west-style symbiotic relationship?"

"No," responded Harry. "The difference in my deal is that I'll not betray you."

Harry then explained his plan. In brief, Fedor was to be Harry's captive to draw Armstrong and his men from the house so Harry could deal with them. Then, whosoever was with Tom would have the choice of killing and be killed, or leaving.

Fedor looked at him, first in disbelief. When Harry kept up his serious face, Fedor laughed. "It's crazy. I love it!"

"That's settled. Can we see what's cooking in the kitchen? I'm starving."

****

Lunch was a mish-mash of leftovers made into a thick and tasty soup with a loaf of crusty, home-baked bread. Harry marvelled at what Michael could with food from a standing start.

Between mouthfuls, Harry told the group that he and Fedor had agreed on a course of action, but without sharing anything of their plan.

"After lunch, I have to head back to my hotel and report in to confirm all's good here. I shall leave Fedor with you. It's what people expect. Viktar and the driver also need to leave the house and remain in the car outside until Fedor is finished here. So, as far as anyone's concerned, it's business as usual."

"And tomorrow at 7 am, earlier than scheduled, I'll pick up Jacob and bring him back to the Manor. Fedor will meet us en route." He explained where they'd stop for them to have a final catch-up. "I expect it'll be the last time these friends will see each other in a long time. Leaving so early gives them some time together."

"Are you going to come back to visit?" asked Natalie of Harry.

"Of course. I'll be back tomorrow to pick up Jacob."

"Yes, I know that. I meant afterward."

"We have some catching up to do." He lied. What else could he do? There couldn't be questions and challenges raised at this juncture. He would tell her when the time was right, hopefully soon. Harry glanced at Jacob, reminding him that their understanding, more like a deal, regarding Natalie was still intact.

Jacob remained blank-faced.

"Natalie and Michael, do you think it would be OK if Viktar could stay overnight? I'm worried about Jacob."

"Of course, we have a spare room." Sizing up the big man, she had to add, "Oh, dear, I do hope the bed is big enough?"

"Not worried about the size. Is it strong enough?" piped

up Michael.

That last comment brought laughs from the others. The remaining tension had somewhat eased.

There were some more exchanges between the three Pallarusians. And again, one didn't need to know their language to understand their worries about Fedor. Eventually, it was all good, with smiles all around.

"And then what?" she asked.

"I'll see you on my next day off," Harry replied, trying to be as convincing as possible.

"Liar! I know something's going on, and it's dangerous and secret. Otherwise, you'd tell us."

"Yes, we have some follow-up meetings, but they're not dangerous, for us at least. Once we get Jacob safely in the Manor, all will be well. I promise."

Harry had to add. "If you value the safety of Jacob, all this never happened. If it becomes common knowledge that Jacob has even the slightest memory, he will be a target. And that could mean you both as well. That's the problem we need to deal with."

Even regarding the Jacob secrecy part, he was only partially truthful. Everything else was a lie, and it killed him to deceive her like this. His plan was dangerous, but he could never admit that. And, yes, he may not return. He also had no plans to see Natalie again. Unfortunately for both of them, he honestly did like her.

Two hours later, at the front door, when Fedor was leaving, Natalie asked him, "please look after Harry. I don't think he's as strong as everyone thinks. There's more to him than meets the eye, and I would like time to learn what that is."

"My dear, I'll do my best, but I think it will be the other way round. He is one of the few men I believe in and trust."

252

"I know."

"Whatever will happen to him will be of his own doing. He is an honourable man on a rescue mission."

Fedor was driven away.

Viktar returned sometime later when it was dark, entering discreetly via the back of the house.

****

Back in the hotel, Harry called in at the appointed time.

"Armstrong," came the acknowledgement.

"Logan, here."

"I can see who you are. Your number's showing on my phone. I'm losing patience. I believe he's been to the Manor. Why wasn't the deal concluded then?"

"Be realistic. You know there's too much security there. I can't afford to fail and lose everything."

"I'm not interested in excuses or what happens to you. I need Kotova dead, and I don't care how or if there are casualties. Got it!"

"I'm not taking any chances with Tom and Jess. If I fail, and even worse, if I'm taken or killed in the process, I know what will happen to them at your hands. So, the plan and its execution needs to be 100% successful. You set the rules. This is the consequence."

"OK. Maybe. So, what's the plan?"

"I'm using Jacob Collins as bait to get Kotova into the open tomorrow and unprotected. It's taken some time to set up."

"You'd better not be playing a game."

"You know I can't deviate. Now it's your turn. I need to speak to Jess and Tom as proof of life."

"As I told you, neither is with me. And I'm not sharing where she's secured. I know how good you are, but you're one person with multiple choices and cannot be everywhere at once. That's my ace, as you are well aware, and I'm not giving up that. Remember, a message from me, and they're dead. Anyway, as you said, the traffic through the BnB proves Tom's still alive, for now at least."

Armstrong cut the line.

****

Harry sat with Fedor in the empty lounge of the small hotel in Shawbury Heath, where they'd both booked in for the night. They planned and rehearsed. Harry liked to plan, to make sure all the angles were covered. He hated winging it. He needed to be in control of events.

"Are you OK with this?" Harry finally asked.

"You're a strange man Mr Arthur Fox, or whatever your name is. And yes, I'm good."

34. AMBUSHED

A smidgen before 7 am the following day, Harry returned to Jacob's niece's and nephew's Shawbury Heath house. The mood was sombre, and no one said anything when he entered the kitchen except Viktar. He stuffed what looked to be the remnants of a bacon and egg sandwich into his mouth and muffled, "goodbye," to everyone. Harry and Viktar effectively performed a changing of Jacob's guard; the big man exited through the back.

Natalie and Michael were tense.

Jacob? Well, Jacob was back to being his plain old unreadable self.

Harry had to say something. An open wound needed to be treated. And he liked this woman. "I did not mean for this to happen to you all," he meant her.

"But it happened," retorted Michael.

"And it brought you here," offered Natalie to soften her brother's less-than-polite response. "Maybe that's the good thing out of all this."

Harry didn't know how to play this, so he evasively dissembled. "Mmm, if nothing else, it's been an interesting time." Looking directly at her, he added, "some of which has been lovely."

"It has indeed," she replied.

As a parting shot, he had to add, "after I leave with Jacob, I can assure you, it's all over for the three of you."

"And will you come back?"

"I keep my promises." He glanced at Jacob, overtly as a view to leave. It was also a reminder of his unforgotten promise to Jacob.

Natalie fussed over Jacob's things and re-checked everything in his overnight case.

In the meantime, Harry enjoyed a cup of tea and a bacon and egg butty offered to him. He was right about what Viktar had stuffed in his mouth.

Once Natalie was satisfied that Jacob was good to go, she, with Michael in tow, followed them to the front door. There, they said their goodbyes. It was too cold at that time of the spring morning to spend time hugging in the street. And it was drizzly.

Harry, with Jacob next to him in the front passenger seat, waved goodbye and drove off.

****

The traffic was quiet so early in the morning, and they reached their scheduled meeting place in good time.

Harry had again chosen well. The parking place, or rather, an entrance into a wood with a gate several metres further in, was better for their purposes than the lay-by, where two men died yesterday. Any innocent passers-by would miss them. It also had lateral and overhead cover, meaning almost zero opportunity to be watched. Harry parked up alongside Fedor's car, which was already there.

Fedor and Viktar stood behind their SUV. Yuryi, his driver, stayed by the wheel.

Harry helped Jacob climb out of his car, then escorted him to the rear of the SUV where Fedor and Viktar waited. After the three men completed their aggressive hugs, Fedor turned to Harry and shook his hand warmly.

Jacob pleaded to Fedor, "please come back to me this time. I'm no longer the strong one. I'm not too sure if I can continue without you, now I've found you again. I know you don't feel the same way as I do, but I can't lose your friendship again."

"You're right, I don't. But a friend can feel as much about another person as a lover. So, I shall be back. And, when this is finished, we'll again be best friends, and the three of us will do everything together again. It will be like before." While it felt good saying those words, he knew they could never be the same again for a long time; if ever. He had a job to do in Pallarus.

And Jacob was not like before. Yes, he was visibly better now than he displayed two weeks ago at the Manor. But, he was still a broken man, damaged beyond repair. Also, the abuse, drugs, interrogations, and worse had taken its toll. Finally, there were the years of strong medication back home, which, for the best of intentions, had further damaged his already weakened mind and body.

Harry wished them well. Heaven only knew what would be in the next chapter of their relationship.

Viktar looked at Harry. "Shall we make tracks, as you British say?"

"Isn't that just sweet? Just touches the heart." A disjointed, out-of-place voice emanated from the shrubbery. A gun appeared, followed by a woman's hand, then an arm. Finally, Helen Welsh appeared.

"Thank you for bringing them to me."

Fedor glared at Harry. His fists clenched as his fight-or-flight adrenaline kicked in. "I trusted you!"

"Not him, you idiot. He's just a stupid, albeit hunky, pawn in all this. I was thanking Yuryi."

Fedor turned to his driver who'd quietly exited the SUV and had his gun trained on Viktar. "You were right Harry," he groaned in disappointment.

Then to Yuryi, he challenged, "why are you in league with the Russians?"

"I am Russian you fool. We've been watching your every move. Miss Welsh is very good at this, isn't she?"

"You two can bicker later. Now, Mr Kotova, you and your friend, Jacob Collins, are coming with us."

"If we refuse?"

"Ah yes, I cannot kill you both, but I can hurt you, and you can watch each other suffer. Knee-capping is such a painful yet non-life-threatening exercise. It's so fun to watch, even better to do the deed yourself."

After letting that settle in, she added, "as Harry can tell you, I mean what I say."

"Yes, she's right," responded Harry, barely controlling his laughter.

"What's so funny!"

"I can't tell you." Trying to remain serious, he forced himself into a form of affected composure that looked like he was about to explode. "If I told you, you'd be angry with me, my darling love." He felt the need to play her game of pseudo-affection.

Helen walked forward and placed the cold barrel of the gun onto the centre of Harry's forehead. "The reason you're still alive is that some in the organisation would like to have a word with you before you die. Others, well they would just like you dead. So, if I killed you right now, I'd win so many gold stars. I'd be their hero. My boss has left the decision to me. So, what'll it be?"

Harry had no opportunity to address the humour all over his face. There was a click of a hammer onto steel, but nothing else followed.

After hearing the cocking of an automatic, Helen felt

cold steel on the back of her head.

Fedor announced, "stalemate."

Fedor reaching for his gun had prompted Yuryi to fire a warning, but nothing happened. There was another click of steel-on-steel as Yuryi again pulled the trigger. He re-cocked it, and it clicked for a third time.

Helen, at last, realised what was so amusing for Harry. "How did you know?"

Still, at the business end of her gun, Harry replied, "no, not knew, but suspected. If I was wrong, no harm done. And, if I was right, well, here we are. When you told me you were tracking Fedor and knew what was going on, I suspected it had to be more than one of your tracking devices. It had to be an inside man, perhaps both. We checked Fedor and his car. All were clean."

Harry always thought the expression, 'staring-down-the-barrel-of-the-gun', was strange unless the barrel pointed at an eyeball. What he saw was the trigger guard, and behind it, a slim finger resting gently on the trigger.

He looked behind the gun into the resignation on her face. He slowly lifted his hand and placed his finger between the hammer and the gun body. It would be such a shame if it went off by mistake. His other fingers wrapped around her hand that held the small automatic gun, and he gently moved it sideways, out of danger.

Helen offered no resistance as he took the gun from her. He then handed it to Fedor, who'd already put on the long washing-up gloves they'd brought.

It was Fedor's turn to explain. "We took precautions. You should have done the same," he snarled at Yuryi. "I always warned you that sloppy gun management would one day kill you."

He shot Yuryi in the head. "I was right!"

Fedor emptied all but one bullet from the gun. He

259

grabbed a hold of Helen and stood behind her. He placed her gun back in her hand.

In the meantime, Viktar held his gun to Helen's head in case she tried anything foolhardy out of desperation.

Helen was sharp enough to know what was going on. They were going to pin Yuryi's death on her. A third gunshot fatality within fifteen miles of the other two would raise suspicions. With any luck, it would keep her incommunicado for the next day or so, perhaps longer.

So she fired into the dead man's body. If Harry was in the mood for admiring someone's shooting skills, he'd have congratulated her on a dead-centre shot to the heart with such a small gun; and under the circumstances. He wasn't, so he didn't.

"Car and keys?"

She pointed further up the road to where they were heading while slowly extracting her car keys.

Viktar handed his gun to Harry, then loped off to make sure it was closed and nothing, of any use to her, was inside.

Harry searched her.

"I love it when you caress me like that. It's sending a shiver down my spine, lover-boy."

He ignored her. He found her mobile in her inside jacket pocket.

He held his phone to her mouth. "Say joyfully into my phone, oh my god, I've just killed another man, it's such fun isn't it? If you want me, come and get me, I'm just north of Bishops Ford."

She sweetly smiled and complied. She had no choice.

Harry demanded, "pass-key."

She held out her erect middle finger. Her phone was fingerprint-activated. It was also a gesture of defiance.

"Useful, so just need a finger then."

Harry used her fingerprint to open the phone.

He dialled 999 from her phone. Viktar had by now returned and clasped his hand over her mouth, holding a handkerchief in between.

"Emergency services," announced a voice at the other end.

Harry replayed her audio message that was on his phone into hers. The emergency services' telephone agent got her message admitting murder. After closing the call, he threw her mobile, car keys, and gun in different locations, deep into the shrubbery.

She wouldn't have time to retrieve any of them before the police arrived.

Harry then pointed his gun at Fedor, "sorry chap, but I need you in exchange for two people I know."

"They'll kill me."

"I know."

To Viktar, Harry ordered, "I have no issue with the hired help. Your contract's ended."

Viktar glowered at Harry. He wasn't planning to go anywhere.

Fedor was resigned to what was about to happen. "Viktar, my friend, it looks like my rebellion-leading days are over, but yours is now about to start. Take over and finish it for me, for us all. Our country is more important than one man."

"The big man turned to Harry. "You and I have some unfinished business. One day, I shall find you and end it, end you." With a fist-up salute to Fedor and a wave to Jacob, he left in the SUV.

Helen had to have a final try to make Harry see reason. "You know they're dead, don't you."

"If they are, Fedor's a free man."

Harry ordered Fedor, "you're driving, and Jacob's next to me in the back. Any funny stuff, I first kill Jacob. Got it!"

Fedor nodded in compliance.

Helen sat cross-legged on the ground, watching Viktar depart, then the three others. All she could now do was wait.

.

35. RE-NEGOTIATION

Harry called in, saying he needed to speak with Dr Barclay. He knew the doctor wouldn't be there so early, and thankfully he wasn't. Eventually, Pato came to the phone. In a distraught voice, Harry announced, "sorry, Pato, but that family issue brewing before the weekend, it's all blown up. I've got Jacob Collins with me. Can you meet me at the gatehouse in thirty minutes? I need to drop him off, then dash off fast."

"Are you OK?"

"No. Well, yes, I am, but my father…"

Pato cut him off. "If it's family, keep it to yourself. This place loves its gossip, and we all need privacy."

"Thank you. I hope I'll only be a few days."

"Just keep Bulldog updated, and I'll let Dr Barclay know what happened when he gets in. See you at the gatehouse in thirty."

"Thanks."

Thirty minutes later, when Harry arrived, Pato and Krish were already waiting for him. They gave Fedor a look of concern, wondering why he was there and especially why he was driving.

Harry put on a display of emotional distraction. "Thanks, sorry, I'm not in a good place. Pato, Krish, I'm sure you remember seeing Mr Collins' old friend, Mr Leanid Kozlov, with his niece and nephew last Saturday. He'd permission from security and the doctor to visit him at their house yesterday. All's good."

"The thing is, he was there when I got the call about my father this morning. I wasn't in a good place a couple of hours ago. He insisted that he drive me here after dropping off Mr Collins. It's such a kind thing for him to do."

Fedor, feigning a little embarrassment at the compliment, shrugged. He helped his old friend out of the car and into the waiting golf buggy. He gave Jacob a final, enthusiastic hug. Jacob barely acknowledged it.

Pato nodded to Fedor in appreciation for his helping Harry. Seeing Fedor's behaviour and Jacob's lack of reaction, he couldn't help adding, "I'm so sorry."

Fedor replied, "While there's a will, there's hope, and I have both."

Fedor turned his back on Jacob. With bloodshot eyes, he challenged his captor with, "OK Mr Fox, I'm all yours now."

They both got back in the car. Fedor, in the driving seat, gunned the engine. They sped off to make the exchange to save Harry's family.

****

After a couple of hours driving and well away from the environs of the Manor, its security, and that of the secret services, Harry ordered Fedor to pull over. He needed to make a call.

"Armstrong," came the acknowledgement.

"I am with your Pallarusian friend." Armstrong and Harry agreed to be careful what was said over the phone, even though they were using burners.

"What do you mean? The agreement was you deal with my problem, and I do the same for you."

"You still don't get me, do you? I don't 'deal' indiscriminately." He emphasised the word 'deal'.

"That was not the agreement!" uttered Armstrong. He was not a happy man.

"Accept it. You've lost control of the deck. Now, I hold the same hand as you. You want something I have. And I want something you have. So, I have a new deal. Since Tom is at Taigh Locha, I'll take your friend there. We'll do the exchange there. It's out of the way. You get what you want, and then you can 'deal' your hand as you see fit."

Armstrong, fortunately, had the sense to keep Tom alive. He knew he'd have to wing it about Jessica when the time called for it. Armstrong hated not being in total control. His plan had somewhat back-fired, but at least he was going to achieve his objective and that of his customer.

Then Armstrong laughed inside.

'Hey-ho, it's what I'd have done.'

"OK, agreed," was all he could say.

Harry continued. "Bring one man only. I'm sure you and one man can manage a slip of a girl and the weakling you've already beaten up. So, if I see more than one man with you, the deal's off."

"You don't give the orders!" Armstrong snapped back.

"OK, your suggestion then?" Harry knew he was taking a risk with that question but had to give him something in exchange for agreeing the new deal.

Armstrong thought about it. A plan to redress the balance was building in his head. He needed to check if it would work. "I'll call you back in 10." The line went dead.

He called Harry back after 5 minutes.

"I already have two of my friends there with Tom. I'll bring Jess with a driver. That's the deal, the only deal."

"No, too many. That'll be four of you and one of me."

265

"That's my counteroffer. Take it or leave it!"

"I'll think about it. I'll call you in 5." Harry then closed the line. Harry had pushed back, but not because he was unhappy with the deal. He needed to offer considered anger and uncertainty about the arrangements. Otherwise, Armstrong might think he could get away with some later adjustments.

Four minutes later, Harry called back. "OK, I can be there by about 6 pm this evening, assuming the traffic's OK. I'll park up on the road before the house. I'll place Kotova in the road in front of the car in full view of the house."

"When I see Kotova, I'll bring Tom and Jess outside onto the road. Once all the cards are on the table, we can make the exchange."

"Works for me. By the way, your Fedor Kotova's a bit of a fighter. He's not the flabby politician/academic now. He's a big, powerful lad."

"Yes, I'm aware of that. But I'm sure the great Harry Logan has him under control. So, your point is what?"

"He'll be a bit dozy, had to drug him. Better he stays that way, eh? But, your choice. After I leave him in the road, I'll reverse away, and you send the kids over. When they are past Kotova, you can deal with him as you see fit."

"That works. I'll be waiting," replied Armstrong. "Any change to the plan and the deal's dead. Might even have a bit of fun with the girl."

"Whatever happened to 'officer-and-gentleman?"

"That's in the old films." The line went dead.

Harry looked at Fedor. "Here goes nothing." At that, they were off to visit Bonnie Scotland.

36. EXCHANGE

At 6 pm that evening, Harry parked the estate car about 200 metres before reaching the large house. He was far enough for Armstrong and his lot not to rush or fire on him, and he could still get away with Fedor if required. However, he was close enough for Fedor to be seen and verified. And as far as Armstrong was concerned, close enough for Harry to view Jess and Tom.

He called Armstrong on the mobile. "We're here."

Armstrong came out of the house and replied into the phone, "I can see that. Show me."

Harry opened the back hatch of the estate car and removed a blanket that covered something large. He then hefted Fedor's hooded body onto the road and half-dragged, half-carried the partially drugged man to the front of the car. He sat the man upright, propping him against the bumper.

'Shame about ruining the suit.'

"Remove the hood. That could be anyone."

"Unlike your lot, I don't drag people onto the street, hood then shoot them." Harry ceremoniously removed the hood and made a play of tidying the suit and his cravat. "Now, you have the kids there. I need proof-of-life. I'll let this man go free if I don't see Jess and Tom alive."

"OK, give me 2 minutes." Armstrong went back inside the house.

A few moments later, two shots, in close succession,

rang out from the trees just past the house from Harry's perspective. Both smashed into Kotova's head.

Harry dashed behind the car for cover. The now-dead body had slumped to its left-hand side, partially face down into a widening circle of red. From where Harry lay, he could see what remained of the back of Fedor's head.

He looked under the car, in the safety of the slumped Fedor, who was blocking further gunfire. Harry's insurance had disappeared with those two shots. He called Armstrong. "What the hell was that! Where's the kids?"

"Insurance, my friend."

"If you don't show the kids, I'm coming for you."

"I don't think so." Remember, I still have them. You've played your hand and lost."

When Harry tried to look around the car, another shot rang out from the direction of the trees. He felt the wind of the large calibre round as it whipped by his cheek. Fortunately, he expected that shot, testing the sniper's skills and his location.

"You're pinned down. My man is a trained sniper. You can't move. And now, we're coming for you."

Leaving one man with Tom as a contingency, Armstrong ordered to the two others, "let's go."

The three men cocked their automatic guns, then walked out to the one-sided gunfight at the Taigh Locha roadway. Harry had been a pain in the butt and wouldn't take orders. So, now he'll pay the price of that insolence.

'I'm going to enjoy this easy shit hunt.'

They had Harry pinned down, and he couldn't return fire. He again looked under the car and peered past Fedor's body. In the distance, and exiting the gate of the house onto the road, he saw three pairs of feet coming towards him.

Harry crouched and peered through the open tailgate.

He caught sight of Armstrong and two men, one of whom he'd recognised from earlier. He ducked before the next sniper round smashed through the windscreen.

In that brief moment, Harry glimpsed Armstrong sauntering toward him, a wide grin plastered across his face. His two companions displayed self-satisfied, serious smirks as they nonchalantly approached the car. Guns drawn, they were coming for their prey, and Harry could do nothing. And they knew it. So, they took their time.

Harry quickly looked out again and, boom, yet another close call. The bullet struck the ground several feet behind him. He now knew the location of the sniper.

Harry ducked under the car to check on the three pairs of feet who continued their approach.

Another shot rang out, and a second in quick succession, followed by a clatter.

Yet another shot rang out. The man to the right of Armstrong fell. His feet disappeared, replaced by the lower half of his face. The man's still-open eyes stared at Harry as if he couldn't believe what had just happened.

"What the fuck! The cheating bastard's got a sniper," screamed Armstrong. "

"Find cover!" Armstrong shouted to the one man still with him. They dived into the verge. They hid behind a tree as best they could from the sniper behind and Harry in front of them.

Armstrong looked behind and realised the earlier two shots had taken out his sniper, whose gun had fallen to the ground. The third shot hit one of his companions. He looked over to where his man lay in the road. There was a bullet hole in the back of his head. Without any scream, the man was dead before he hit the ground.

Harry again peered through the open tailgate, over the back seat to where he knew the sniper would have been if still active. He quickly ducked out of sight, just in case. He needn't have worried. That glimpse offered him a man hanging upside down from a tree, held by his harness, and a large calibre sniper's rifle lying on the ground.

As a final check, Harry looked again from under the car toward where the three pairs of feet once approached.

The two remaining pairs of feet, owned by Armstrong and Co., had disappeared.

Harry peered past the car and saw Armstrong and one of his men crouching at the side of the road behind a tree.

Armstrong ensured he had the safest spot. He was correct to do so. His companion leaned out a little and fired at Harry. Wrong move. Another shot rang out from the trees on the other side of the road just past the house. The man next to Armstrong fell into the road.

Armstrong ducked into the shrubbery out of sight. He called Harry, "Your boy's dead. You've just killed him!"

He shouted into his handheld radio, "Paddy, kill the little shit!"

A few moments later, the sound of two shots came from within the house. Then silence.

37. KILL TOM!

Armstrong was ready for Harry's arrival with Fedor Kotova. There'd be no witnesses, and everyone was going for a permanent swim in the loch when it was finished.

A lookout had already notified Armstrong of Harry's arrival, so when he got Harry's call, he already knew. He peered out of the window. Harry wasn't stupid. While a good rifle shot away, he was too far to be stormed.

Once the semi-conscious Fedor Kotova was in position in front of the car, Armstrong laughed at Harry. Although Harry was well out of earshot, he had to comment to Harry for the benefit of the others around him, "you mug!"

Into his handheld radio, he ordered, "kill Kotova, then Logan."

His sniper, who hid in one of the trees just past the house, opened fire with lethal accuracy. Unfortunately, Harry moved just after he made his first shot at Kotova. By the time he'd taken the third shot, Harry had dodged back behind the car.

Armstrong ordered one of his men, "Paddy, stay with Tom." While Armstrong suspected Paddy didn't have the balls to kill Tom in cold blood, he knew Paddy was a good soldier and followed orders. He would make sure Tom stayed captive. Killing Tom could be done later. Tom, for now, remained his bargaining chip, if the worst happened.

He gestured for the other two to follow him. "Let's go and have some fun with our friend Harry, shall we?"

Both nodded with enthusiasm, following their boss

outside.

After they left, Tom spoke up, "you know they're going to kill me, don't you."

"Yep."

"And you're going to let that happen!"

"That's their business. Now shut up."

Tom asked, "OK if I go to the window to check what's happening?"

Without any enthusiasm, Paddy replied, "knock yerself out." In reality, he was desperate to know what was happening, but the professional in him demanded he watch Tom intently. As it transpired, he could do both. Tom relayed what was happening outside.

After the tables had turned against Armstrong, Tom challenged Paddy. "Those two men with Armstrong are dead. Harry'll deal with Armstrong, and then he's coming for you. Give yourself up while you can. I've watched you these days. You're not like them. You're too professional."

When Paddy received Armstrong's kill command, he cocked his weapon.

"Really!" Tom challenged him from the window. Paddy had earlier glanced out and had seen the hanging sniper, then the dead bodies of his colleagues. He knew Colonel Armstrong was on his own and up against Logan.

Paddy fired once, then again. Into the walkie-talkie, he announced in a downbeat tone, "it's done, boss."

Tom whispered, "I'm sure we won't charge you for the damage to the ceiling."

Paddy grinned back, "I don't do non-combatants."

"Aren't you the lucky one," piped up Fedor from behind him. He and Viktar had been watching events in the living room and were ready just in case Paddy wasn't the person they and Harry thought he was.

Paddy raised his arms, and Viktar took the gun from Paddy.

"Sit. Not a sound."

Paddy complied.

"I'm fine," shouted Tom after opening the window. He kept himself out of sight in case Armstrong decided to fire at him.

Fedor held out his hand to Tom, and the young man shook it warmly.

"From your accents, I take it that one of you is Fedor Kotova."

"Me. Viktar and I travelled here to support Harry. We let ourselves into the back door with Harry's key. Looks like we were not needed."

Watching events through the window, Fedor added. "Saying that, I have a job to do on behalf of Harry."

"Viktar, keep an eye on this man," he gestured in the direction of Paddy.

****

After hearing Tom's announcement from the window, Harry called out to Armstrong. "You've lost. It's over. Throw your gun out. I'm not going to kill you unless you make me."

An automatic handgun landed in the middle of the road. A few moments later, Armstrong stepped into view, a smirk engulfing his face. He taunted, "I know you. You don't kill indiscriminately. But we'll meet again, I assure you."

"Somehow, I don't think so," replied Harry.

"What, your sniper will shoot? No way. As I said, it's not your style. And that's your weakness."

Harry slowly lifted his gun.

"Are you trying to scare me? You don't have the balls, missionary boy."

Harry hadn't heard that phrase for years. However, he was neither aiming his gun nor threatening Armstrong. He was pointing with it. "Yep, not my style, but I can't talk for him."

Armstrong heard a loud voice boom out from behind him. "Hello, my friend, it's been a while?" The happy smirk slid from his face, leaving it a deathly white. He slowly half-turned around. He had a double-take when he saw Fedor Kotova walking towards him. He recognised that voice, and now the man, "but we shot you!"

"Your dead sniper was a pretty good shot. See." Harry pointed to the bullet holes in the man's head. Yep, only a couple of inches apart; not bad. Unfortunately, he shot the wrong man. Now, look at ours. That's what you call shooting. He gestured to both dead men who enjoyed bullet holes smack in the middle of the backs of their heads."

Armstrong gasped at the sight. He didn't care about his dead men. He gawped at the man lying in front of the car. He wasn't interested in the accuracy of two bullet holes in the middle of the dead man's face, still oozing blood. It wasn't even the lack of the back of his head. It was the shock that it wasn't Fedor! He pointed to the dead man in front of Harry's car. "So, who's that?"

Then a dawning came. "Is that...? No, it can't be!"

"Yes, it is. You're so slow on the uptake. It's Colin, one of your men who attempted to kidnap and rape Jess. He's about the same size as Fedor. A shave, a haircut, a smart jacket, not forgetting Fedor's jazzy cravat, and finally, Jess's loving touches with make-up. And guess what, at 200 metres, he's Fedor's double."

Even close up, Armstrong could still see a resemblance.

Harry continued. "The other one you sent, I seem to remember the name Barys, wasn't in a good enough condition to use after Jess had finished with him. Had to be euthanised."

"As you've by now noticed, your man, your inept sniper, was up against and outclassed by a better one."

Armstrong shrugged his shoulders, resigned to what was to come. Suddenly, he spun back and dived toward the gun he'd earlier thrown onto the road. Cocking it as he raised it toward Kotova, he was too slow. Kotova didn't need any excuse to kill this man. But, he knew of Harry's distaste for blatant murder. He shot Armstrong twice, then several more times, slowly, because he could, and maybe, just to make sure.

"Finished?"

"Yes, and thank you, Arthur Fox, or whatever your name is."

Tom ran over and delivered a man-hug to Harry. Harry responded equally enthusiastically. After a moment, he looked over the smaller man's shoulder to Fedor and mouthed a thank you.

Shortly afterward, Harry drew Fedor's attention to a tree ambling toward them as best as it could. Twigs and branches started to litter the road behind as it approached. It wasn't long before the tree metamorphosised into Jess after she'd extracted the final remnants of foliage from all around her body.

"It's you!" remarked Fedor. He bellowed with laughter. "Love the camouflage. It becomes you."

To Harry, he commented, "She is some lady!"

Tom let go and looked around. He and Harry laughed at the sight approaching them.

No longer encumbered with half a tree stuck in and around her various bits, Jess ran the last few metres toward her family. She leapt on them, making a tightly entwined threesome.

Fedor and Viktar left them alone for as long as they needed.

Tom was the first to surface. "What's about all this mess," he asked.

They broke the circle. Harry responded, "sadly, I have to use that ace up my sleeve…"

38. A SETUP

Harry had no option but to call Ms Smith, his ex-controller. She wasn't really his ace in his current circumstances, more of a Get-Out-Of-Jail-Free-Card. He didn't look forward to her response after their parting of ways some six months earlier. It wasn't exactly a mutual agreement to terminate their relationship. In truth, Harry had absconded from under her quasi-governmental department's control.

Their relationship, while lucrative to Harry, was coercive and manipulative from her side. Until he left, he was under their control, previously doing a job that eventually disgusted and appalled him.

Ms. Smith wasn't her real name, but just one she accepted being called by Harry. Harry had other names for her, which he didn't share for obvious reasons. His favourite was Dragon-Lady because that's what she was to him.

I know, a bit childish, but she had that way of dragging the parent-child response from him. However, given their history and that of the governmental organisation she represented, most people would feel the same way. After their briefings and exchanges, he was always left angry and frustrated. He wasn't actually looking forward to this re-kindling of their relationship, but needs must.

After this call, he knew he'd be hooked again. Now his masters would be more vigilant. So the next time, it was not going to be so easy to extract himself.

Saying that, they trained him well to be invisible in plain

sight. Perhaps there was hope after all. However, for now, he'll have to frown-and-bear it.

So, Harry called Ms Smith.

"You took your time," was her first words after six months. "We were beginning to think you were going to fail. But I was rooting for you. I knew you'd follow through."

"You were on my side of what? What on earth are you talking about?" Harry was gob-smacked. He'd expected her usual caustic response after his six-month silence, perhaps followed by a tirade of comment worse than abuse. But he didn't expect this. Was this her being nice? Did she miss him?

"Can I assume you are at last calling because you've left some items of rubbish strewn around your little retreat in Scotland? And, are you looking for someone to collect the waste, perhaps even sanitise the area?"

"How do you know? What do you know?"

The controller, as usual, followed her conversational agenda. She ignored his question. "How is Colonel Armstrong? We need to debrief him. He is not to be interrogated by any of you. Understood!" What Armstrong knew, and if he let drop, could have pushed Harry over the edge from which there was no coming back. She had to handle that partial information sharing with Harry.

"Absolutely. Enjoy the chat."

"What do you mean?"

"How do you know about Armstrong!" Harry also ignored her question and was equally evasive. It was the game they played, which she invariably won. But he always had to try to get one over on her.

It at last clicked.

'Of course! Idiot!'

If she knew about Armstrong and Scotland, it meant she was in the know about all of this. No, it was worse. "You arranged for him to find us!" He screamed at her. "They could have killed Tom and Jess. They almost raped her before I could get there! You bitch, you evil bitch!"

"Tch, Tch, Logan. This was all down to you. You chose to resign and hide among the northern natives. You gave us no choice, forced our hand!" she retorted. "Oh, and remember, you're on a phone, and conversations can be overheard, even recorded."

"Fuck conversations being overheard!" Harry rarely swore, even to her. "You could have asked, even threatened, as is your style."

"We suspected you were planning to run again since this would have been the obvious next step. We were on the verge of popping in and saying hello, and this perfect opportunity came up. You were the ideal person for the job, and we could kill both problems with the same stone, as they say. And, you could have the pleasure of resuming your employment with us."

"Piss off," was all Harry could think of to say at that juncture.

"Now, how's about you answering my question about Armstrong? How is he?"

"Ventilated."

"Stop playing games. Is he able to help us with a few questions?"

"No."

Then it dawned on her. "You?"

"Can't say for sure. All a bit of a blur. Bullets flying around and all that."

"Won't say, you mean."

"Whatever."

"I'm getting tired of your games…"

Before she could continue, Harry shouted. "My games! You set all this up, and you're accusing me of playing games…"

It was her turn to interrupt. "Stop before you say anything you might regret. And trust me, you will regret it. I assume you're at Loch House?"

Harry took a deep breath and calmed himself down. This woman always managed to get under his skin. "Yes, I'm here."

"Thought so. I'll be there in three to four hours. I've just requested a clean-up team. They'll be en route in minutes."

"When will the cleaners arrive?"

"Soon. Stay."

"You're not talking to a dog," Harry remonstrated.

"You're correct, sorry. A dog would obey without question. So, stay there, or else there will be repercussions! Is that clearer?"

She always seemed to have the last word, which left Harry speechless and fuming.

The line went dead. Harry had to walk away from the group. He went to the water's edge and stared out across the loch. It was all coming back, all happening again. He knew it would. Even after six months, his feelings of anger towards his masters were still there. The three of them were so close to the next phase of their escape, putting more miles and confusion between them.

It wasn't the first time he'd mulled over his fate while looking over the calm blue waters. The sky was still clear, but dusk was coming. The shadows from the western hills pushed the sunlight up the eastern ones.

Tom saw the tension build within Harry with every word exchanged with that woman. When Harry ambled towards the water's edge and stared out over his favourite view, Tom knew Harry needed time out.

"Right guys 'n' gal," piped up Tom to the others. "Let's at least shift the bodies out of sight before whoever they are, arrive." He'd overheard enough. "We need to get the car off the road and into the driveway. It'd be disastrous if some lost tourists saw this scene from a Zombie horror movie. It'd bugger our reviews."

Tom had to ask, "So, Viktar, what are, or who are you in all of this?"

The big man paused and thought about his and Fedor's relationship, "I suppose, second in command, social secretary, tea-maker, you name it."

Fedor interjected. "Bollocks, as you say here. He's my close and trusted friend, and I suppose he's also my bodyguard."

Tom laughed, "and he's ours," he motioned in the direction of Harry while still hugging Jess. "That's when we're not protecting him from himself."

Harry heard the voices from behind him and looked back at them. He wondered, after all this, what could be so funny. But that was fine; everyone eases tension in their way.

****

After she'd come off the phone to Harry, her 2nd in command piped up, "OK, you were right, but you took a risk. We might have lost him."

"And, he delivered as usual."

"I must admit it was a master stroke arranging for Armstrong to know about Tom and Jess being with him. Their abduction was all he needed to push him into action.

281

Weren't you worried about them being killed?"

"Don't be silly, Mr Jones," she replied, using Harry's mock name for him. "This is Harry Logan we're dealing with."

But deep down, she knew she'd taken a risk with innocent lives.

'But the ends justify the means.'

At that, a roar of whirring rotors filled the house. Their transport to Scotland landed on the lawn at the back of the mansion where she and Mr Jones' department had their headquarters. After a few moments, they were off, flying north.

39. SPRING CLEANING

Almost two hours later, an RAF Puma helicopter landed across the road, about 200m from the house, on the village side.

Four large men immediately got out on the far side, wearing lime-green jackets sporting Scottish Gas insignias. They erected barriers and tapes a further 200m toward the village from the helicopter. The signs warned of a dangerous gas leak on the road to the house. The four men were also big enough to intimidate and deter any nosey locals or visitors, should any appear.

Once they'd secured the access, six more hooded occupants jumped out on the side facing the house and waited by the helio's doorway. They were not the big, imposing muscle of the gas men. These were a more specialised breed, lean, sharp, and followed orders to the letter; unlike Harry. They wore no markings, insignias, or ranks. They only wore handguns for this operation, leaving their larger weapons inside.

A seventh, slighter than the others, exited and walked over to the house, followed by two of the men. This one, a woman, was clearly in control of this operation. She met Harry on the road.

He suspected she held the rank of sergeant, perhaps even a lieutenant.

She recognised Harry. Without exchanging pleasantries, she formally requested, in a voice loud enough to be heard above the noise of the still fast-spinning rotas, "are you armed?"

Harry lifted his arms and signalled he had a weapon inside his jacket.

She and the two with her pulled out their handguns and pointed them at Harry. She motioned him to extract it.

At that visual command, Harry carefully removed the gun from its holster. He ejected the magazine, cleared the chamber, then handed over his gun, handle first.

Now that precaution was completed, her next question was, "how many bodies and where?" They re-holstered their handguns.

Harry pointed to the boathouse where Tom had arranged the storage of the four bodies that had littered the road. "Four," he shouted to the person in charge, displaying four fingers as confirmation.

She signalled to two of the two men by the Puma, also lifted four fingers, then pointed to the boathouse. They picked up four body bags and did the necessary.

"One in that tree, a sniper," Harry said loudly. He pointed to the heavily foliaged tree just past the side of the house. Tom, with Viktar's and Fedor's help, had pulled the not-so-good sniper back up into the tree cover.

She signalled the tree location to the two remaining men, lifting one finger; one body. She looked back at him for the next update.

"Live captive in the house."

"Bring him out."

Harry made the call on the handheld radio he'd purloined from Armstrong.

Paddy walked out of the house, followed by Viktar holding a gun to his back.

The sergeant re-drew and readied her handgun, as did the two men with her, and walked toward Paddy. Her two men disarmed Viktar while she hand-cuffed Paddy.

"Any more weapons?"

"In the house, one sniper rifle and three handguns." He could have gone into further detail about the guns, but that information would have been superfluous. He'd squirrelled away their own guns from the environs of the house.

She ordered her two men to retrieve the weapons from the house while keeping her gun trained on Paddy. When they returned, the two soldiers, plus Paddy, strode back toward the helicopter. She'd peeled off to speak to Harry, and sighed, "any more bodies and/or weapons?"

"Just one more body." He explained about Barys and the car in the loch and gave its location. "Not a pretty sight. Better not use a civilian team since they might ask uncomfortable questions of your masters."

"Good. I'm running out of men and body bags. I'll alert a specialised recovery team for the car and occupant. Now, are we all done?"

"Yes, that's it for today." Then in a mock American accent, he commented, "thank you for your service."

Trying not to be amused at his last comment, she nodded, turned on her heel, and strode back to the Puma. Out of sight, she allowed herself a smile at Harry's last quip.

Within an hour, the cleanup was complete. After their thorough job, there was no evidence of any foul play having taken place. Even the blood-covered road surfaces had been pressure washed by the extraction team.

With the five dead bodies, Paddy, and all the weaponry (the assumed sergeant wasn't leaving any guns around for the next visit), the pilot fired up the helio's Turbomeca Makila engines, and they were off. The four large Scottish Gas men remained at post to prevent all access to the dangerous gas leak by the house.

From the Taigh's driveway, the five of them watched

the cleaning team lift off and head away, disappearing behind the trees.

Jess had to ask, "Harry, did you get her number?"

"Not my type."

"Not that! Just thought it'd be useful to have her and her team pop around after one of Tom's baking sessions."

Tom growled and swung his left hand toward the back of her head, to which she ducked. However, the right hand didn't miss. It smacked her on the exposed buttock, which resulted in her chasing after him.

Tom, still out of breath from dodging Jess, had to comment, "bet those fancy road cleaners aren't paid as much as our council ones?"

Harry announced, "I need a drink!"

They were no dissenters. All eagerly followed him into the house.

40. FULL CIRCLE

Just over an hour after the cleaners departed, another helicopter landed in the same place as the earlier one. Four heavily armed members of what Harry referred to as the Balaclava Brigade exited the machine. They took defensive positions around the open door.

"All clear," shouted the team leader.

Ms Smith and Mr Jones alighted. There was no welcoming party for this group, nor sign of anyone around. They could smell smoke from a log fire, which they assumed came from the house. Dusk had settled, and they could see lights and shadows moving behind the curtained windows.

"Where's Logan?" shouted Jones into Ms Smith's ear to be heard above the slowing engine and rotors. "He's an ignorant sod. He should be here."

Ms Smith shrugged her shoulders. She never expected a warm welcome, and that's exactly what she didn't get.

Smith and Jones waited by the helicopter with two of the men; their bearing suggested these were all men. The other two strode to the Taigh. Not knowing what to expect, they cautiously entered, without knocking or permission, what they understood to be the living room.

Holding the five occupants at gunpoint, one of the balaclava-covered men ordered, "stand!"

The five complied.

The other soldier searched them and around where they

sat for weapons. He then checked the rest of the room.

"Sit," the same man ordered, to which the five yet again complied. People find it more difficult to attack from a seated position.

Satisfied, he left and clumped around the house, searching for whatever they searched for in these situations.

He returned after about 10 minutes and notified his colleague, "all clear."

The other man covered his radio mouthpiece and talked into it. He nodded, obviously having taken instructions in response.

By the time Smith and Jones walked into the living room, the two armed men had taken up textbook positions. Any of their gunfire would not hit each other or their two wards.

Harry assumed the other two men would have accompanied them to the house and had taken up position outside and/or in the hallway.

Ms Smith left Mr Jones just inside the doorway and walked into the room. She made a play of fixing her hair in the mirror, then turned to face the occupants. All was for dramatic effect to emphasise she was in control here.

Harry couldn't help himself. He had to comment, "Ms Smith, love the entrance."

In response, she looked at Harry for a few moments before she spoke. "You were having a girly-hissy-fit earlier? Calmed down now?"

He made a play of bowing to royalty; quite difficult from a seated position. "As ever, I mirror your lead, my liege." He couldn't stop himself from acting like an adolescent with her. She drew out the worst in him.

Smith always maintained an abrupt behaviour with her operatives. No way could she allow herself to feel any emotional attachment to them. That would be a dangerous play when she knowingly sent them into life-threatening situations. Sometimes their chances of return were slim. In their game, they lost people. Emotional attachments left scars. With Harry, it was worse. If she'd only but admit it, she had a deep respect for this complex one.

"In that case, I'm in a lovely humour." Her mouth contorted into a smile of sorts.

To the other four people, she challenged, "are you going to behave?"

It took Harry to respond. "As we're all friends here, how's about a nice cup of tea?" This was his way of saying yes.

She got the message. Ignoring his question, she studied both Pallarusians in turn. "Fedor Kotova?" she identified the correct one.

"And you're the infamous Ms Smith," he responded wistfully. "Harry's told me so much about you. The image he voiced doesn't do you justice."

"I imagine it didn't."

She turned to the big man. "Viktar Maroz?"

He nodded.

She ignored Tom and Jess. She knew perfectly well who they were and assumed likewise from their perspective. There was no reason for her to acknowledge them, so she didn't.

Back to Harry, she at last responded to his question. "Tea? Don't you have anything stronger?"

"That's reserved for welcome guests. You're not welcome. But you're here. Tea or coffee? The water for tea is lovely here. Straight off the mountain. In this place, they don't add any of that shit to whatever passes for water in the cities."

Ms Smith shook her head in dismay. After the helicopter ride, she really would have welcomed a decent whisky. She wasn't a big drinker, but now was one of those times when she would have appreciated the warm nectar burn. The bottles in the cabinet, which housed the mirror, had stared at her, beckoning her to pour herself one.

Sadly, from her perspective, she'd promised her boss, Sir Archibald, to be nice. So, she held off. There was no point in further upsetting the already strained situation.

Harry could see that the lady wasn't amused, which pleased him no end. He pointed to the settee they'd kept vacant for Smith and Jones to sit.

"Tom, Jess, this is Ms Smith." He wasn't about to stand by while she ignored what was effectively his family. "You'll remember that I've talked so much about how this lady and I have worked so well in the past together."

They knew all about her and her nickname, the Dragon-Lady. And now, at last, they were meeting this infamous woman.

"And, this is Mr Jones, and heaven knows what he does," added Harry.

When the two were comfortably seated, Harry demanded, "right, what's this all about, and why suck us into your shit again?"

"Before I answer, I must ask Mr Kotova and Mr Maroz to step outside with my friends. Oh, and the children can stay, for the reason that will become very clear."

"In that case, my dear," Fedor addressed Ms Smith as he and Viktar stood up, "I bid you a temporary farewell." Both were followed out by her balaclava'd 'friends'.

Leaving Smith and Jones alone with Harry and his 'kids' suggested all were satisfied they'd be safe. And, it was also likely that whatever was about to be discussed was not for the ears of the special services team.

She opened. "Right, I'm giving you all this explanation, not because I owe you, but later you'll understand. So, I'll be brief. We chose you because you work well on your own, and we needed this done quietly and off the books; no trail to us. Can't be any political repercussions. You're a highly skilled lone wolf, we've not heard from you in six months, making you completely deniable."

"And, we had a little further incentive for you, should you have needed encouragement."

"What more incentive did you need?" snapped Harry while looking over at Tom and Jess.

"Well, the worst could have happened. You might have lost those two as incentives." She gestured in Tom's and Jess' directions. "I thought you might have reached out to us sooner and I was going to let you know that Lieutenant Colonel Gerard Armstrong was ATS' head of station in Afghanistan while you were in front-line army duties."

"So, are you saying he was behind the Op that went south?"

She pursed her lips and tilted her head to one side, signalling that was the likely case.

Harry always suspected there had to be someone else, but there was no way for him to be sure. It was the result of that Op that drove Harry into the hands of her masters. So, now he had a name, albeit a dead one. However, he also knew she was an evil, conniving cow who couldn't be trusted. And dead men cannot confirm or deny anything.

"So, you told them about me and where I was?"

"No, no. You should have discerned by now that we don't like to be visible."

"Yes, you lot live in the political sewers."

"Excellent analogy, couldn't have phrased it better myself." She surprisingly grinned at Harry's accusation. "I'll remember that one. Yes, our political masters gorge themselves on politically dodgy ideas. The ones that go bad get flushed down to us. We are the people who live in and have to navigate through those proverbial sewers."

"Anyway, to get back to your question. As you know, his lot knows all about you and how useful you can be." With a wry smile, she continued. "As I said, we never directly said anything about you. Can't leave a trail of information, can we? But you know what it's like. Someone who knew someone, who knew someone, saw a document about you and where you were. Chinese whispers are such terribly useful devices, but we had to handle those whispers carefully. We don't want everyone to know where you are, now do we?"

Harry laughed. It wasn't actually funny. It was more due to the cruelty of the games these people played.

"So what was this all about?"

"Politics my dear boy, it's always about politics. Here's what I can tell you. And, knowing the sharp operator that you are, I suspect you know or assumed a lot of this already."

She took a deep breath to collect her thoughts. "Whether we like it or not, what we call the West is embroiled in the Russian invasion of Ukraine. Russia escalates, and Ukraine responds with our backing. We are desperate to stay out of the direct fighting, officially anyway."

Harry nodded and waited.

"Russia has many allies dotted around the world. Almost all are indebted to them, one way or another, so they have no choice but to support them. There are others, some of whom are in Eastern Europe, that actively support Russia, again partially due to their indebtedness. They need Russia's prop up their governments and their economies. ses them as its barrier to NATO's alleged aggression."

"OK, so far?"

Harry and the other two had been keenly following developments of this invasion.

She continued. "Now, if these countries became actively involved with feet on Ukrainian territory, the direction of the war would change. A bad scenario would be the Ukraine government and infrastructure brought to its knees. Worse still, we'd be drawn into the battle of Eastern Europe. Whichever the case, Russia wins."

He'd suspected most of what had now been confirmed by Ms Smith. "So you destabilise one of Russia's allies to make a point to the rest."

"Mmm, partly. As I said, it's about politics. Our masters held informal and very secret discussions with Pallarus along the lines that if they were naughty and got involved, even indirectly, we might not like it. We had hoped that would be the end of that. However, the kid-gloves came off when Pallarus hosted Russia launching its attack on Kyiv. We'd warned them about active support like that and its consequences. They, in effect, turned their noses up at us. That was the last straw. Even those earlier dissenters within our glorious government agreed. They gave us the go-ahead to play politics with Pallarus. As a direct result, the Israelis set Mr Kotova free."

"Surely you could have seen this coming a decade ago when Russia invaded Crimea."

"Possibly. However, we work to what we believe to be the right balance. The West, at that time, needed to stop Kotova's revolution in Pallarus since it would unbalance the power in Eastern Europe. If the pro-West Fedor took power, there was a fear Russia would invade Pallarus in response. It is why they are invading Ukraine now and Crimea earlier. There needed to be stability. Now the West

293

is in the Ukraine war, its sentiments have changed. The potential for Pallarus' direct involvement has changed everything. So, anything to de-stabilise Pallarus is a good thing now."

"So, those powers, who turned on the Pallarusian people eleven years ago, leading to the capture of Fedor, have now done a strategic U-Turn. They've arranged for the Israelis to free him to do whatever he wanted."

Her blank face neither confirmed nor denied his analysis.

"You allowed a man onto the streets in the UK, with a belly full of revenge, to go after one of your own." In other words, they allowed Fedor to enter the UK to attack Jacob, one of their ex-agents.

"Not exactly. Our American cousins negotiated that part with Mr Kotova and never told anyone. And once we realised what was in play, we ensured you got engaged. As you know, Pallarus hired Colonel Armstrong to kill Mr Kotova. All we did was lubricate the path for him to choose you since you had those two young incentives." She glanced at Tom and Jess. "So, the colonel engaged you to do his dirty work. We knew he was after you anyway. And this would be a perfect solution for him to finally deal with you. So, it was the perfect operational fit."

"You have the resources. Why didn't you just stop Armstrong and his men?"

"Ah, you still don't get it. We officially don't know anything about anything. We are the innocent party in all this. The Russians and the Pallarusians don't know that we know what's going on, and that's how it needs to stay."

"She gave Harry what looked to be a maternal look, one she'd probably never use again. "I also knew that you'd never agree to kill anyone in cold blood, so I knew Kotova and Jacob were as safe with you as anyone I know."

Then, back to her normal school ma'am demeanour, she added, "and, let me reinforce what I said earlier, we have not contacted or spoken with Mr Kotova. And it stays that way!"

Tom had to jump in at that point. "Yet, here you are with him and talking to him. And I expect he'll be leaving with you, and he'll be under your control."

"As I said, we've officially never met. End of!"

Harry continued. "The West suspects Fedor has the ability to restart the independence movement in Pallarus even without the key that Jacob's hidden."

"We believe so yes."

'She still believes Jacob had, or has, the key. And no way am I contradicting that belief. That'd put Fedor in danger.'

"So, with Fedor on the loose around Europe, Pallarus has now to focus inside its borders rather than outside," observed Harry. "And by implication, this was a warning to other countries that might support Russia."

"Now you've got it. The ex-colonel was very close with Pallarus, having spent a lot of time there. Now, we don't know if they have something on him, or he was bribed, or even both. However, in a nutshell, he was working for them."

"So, the killing of Kotova, on sight, would send an upwards pointing middle finger to the West."

"Absolutely. Now what's been missing from the mix was our Russian friends. It has its little beady eyes everywhere. And it is most adept at politics. If they captured both Mr Fedor Kotova and our Jacob Collins, they could use them as a bargaining chip to ensure Pallarus played their game, Russian-style. Also, they had the forlorn hope that bringing them together might even release those memories of the key that are in Jacob. That would also be information and a bargaining chip Russia could hold over their friend and close ally, Pallarus. Enter your darling Miss Helen Welsh."

"So, you know about her!" blurted Harry.

"Who's she?" interrupted Jess.

"Quiet young lady! The adults are talking."

Harry turned to Jess, took hold of her arms, and spoke to her face-to-face. "Jess, Helen Welsh works for the Russians via another part of ATS. She'd been sent to play me. I later found out that she's a nasty piece of work." Harry wanted this out in the open from him rather than Ms Smith. It would be easier for him to manage any fallout. And knowing how Jess felt about him, there would be serious fallout.

"You screwed her!" she hissed the accusation. "You fucked the enemy. You were alone with her and could have been killed!" She didn't know whether to be more angry at his stupidity or giving another woman what she'd been so desperate to have; himself.

Harry grimaced a yes.

Jess glowered at him. "We'll deal with this later," was all she said.

He groaned inside.

Jess then turned back to Ms Smith. "The geriatrics can now continue their ramblings. Please carry on."

"Can you please get back on track?" demanded Harry of Ms Smith before she could deliver one of her cutting responses to Jess, which would have ignited all hell's fires.

Instead, Ms Smith delivered her best teacher-to-naughty-girl look. Jess responded with her best insolent-pupil-to-teacher look. She won the round, being the expert at this sort of game.

Harry grinned and threw Ms Smith an I-told-you-so look.

Harry's ex-controller was about to respond again but thought the better of it. She could see Jess was sharp and not to be verbally trifled with.

Instead, she continued. "Thank you for supplying Miss Welsh to us, all neatly wrapped up like that. We're in the process of discussing her future and what she'd like to tell us. We do have her over a barrel. As you know, the Russians don't like people spilling beans or potentially doing so."

"So, yes, we played you and your little team here. I do not apologise for doing what's right for our country's and Europe's interests. You are one of a kind, Logan. If anyone was going to fix this, it could only be you."

Ms Smith reluctantly felt she had to add, "and, you did, I must say, a reasonably good job."

"And what happens to Fedor?"

"Mr Kotova is under our discreet protection. And whether he likes it or not, he is now a key ally of the West. That's all you need to know. You can imagine the rest."

"And you lot are going to start a rebellion in Pallarus."

Ms Smith said nothing more on the topic. Her poker face perfectly hid anything she might be thinking.

Harry did have to ask. "And Jacob Collins, you owe an explanation to that man. He's only done what was the right thing and for the right reasons."

"Don't give him too much sympathy. He was a trained killer like you, but many years before your time. He was good, perhaps even as good as you."

"He talked about New-Me. Now I understand. You lot had him under your greasy thumb, and I wouldn't be surprised if you forced his compliance. He has my full sympathy. Anyone, everyone who gets involved with you, has my sincerest sympathy. The poor man needs to know what happened to him, and so does his doctor. He deserves the right help. It's because of you and your kind that he was so badly abused."

"His downfall was that he made mistakes and trusted the wrong people. Logan, you get angry and are easily dealt with. However, Jacob could be a pain in the arse. He had the habit of irreverently winding up his masters. Sometimes, he even liked to use cryptic stories and messages in his reports under the pretext of security. That behaviour didn't endear him to those above me."

"So, people took the huff."

"That's not what got him taken, but it didn't help him later. Messages allegedly from him were misinterpreted, and that was his downfall. He was a loss to the team, but we recovered. Politics and people move on."

"That's not good enough," Harry pushed back.

"OK, this is what I can tell you. I owe him at least that. You cannot say anything to anyone. That is a Breach of the Official Secrets. If I find this getting out, I know it will be you and I'll have to deal with it, and you. What you do or say next is up to you."

Did Harry see a bit of remorse in her eyes? Nah! The poker face was back in position.

"On that fateful night of the weapons exchange, several things happened. Yes, and in hindsight, sadly, we betrayed Kotova and his uprising. We needed to maintain the status quo in Europe. Fedor was whisked away to Israel. As I said, politics is politics; people, sides, and positions change. So, the West kept him on ice."

"Regarding Jacob. All I can say is that the Russians, who were on the periphery, took Jacob because of that damned key in his head. Once in their hands, on foreign soil, we could do nothing! From what I can gather, their internal politics demanded Jacob be given to Pallarus. Jacob had evidence about a mole. But, he was taken before he could name names. You've seen Jacob. Any information he once had, is lost."

"The third major thing that happened was that a village on the Libya-Egypt border, where the exchange was about to be made, was wiped out by a US drone strike. Those not killed in the drone strike were subsequently murdered; every man, woman, and child."

"At the time, we thought Jacob had supplied the wrong strike coordinates in his encrypted way. One doesn't go in later and wipe everyone out after a mistake. Because of this cover-up, we knew it wasn't Jacob's error. This was down to MI6."

"But, aren't you MI6 or SIS or whatever you call yourselves these days?" interrupted Jess.

"Silly girl, of course not. We are more strategic."

After listening to all this, Tom decided to intervene. "Her lot is the politicians' dodgy-deal strategists. When a deniable job needs done, it executes, in more meanings than one."

"My word, you are a sharp little cookie, aren't you." She neither confirmed nor denied what Tom had outlined.

"Right, back on track if you two don't mind? Only Jacob knows the truth, or rather, he knew the truth about what happened then. As well as the key lost inside his head, we'd an atrocity for which we'll never, officially, know who was responsible."

"So, Jacob was tortured by Pallarusians until they concluded he'd locked the key so far away that no one could find it. And now it seems everything else has been lost," added Harry. "How convenient. So, once stripped of his mental and physical faculties and no use to them, you eventually decided to bring him home. How big of you lot! You haven't even told the medical staff at the manor what happened to him so they could help him. They're working

299

in the dark."

"We cannot tell them anything. I cannot tell them anything. I am under the strictest orders not to."

Harry thought about what she'd just said.
But, I can bitch, and I will!'

Ms Smith finished with, "lesson over."

"So what happens now?"

"You mean the yet-to-be-discussed business of what happens to you. As I alluded to earlier when I started my explanation, I wanted the three of you to know this background for good reason. We'd like to make you an offer. It's one you cannot afford to refuse."

She had the threesome's full attention.

"We know you will run again, eventually, no matter what constraints we put on you. It would be most inopportune if you ran when we needed you. It took almost five months before we found you. And then that was only by luck. Your plan was a sound one, and you almost made it. I do not doubt that you'll have learned, and the next time will be even harder for us."

"So what are you threatening?" accused Jess.

"Heaven forbid, we are not the Russians or the Chinese."

"True," replied Harry. "You're worse."

"Tch, tch. The offer is that you work for us. No kill-on-demand requests. You and your team will operate to fix problems like this one."

"What team?"

"⸻ of course," piped up Tom, nudging Jess.

⸻arp," Ms Smith acknowledged. "You've And, as consultants, you'd be well paid."

⸻ou the bill for this mess you created?"

"Don't be silly. You were never working for us. Remember deniability?" She gave Harry a rare smile. "Oh, and by the way, this is a wonderful safe house. We might even send you the occasional very-well-paying government-sponsored guest to look after."

"What's about Paddy? He knows about this place. He could talk."

Ms Smith looked at him knowingly. "Paddy who?"

'She's either got Paddy by his balls or he was insurance.'

Harry looked at Tom and Jess. They looked enthusiastically back at him.

"Two years from today we're done. We walk, and you forget about us."

"Five years, sixty months."

"Forty months."

"Agreed."

"Oh, while I have your attention, we have some unfinished business for which we need your help. Let's call it your gesture of goodwill."

"OK?" she hesitatingly asked.

Harry filled them in on the request.

"Deal!"

They never shook hands on any of it. None of the three wanted the smell of those sewers on their skin. However, Harry did capitulate in offering Ms Smith and Mr Jones their well-deserved, very large, glass of his finest malt.

After the pair and their entourage left, Jess giggly commented, "can we soak their glasses in disinfectant?"

The other two laughed.

Tom raised his glass as a toast. "To us and whatever that lot throws our way." The three then clinked glasses.

41. NOTICE

For Harry, there was unfinished personal business arising from this mission. If he thought about it, perhaps it was even Dragon-Lady's one, although she could never admit it.

The following morning, Harry called the manor. "Mrs Matthews please?"

"Matthews," Bulldog announced when he was put through.

"Hi, Arthur Fox here. Unfortunately, my family problems have come to a head. I need to resign. I'm so sorry. I've a temporary fix, and I can work my notice. You've all been so good to me. I've loved my short stint there."

"My goodness! Shame to lose you. Hard to find good people."

"Is two weeks OK?" I've got that cover for my father. Then it's all down to me."

"You'll do a good job with him. I'm sure. When will you be back?"

"Thanks. I expect to arrive after 9 pm this evening."

"Sadly, I'll not be here. I'll notify the gatehouse and Pato. Bye."

The line went dead. She wasn't the greatest of conversationalists.

Harry arrived before 9 pm to an enthusiastic welcome from his erstwhile teammates. It was their turn on night duty.

It was early afternoon when Harry and his team surfaced from their night shift. Harry had left a message asking for a meeting with Dr Barclay. In return, a note from the doctor awaited him in reception at the start of his shift.

Harry addressed Pato while waving the slip of paper. "Gotta see Dr Barclay, that OK?"

"When the boss calls and all that. Good luck. I'm assuming he'll want to try and keep you."

"Sadly, he can't, and I can't. See you when finished with him."

At that, Harry bounded upstairs and headed to see the boss.

"Sit," said the doctor, pointing to one of the comfortable armchairs. He sat opposite Harry. "So, what's this all about? Why the urgency to see me?"

"Can I trust you?" Harry was breaking official secrets and all that legal government shit, but he had to do the right thing. He trusted this doctor. "What I'm about to tell you is in confidence and cannot go outside these walls."

"Patient confidentiality and all that," replied the doctor. "Lips are sealed. If it's who I think it's about and whatever you're about to tell me could help him, nothing will get me to talk. Anything to help me with his treatment, I'm all ears and completely forgetful. Does that make my position clear?"

Harry rocked both head and body as an enlarged nod.

The doctor had picked up on the obvious. It could only be one patient. Only a couple of days ago, Harry was with Jacob and hadn't worked back at the manor since. Then there was how Harry had dropped Jacob off and the urgent matter of Harry's family issue. One and one always made two.

"So, as you've already guessed, it's about the well-being and possible treatment of Jacob Collins."

Dr Barclay leaned in and waited.

Harry kicked off. "What I know is this. His condition is not mission-induced PTSD. Before Jacob came here, he'd been held by the Pallarusian government for almost one year. He'd been brutally and repeatedly tortured for information. He'd been drugged, degraded, and abused in every manner conceivable. That's only a part of what destroyed him. Then, the Russians had a go at him using whatever means they had at their disposal. They also were desperate to extract information from him. The brutality lasted over one year."

"Wow! It helps enormously. I'm aware how the Pallarusians operate, their methods, preferred drugs, and cocktails. We are a small community of specialists, and we help each other. Any gaps in what I have on the Pallarusians, I know some colleagues I can ask to fill; all discreet. We do this all the time. The same applies to our friends in Russia. Every country has its interrogation preferences."

Harry relaxed. It was a relief there may be some hope for Jacob. He wasn't naive enough to think Jacob might make a full recovery or anything close to it. However, anything or any improvement would be a miracle after the last ten years.

"You are brave in telling me this, thanks."

"I owe the man. We all owe that man for the service he gave us that brought him here."

"I cannot guarantee miracles, but what you have told me is extremely helpful. Thank you."

Harry stood up to leave, and the doctor also stood up

and shook Harry's hand.

"Arthur Fox, or whatever your real name is, if ever you want your job back, I'll do whatever I can to help you return. You've done so much in the short time you've been here."

At that, Harry took his leave to continue his duties for the next two weeks.

He was and wasn't looking forward to returning to the Taigh. He missed the siblings. He also knew Jess had a long memory, and there would be consequences regarding Helen Welsh.

****

Saturday came, as did Natalie and Michael. Harry kept himself busy, but work required him to enter the lounge where the two sat with Jacob.

Harry did his best to ignore them, but Natalie wasn't having any of that. She came over to him when he was free. "You haven't called or visited. Have I done anything wrong? You promised you'd come."

"Of course not, and sorry."

"I know what's about to come. So, before you start, don't give me the it's-not-you-it's-me bollocks."

Harry chuckled. "'fraid you've got me there." Then he thought about his inappropriate response. It was an involuntary action, a release of tension, but the words were wrong nonetheless. "Sorry," was all he could think of to say.

"I thought we had something?"

Harry would have loved to have said, "yes, we do, and I'm also fond of you," and other words. But he couldn't. He looked over to the man he'd promised to protect

305

Natalie.

"Listen, all that stuff about me being a killer, it's true. I killed indiscriminately. I could hide under the mantle of doing it under orders, but I knew what I was doing." He took hold of both her forearms. "There were times at the beginning when I enjoyed it. I'm sick, Natalie." He sighed and breathed out long and hard. "I'm sick, and I'm dangerous for you."

"But you are not that man any…"

He cut her off. "You are too good a person for the shit that would come your way if we enjoyed any relationship. My two closest friends almost died because of me. I couldn't protect them, and I cannot protect you as well." Then, he used that same metaphor from that discussion with his controller. "I'm about to climb back into the sewers, and that stench gets everywhere, contaminating everything and everyone around."

"What are you talking about?"

"You now have an idea of the sort of work I have to do. I'd have loved it to have been different. But it can never be. For a short time, I'd been living a utopian dream. Then reality kicked in after I left you. When I again had to face what is my life. This is not the life for you."

She didn't know what to say.

He had to leave before he'd display the emotions that were welling up from within. "I have to get back to work." At that, he departed to help a nurse who, thankfully, needed assistance.

"What was that all about," asked Michael when she returned, more upset than she wanted to show.

Jacob intervened. "He is a good man, one of the best I know. But he is bad for you. The baggage he carries is corrosive, toxic, and dangerous. Leave that one well alone." And that was all he said the rest of the afternoon. Harry had kept his promise.

****

On this last day of work at the manor, Harry sat with Jacob outside, in their usual place, looking out over the rolling hills.

"This is my last day here. I'll miss our time together. Will you be OK?"

"I am safe in their ignorance," Jacob whispered while staring into the distance.

For once, Jacob looked at Harry and frowned. There was a glimmer of brightness in Jacob's eyes that Harry hadn't seen since Fedor was with them. "Never trust our masters. That was my downfall."

Harry didn't need to say anything. That much he already knew.

Soon, it was time to take his leave. It would be the last time he'd enjoy this view with this patient/friend/predecessor/confidante, or whatever their relationship was. He struggled for the word to describe what Jacob was now to him.

Harry took Jacob's hand and said, "goodbye, Old-Me." At the same time, he surreptitiously pressed a note in Jacob's palm. It was the telephone number of his messaging service. "Just in case," he whispered.

At that, he started his journey home.

42. PAYBACK

"Uncle Nev, oops, I mean Mr Davidson. Susan always called you that. Anyway, good evening. So sorry to bother you. I'm a friend of Susan's, and I need your help."

Neville looked at the sweet-smiling, elfin-beauty standing in front of him. "How can I help you, doll?" He responded in his usual charismatic and sexy manner when confronted by such as her, which wasn't often, more like rare. OK then, never.

Jess continued. "Susan's told me so much about you, but I lost contact with her after university and her address. I asked around, and she was right, everyone knows you. So, you were easy to track down. I've got some of her documents that were sent to my address when she made a job application. I need to give them back to her. I think one is a job offer, and it looks important," which she showed for Neville to read. "I remember her making the application and using my address."

Neville didn't get the detail, but it looked genuine enough. Then, referring to the greying older man standing behind her. "Who's that with you."

"My dad wanted to bring me. He said this was a rough area, and I shouldn't go alone."

"And he was right darlin'. Please come in," he gestured to the two of them.

Jess followed him to the living room while Harry hung back a few paces behind; it was Jess' play after all.

Inside were four men, still in building work attire, sitting around a table playing cards. The fifth empty place was obviously Neville's.

"She says they've got some documents for Susan." Then he grimaced at Jess, "but I don't believe a fuckin' word you say. Who the fuck are you?"

Her sweet smile changed to a smirk. "I'm Tessa Greywell, and this is my dad Barrie. Susan is leaving the country tonight."

"Fuck, I know you!" exclaimed Neville. "She told me all about your dad and what to do if he came around."

One of the men had quietly left the table and grabbed Jess from behind. He wrapped his arms around her. Unable to control himself, he had to have a grope of her pert breasts. He lifted her high off the ground. Adding insult to injury, he pulled her close and droolingly muttered in her ear, "you smell nice, little one."

The others laughed. Two of them arose to bar Harry, who stood in the doorway, preventing him from helping Jess.

Harry ignored them. He remained there unperturbed at what was happening with Jess, that is until he saw all that had happened. Then he joined in the laughter but for a very different reason.

He laughed at the man holding Jess. "Poor bloke!" he exclaimed in between giggles.

One of the two men barring his defence of Jess, growled, "what's funny tosser?"

Harry chuckled, "if there's one thing he shouldn't have done, it was that."

"You'll be laughing at the other side of yer face when we finish wiff ya."

Jess pleaded with the man to let her go.

He leaned close in. His half-day stumble rasped her skin

as he rubbed it against her.

The smell of him belching beer alongside her made her go limp and pull away with fear, or so he thought. He lifted his head and laughed with his mates. "you're a little beauty, ain't you?"

She snatched at his topmost thumb and rolled the hand sufficiently away to give her a little wiggle room for what she was about to do. And now she had enough distance to backward-head-butt him, then a second time for good measure. Stunned, his hold had reduced enough for her to squirm downward and bite into his arm, drawing blood.

"Cunt!" He pulled his arm away from her. Partially released, she tore downwards with her heel, on one of his knees, then the other, kicking and scraping. Jess and Harry wore stout walking boots in case something like this might happen. Groping-man buckled, collapsed to one knee, and released her. With his head at her shoulder height, she spun and elbowed him hard in the face, then untwisting like a coil of steel, she spun the other way and elbowed him on the other side. He went down hard. He was out.

It wasn't only Jess who needed to demonstrate the predicament these men were in. Harry wasn't so aggressive. He didn't need to be. After checking she was OK, he delivered his measured and practiced response.

Hearing Jess and her groper, the blocking man on Harry's left partially turned around. While Harry didn't need any edge with these bar-room brawlers, it made matters simpler. He delivered a low side kick to the side of the man's knee. There was a grating of tissue, and the man went down. The right-hand man couldn't get off a right punch because his friend was in the way. So he used his favourite blow for close-combat barroom fights; he head-butted Harry. Harry expected that response. He merely crouched a little, and the man's face struck Harry's forehead cleanly and hard. Dazed, the man collapsed to the ground.

As closure, Harry delivered a snap-jab to the first man's face. Theirs was, after all, just a 'gentle' warning. They crawled away.

Harry reverted to standing at the doorway, arms crossed. It was still Jess' deal.

Jess looked down at the unconscious man. "Thanks for the real-life self-preservation lesson." While her practice sessions with Harry and Tom had prepared her for this eventuality, there was nothing better than the real thing; with Harry there as backup, in case.

She remembered the final part of Harry's 'don't let them get up' lesson. You're not judge, jury, and executioner. Remember restraint. And she did.

Harry winked back congratulation, not only on the fight but more about her 'control'.

Harry said to Jess, "foot on him, champion-style." And to the man with a smashed and bloody nose, "hold her arm up, winner-style."

Harry took a photo. To Neville, he said, "you're coming with me to Susan now."

"And if I refuse, and we call the police?"

"Ah, that'd be a funny conversation. Your friends were beaten up by an old man and a slip of a girl after you sexually assaulted her. This picture goes on social media. You'll all be the laughing stock."

Harry clicked his fingers, "I've got a better idea. Let's go down the pub to explain, shall we?"

At that point, the bell rang. "Better answer it," said Harry to Neville. He stepped to one side to allow the man to pass.

"What do you want," growled Neville to whoever stood at the front door.

From the doorway, they heard the reply, "Detective

Inspector Chalmers. I've a warrant for the arrest of a Mr Neville Davidson for conspiracy to rape and attempted murder."

"How'd you know what was going on? But nothing happened. Errol just grabbed her in self-defence, and she attacked him. Come in and see."

DI Chalmers followed Neville into the house. "Are you saying this man also attacked Miss Tessa Greywell?"

"What do you mean also?"

"This young woman has pressed charges against you and Miss Susan Davidson for an attack in the Scottish highlands last month."

Jess interjected, "if he takes us to Susan and gets her to agree to the deal, I'll withdraw my allegation."

"Fuck you." Neville grabbed his jacket. Then, to his friends, "get Errol to the hospital."

The policeman and his two visitors followed Neville out.

When they were in the street, Neville addressed the policeman, "I don't know what shit's going on here, and I don't want to. But I can tell you now, they're both mental."

Then to Jess, he growled, "she lives round the corner, then I'm done OK?"

"We'll see what Miss Davidson has to say, shall we?" responded Detective Inspector Chalmers. "Please lead the way."

Following up behind, Jess whispered to Harry, "are you sure we shouldn't have gone directly to Susan's? Seems an awful roundabout way of doing things."

"I know, but from what you said, she worships her uncle. She'd have refused. Then she'd have called him to her defence. And if he came mob-handed and prepared, some of them might have been badly hurt. Our little shock-tactic forced his hand on our terms. Once she sees the

312

futility, she'll cave, you'll see."

****

Susan Davidson heard the urgent knocking on her front door. It was late, just before pub closing hours, but she wasn't worried about any problems. Her Uncle Nev and his mates were well known, more like notorious, in the area. She opened the door and stood to one side to let him in when she saw him standing there. "What're you don' here so late? Isn't this your cards night?"

Her friend, with whom she shared the two-bed-roomed house, had stood behind, just in case. Seeing who it was, she headed back upstairs.

Normally, Neville Davidson would have been happy to walk straight in since they were close family, but not today. The door opened onto the street; no front gardens in this neighbourhood.

"Susan. Sorry darlin', but there's some serious shit going on, and someone you know wants to talk with you."

Illuminated by the hallway light, she saw the look of trepidation on his face. "Anything wrong Uncle Nev?"

"I don't know, you tell me."

Then Jess stepped to his side.

"Uncle Nev, for Christ's sake, what's that bitch doin' here?"

"Susan," opened Jess, "I've been asked to deliver this job offer from a charity dealing with an outbreak of Ebola in Africa. I made the application on your behalf. Good news, you got the job since you fit the bill."

"What the f...fuck!" she stammered, which was unusual for her. "Uncle Nev, why're you lettin' this happen?"

Neville gestured to the man standing under a street light

across the road. She gasped. Fear enveloped her. "It's him. Get Errol! He and the boys'll sort them out. Please, you need to get them," she pleaded.

"Errol can't come. He's on his way to hospital." Nev pointed to Jess. "That bitch took him down like he was nuthin'."

Susan whined, "get the others, he's a professional killer!"

Uncle Nev pointed to Harry. "They were there and that man took down Joe 'n' Baz like they was kids! What shit are you involved with? And what the fuck are you doin' getting' me involved?"

Jess responded to Susan's whine. "My father's a little pussycat." She leaned in. "It's me you need to worry about," growled Jess.

"I promised I'd be back, and here I am." She was enjoying this. Susan knew exactly what she'd done that time several weeks ago. Now was payback.

The policeman came into view on the other side of Neville. "Miss Susan Davidson, my name is Detective Inspector Chalmers. You have a choice of my arresting you on the charge of murdering a certain foreign national called Barys Novik. You will also be charged for conspiracy to kidnap and rape."

"I didn't do anything!" she squealed. "It must have been them," she pointed at them in turn. "They're the killers."

"All the evidence of the murder points to you, and with her witness statement, you'll be doing jail time for many years."

The DI let that settle in. After some seconds, he continued. "You've been given a choice because these two innocent people were in witness protection from the very man you killed. I do not want to go through the process of finding new identities and another safe house. So, you have the alternative of keeping your mouth shut, leaving the country, and never returning. Or, you go to prison and piss me off with added paperwork.

Jess handed over the job acceptance letter and a flight ticket. "Your flight leaves in four hours from Glasgow Airport. Here's your ticket." She pointed to a car that flashed its light. "That's your ride."

Susan took the papers and gave her Uncle Nev a pleading look. "You introduced me to them. I never killed anyone."

Nev responded. "But I didn't know what they were up to. I just made the intro. You could have said no to what you had to do for the five big ones."

"What about my friends, Elizabeth and Karen? What have you done with them?"

In truth, Elizabeth and Karen were no longer friends of Susan and hadn't spoken to her since the incident. They never did finish their holiday together.

Jess responded, "they've secured jobs with Médecins Sans Frontières and are already out of the country." She didn't tell them that their contracts were coincidentally for forty months.

The DCI added to Susan, "if any of this comes to light, you will spend the rest of your life in jail." To Nev, he added, "I don't have to remind you about your precarious position. After all, you are still on probation. Adding the crimes of conspiracy to murder, abduction, and rape with Miss Davidson, you'll be away for a long time."

"We'll leave you to it," smirked Jess. "Have a safe journey."

The three of them walked away.

Susan packed.

****

Detective Inspector Chalmers made a call. He handed the phone to Harry. "That's us done," said Ms Smith. "I think you're safe there for the term of our agreement. After that, you're on your own. That is assuming you play ball."

Harry handed the phone back to Mr Jones, aka DI Chalmers.

EPILOGUE

While Jacob improved, he never fully recovered. Too much physical and mental damage had taken its toll.

They replaced his earlier debilitating medication with a suite of treatments that were more appropriate to the causes of his condition. His revised medication was more targeted and in lower, less invasive doses.

They put a care package in place for Jacob to spend increasing time with his niece and nephew. Harry suspected this was part of the deal for Fedor's support. Nothing further was muted about him being with his best friend once more.

With his improvements, there was enough inside Jacob for him to understand what he could and could not say outside.

****

And Jess did bring Harry, who was again Barrie Greywell, and Tom (aka Ron), to meet Charles and Agnes. Jess fleshed out a vague story that Barrie and Ron were thrown out of the house by her alleged mother all those years ago. It was good enough to satisfy Agnes' interrogation.

And they kept in touch.

****

Back at the Taigh, Harry continued his routine. While he had a deal with Smith 'n' Jones, others would still have loved to have had him in their sights. He unintentionally, but by design, met Auld Wullie on his first run out. There was a lot to catch up on from the herder.

"Where've you been? Missed our blethers."

"Here and there," replied Harry. "Been away for a few weeks. Needed a break from all the work at the house."

"Now yer back, so wot's been happenin' with the gas men two weeks ago. Been talk o' loadsa small explosions by yon place. You all OK?"

"Yes, all fine now. They found what they thought was unexploded ordinance that had to be detonated. But it was all a flash in the pan, as they. A bit of a stressful time, though."

"Ah, that's fine then. It sounded like gunfire down by the Taigh, crazy eh? Were those helicopters or UFOs by your house?"

Harry had forgotten the view that the herder had from where he sometimes grazed his sheep. He stared back aghast.

Then, Wullie let him off the hook. "I'm an old man, and I see things as well. Musta' imagined some o' that stuff."

"He gave Harry a knowing look. "Now, are we all good with saving the sheep?"

"Yes."

"By the way, Gus' 'n' Bob's deal with yon posh bloke never materialised. They complained about English cheats and liars who never paid their bills. He seems to have disappeared."

"Just can't trust the English," Harry grinned at the old man. And they continued chatting as they would do most days.

****

And, Helen Welsh? Ah well, now that's another story.

The End

SMALL REQUEST, BIG FAVOUR

Dear Readers,

Authors thrive on reviews. It's not an ego thing. OK, perhaps a little. Reviews encourage others to read an author's book and spread the word.

So, if you enjoyed 'Kill or They Die', please leave a review where you bought it, plus on Goodreads if you are a member.

And, please tell your friends.

If you have any comments or have a question related to this book or my writing, please email me at maxholden-author@outlook.com, or reach out to me on FaceBook max.holden.author.

For information on my writing, please feel free to check out my website at: www.maxholden-author.co.uk.

I'd love to hear from you.

P.S. At the end of 2023, Harry will again be saving us all in his third book. Afterward, I have plans for future Harry Logan books; so many stories and not enough time.

ABOUT THE AUTHOR

The son of a Scottish father and an Austrian mother, Max spent his informative years as a military brat in Malaysia, before returning to Scotland. He and his wife spent many years living and working in the Middle East and Asia.

Writing was the most enjoyable part of his work as an international marketer. With several thriller and murder novels bubbling around his head and desperate to pop out, the time had come for him to write his own stories.

Now a full-time writer, 'Kill, or They Die' is his fourth novel, and second in the Harry Logan series. He hopes you enjoyed reading it as much as he enjoyed writing it.

He is married with two children, a football team of grandchildren, three dogs, and three cats.

Home is the south coast of England.

Website: www.maxholden-author.co.uk

Printed in Great Britain
by Amazon

30004071R00178